Acclaim for Guillaume Musso's

THE STRANGER IN THE SEINE

"A story that will set your nerves on edge and disturb your sleep!"   —Sandrine Bajos, *Le Parisien*

"Musso takes pleasure in repurposing a news item from the end of the nineteenth century that has intrigued many writers and poets, from Aragon to Proust to Rilke. He uses it as an original starting point for an effective thriller."
    —Isabelle Lesniak, *Les Echos*

"A gripping thriller that flirts with the supernatural."
    —Camille Da Silva, *Ouest-France*

"A clever mix of police investigation and psychological suspense embellished with a pinch of the supernatural...Something to captivate all audiences."   —François Lestavel, *Paris Match*

"Musso successfully returns to a pure thriller."
    —Bernard Lehut and
    Aymeric Parthonnaud, *RTL*

"With his nineteenth novel, Guillaume Musso delivers a mysterious and captivating story...The book still haunts us once we've finished reading."   —Lila Dussault, *La Presse*

"Inspired by Greek mythology and the world of theater... The great French writer Guillaume Musso invites readers... to accompany him in a new high-tension story, *The Stranger in the Seine*. This brilliant, multilayered novel once again proves the talent of the author."

—Marie-France Bornais, *Le Journal de Québec*

THE STRANGER IN THE SEINE

Also by Guillaume Musso

CENTRAL PARK
THE REUNION

THE
STRANGER
IN THE
SEINE

A NOVEL

GUILLAUME MUSSO

TRANSLATED FROM THE FRENCH
BY ROSIE EYRE

BACK BAY BOOKS
Little, Brown and Company
New York   Boston   London

Copyright © 2023 by Guillaume Musso
Translation copyright © 2023 by Rosie Eyre

Back Bay Books / Little, Brown and Company
Hachette Book Group
1290 Avenue of the Americas, New York, NY 10104
littlebrown.com

First North American edition: August 2023
Originally published in France as *L'Inconnue de la Seine*
by Guillaume Musso © Calmann-Lévy, 2021

Back Bay Books is an imprint of Little, Brown and Company, a division of Hachette Book Group, Inc. The Back Bay Books name and logo are trademarks of Hachette Book Group, Inc.

The publisher is not responsible for websites (or their content) that are not owned by the publisher.

The Hachette Speakers Bureau provides a wide range of authors for speaking events. To find out more, go to hachettespeakersbureau.com or email hachettespeakers@hbgusa.com.

Little, Brown and Company books may be purchased in bulk for business, educational, or promotional use. For information, please contact your local bookseller or the Hachette Book Group Special Markets Department at special.markets@hbgusa.com.

ISBN 9780316497305
LCCN 2023933886

Printing 1, 2023

LSC-C

Printed in the United States of America

For Ingrid, Nathan and Flora

PART I
THE STRANGER IN THE SEINE

Monday, 21 December

1

THE CLOCK TOWER

1.

Paris

'This time you've put us all in a tight spot, Roxane. The unit, your colleagues, me . . .'

The unmarked police car had just pulled out of Avenue de la Grande Armée onto Place de l'Étoile. It was the first time Captain Sorbier had spoken since they left Nanterre. With his fingers clenched around the steering wheel, he continued his lecture in a grave tone.

'Given the current climate, if the press get wind of what you've done, even Superintendent Charbonnel's neck could be on the line . . .'

In the seat next to him Roxane Montchrestien remained silent, her gaze turned towards the droplet-streaked window. Paris loomed ominously under the heavy, grey sky. It was the latest in a succession of dismal days since the start of the month, and the whole passenger compartment was thick with damp. Roxane leant over to put the demister on full blast and squinted through the glass. The spectral bulk of the Arc de Triomphe was barely discernible behind the curtain of rain. In a surge of déjà vu, the bleak setting made her think back to that Saturday when gilet jaune protestors had descended on the capital, and the most extreme fringe of them had attacked the iconic monument. The scenes of revolt had been broadcast around the world, encapsulating the toxic environment that was choking the country. Things hadn't really improved since then.

'Basically, we're all in the shit because of you,' Sorbier concluded, kicking down to veer onto Avenue Marceau.

As Roxane was thrown back in her seat, she let her boss's criticism sink in. It didn't even cross her mind to defend herself. She had a lot of time for Sorbier, who headed up the Brigade Nationale de Recherche des Fugitifs – the BNRF for short, the unit charged with hunting down France's most wanted criminals. The problem lay with her. For months now, she'd been wading through a tunnel with no end in sight. She rubbed her eyes and wound down the window. As the cool air hit her face, she wanted to believe that a fresh lease of life was gusting into her and making everything click into place: from now on, her fortunes would be decided a long way from the national police force.

'I'm going to hand in my notice, boss,' she announced, sitting back upright. 'It's better that way for everyone.'

Roxane felt a certain liberation in saying the words aloud. She was someone who had always lived for her job, yet she now found herself incapable of doing it properly. Like many of her colleagues, over time her sense of unease had developed into genuine anguish. In France, and especially around Paris, people's hatred for the police was palpable. Ubiquitous.

'GO TOP YOURSELVES! GO TOP YOURSELVES!' She could still hear the foul chants that had been slung at police officers during the demos. *It's time,* she thought to herself between repeated gulps of polluted air, *time I got out of here.*

A deadly spiral had been set in motion, inciting the public to loathe the very people who were meant to protect them. Police officers were ambushed in housing estates, their stations were attacked, they were lynched at protest marches and hit by mortar fire in the middle of Paris. Their children went off to school with terror in their stomachs. Their family lives disintegrated. And all the while, Saturday after Saturday, demo after demo, the news channels continued to take shameless relish in making them out to be Nazis.

'GO TOP YOURSELVES! GO TOP YOURSELVES!' *It's time I got out of here.* Luckily, she didn't have anything to tie her down. No loans to clear, no kids to bring up, no rent to pay. It wasn't just the force she was turning her back on. It was this whole sick country. She'd find herself a distant rock somewhere, but not so far away that she couldn't sit back and watch, to the painful end, as it all went up in flames.

'I'll get my resignation letter to you by this evening.'

Sorbier shook his head.

'Dream on, Roxane. You're not getting away that easily.'

They were now driving along the banks of the Seine towards Place de la Concorde. For the first time, Roxane let her irritation show.

'Can I at least know where you're taking me?'

'For a little run-out.'

She could almost have smiled at Sorbier's turn of phrase. It made her picture lush countryside, fields stretching out as

5

far as the eye can see, ripe wheat dappled with sunshine, a gently rippling breeze, the tinkle of cowbells. A world away from the reality of Paris: a city cankered by filth and apathy, crusted in pollution and endless miseries.

Sorbier waited until they were halfway across the Pont de la Concorde before revealing what he had in mind.

'Here's the idea, Roxane. Charbonnel has found you a quiet unit where you can lie low for a few months.'

'So I'm getting a transfer, that's what you're telling me?'

'Temporarily, yes.'

François Charbonnel was the chief superintendent in charge of the OCLCO, the central office for combating organised crime that oversaw the BNRF.

'And what about my investigation team?'

'Lieutenant Botsaris will take over duties for the time being. We're giving you a chance to get back on your feet. After that, if you're still dead set on it, you can ditch us for good.'

Roxane raised a hand to her chest, feeling a sudden flare of heartburn.

'What will I be doing in this new unit, exactly?'

2.

'Have you heard of the BUA?'

'Nope.'

'To tell you the truth, until this morning I hadn't either.'

Sorbier was at least decent enough not to sugar-coat his proposal.

The wipers were locked in a losing battle with the sheets

of rain pouring down the windscreen. The car was now on the Left Bank, stuck in a tailback that ran the length of Boulevard Saint-Germain.

'The Bureau of Unconventional Affairs was set up under Pompidou in 1971,' Sorbier explained. 'It's directly answerable to the Paris Prefecture. Initially, its aim was to investigate unusual cases that the judicial police couldn't find any rational explanations for.'

'When you say "unusual" . . . ?'

'Anything relating to the paranormal.'

'You're having me on.'

'No, but you've got to put it in the context of the time. The whole "magical realism" craze was in its salad days. People wanted to study areas that were shut out of "official" science. Flying saucers were all the rage, *The Morning of the Magicians* was selling out in bookshops, the national UFO unit was about to open in Toulouse . . .'

'Why's nobody ever heard of this thing?'

Sorbier shrugged.

'It got a bit of press coverage at the time. They had a dozen or so people working there during the late seventies and eighties. But with the socialists coming to power, and all the changes in society since, over time it's just become a place to crash for cops who've gone through the mill a bit or fallen out of favour after some blunder.'

Roxane knew about the Le Courbat centre in Touraine, which had been set up for CRS riot officers suffering from depression, alcoholism or burn-out, but this particular dumping ground was new on her.

'Over the years the BUA's moved offices and its staff have melted away. It's only a heading in the budget now, and next

June it's being disbanded altogether. There's every chance
you'll be the last cop in the post.'

'Is this the only deathbed you could find me?'

Her skipper didn't let the comment slide.

'I don't think you're really in a position to argue, Roxane.
And for someone who wanted to resign five minutes ago,
you're being bloody picky.'

Sorbier had just turned right onto Rue du Bac. Roxane
lowered her window as far as it would go. Grenelle, Verneuil,
Varenne . . . The streets of the Saint-Thomas-d'Aquin quarter filed past. This was where she'd grown up. She'd been to
school at Sainte-Clotilde's, a stone's throw away. Her father,
an army man, had worked for the Ministry of Defence at
the Hôtel de Brienne; the family home was just opposite
in Rue Casimir Périer. Saint-Thomas-d'Aquin was like
Saint-Germain-des-Prés without the tourists and posers.
Returning here today was unexpected, stirring a flurry of
hazy yet comforting memories – parquet floors crisscrossed
with sunlight, white acanthas-leaf moulding, the tinkling of
an old Steinway, the bronze cat-butler sculpture that always
seemed to be sneering down from the mantelpiece.

A furious taxi horn blared her back to reality.

'How many guys will I have on my team?'

'None. Like I said, the unit's been running idle for years.
In recent months there's just been one person in the job:
Superintendent Marc Batailley.'

Roxane frowned. The name vaguely rang a bell, but she
couldn't place why.

Sorbier jogged her memory.

'Batailley's an old-timer from Major Crime. He had his
moment in the sun at the start of the nineties, when the

group he ran in Marseilles identified and arrested "The Horticulturalist", one of the first French serial killers.'

'The Horticulturalist?'

'The guy used secateurs to lop off every part of his victims that stuck out: fingers, toes, ears, penises . . .'

'Original.'

'After his five minutes of fame, Batailley secured a transfer to the judicial police HQ in Paris, but he never lived up to hopes. Because of his rocky family life, I think. He lost a child and his marriage fell apart. The later part of his career was disrupted by health issues, which is how he came to be posted to the BUA.'

'Is he retired now?'

'Not yet, but he suffered a massive heart attack last night. That's why Charbonnel and his team were able to swoop to land you the job.'

Sorbier turned on the hazard lights, then parked up opposite the railings of the Square des Missions Etrangères. The rain had stopped. Roxane scrambled out of the car. The damp had wormed its way into her clothes, hair and brain. Sorbier followed suit, then leant against the bonnet to spark up.

The wind had picked up. She could breathe at last. A timid sliver of blue sky appeared above the square. Kids were already refilling the playground, squealing with delight as they besieged the swings and slides. Roxane had memories here too: strawberry and vanilla cornets from the olde-worlde ice-cream parlour next door, trips with her mother to Bon Marché and The Conran Shop, Romain Gary's apartment a bit further down. She used to pass it with fascination while studying for her French literature baccalaureate, always casting a hopeful eye in case the door had been left ajar and the ghosts of Gary, his wife Jean and their son Diego might emerge.

'There's your office,' Sorbier announced, pointing heavenwards.

Roxane craned her neck. At first she couldn't tell what her skipper meant, then she spotted a kind of belfry, crowned with a clock. A crow's nest tucked well back from the street that she'd never noticed before and which towered over the surrounding rooftops.

'The building dates from the twenties,' Sorbier began in a teacherly manner. 'It was originally part of the Bon Marché complex, designed by the architect Louis-Hippolyte Boileau when the store was expanding into its Grande Épicerie food hall. The Prefecture got hold of it in the nineties, but the government's just put it up for sale.'

Roxane made her way towards the imposing, blue-repainted carriage gates.

'I'll leave you here,' Sorbier said, handing her a bunch of keys. 'And for god's sake, Roxane, behave yourself.'

'Do you have the door code?'

'It's 301207: the date Clemenceau set up the Tiger Brigades. Followed by "B" for "Brigades".'

'Or "Bureau of Unconventional Affairs",' Roxane mused.

'I hope we've understood each other, Roxane. Keep under the radar. We won't always be here to clean up your mess.'

3.

If the tower was unremarkable from the street, once through the gates its majesty hit her. At the back of a small, leafy courtyard the lighthouse-esque structure soared gracefully overhead, squeezed between two charmless apartment blocks. The clockfaces at the top consolidated its domination over the Parisian skyline. A real-life fortress in the middle of the 7th arrondissement.

Roxane crossed the cobbles to the solid, polished-wood entrance, where a bright-red moped was parked. With the keys Sorbier had given her, she unlocked the double doors. The belfry opened onto a stained-glass skylight that filled the three upper storeys with a warm, churchlike glow. The ground floor gave a taste of what was to come: exposed red brick, oak parquet, metal joists, riveted girders inspired by Gustave Eiffel.

A cast-iron spiral staircase connected the four levels. Roxane began to climb, her eyes fixed on the summit. The heating was purring away nicely. From the top floor she could hear bursts of piano music. Schubert's *Impromptus*. One of the soundtracks to her childhood.

She reached the first landing. The storey was divided in two. The first side was a mass of metal filing cabinets, with shelves up to the ceiling, boxes of paperwork, a fax machine and even an old Minitel. Off to the other side was a kitchen area with a rough wooden worktop, and a shower room beyond.

Near the photocopier stood a traditionally decorated Christmas tree, guarded by a plump Siberian tomcat sprawled on a bed of papers. On seeing Roxane he yowled and scarpered off towards the floor above.

'Come here, you.'

Roxane caught up with the animal on the stairs and bent down to stroke its belly. It was a hefty, muscular creature, with gleaming silvery fur and a cartoonish face.

11

'His name's Poutine,' announced a voice behind her.

Roxane whipped around, feeling for her Glock in its holster. A young woman was standing by the window on the second-floor landing. She was about twenty-five, with an Afro haircut, olive skin, emerald eyes framed by tortoiseshell glasses, and a broad smile that revealed the gap between her teeth.

'Who the fuck are you?' Roxane demanded.

'Valentine Diakité,' the girl replied calmly. 'I'm a student at the Sorbonne.'

'What the hell are you doing here?'

'I'm writing my PhD on the Bureau of Unconventional Affairs.'

Roxane sighed.

'And what right does that give you?'

'I've got permission from Superintendent Batailley. For the past six months I've been sorting out old case files. You should have seen the state of them before I started!'

Roxane watched the student advancing through the cardboard boxes like a princess in her castle. With her black tights, velvet skirt, turtleneck sweater and snakeskin boots, she brought to mind a modern-day Emma Peel.

'And who are you, if you don't mind me asking?'

'Police. Captain Roxane Montchrestien.'

'Are you standing in for Superintendent Batailley?'

'You could put it like that.'

'Do you have any news on how he's doing?'

'No.'

'Poor guy. It's so awful, what's happened to him. It's all I've thought about since this morning. I'm the one who found him.'

'Is this where he had his heart attack?'

'I don't think it was a heart attack. I think he tripped on the stairs.' She gestured at the snaking metal structure. 'It's a real deathtrap.'

Turning her back on the student, Roxane continued to the top floor. The location of Batailley's office. It was a remarkable space, with a ceiling height of at least 20 feet and riveted beams splaying in all directions. A Chesterfield sofa, a striking Jean Prouvé-style oak desk and red-brick walls completed the décor, giving an effect somewhere between a British nightclub and a New York loft. But most arresting of all was the view. A dizzying panorama of Paris, with the Eiffel Tower and the dome of the Hôtel des Invalides off to the west, the Butte of Montmartre and the Sacré-Coeur to the north, the Jardin du Luxembourg and the eyesore of Tour Montparnasse to the south, and the still-bruised shell of Notre-Dame to the east. It all gave a heady sense of cruising above the world, far enough removed to escape its wrath.

4.

Roxane went back to find Valentine Diakité, who'd set up her own office on the floor below. Behind her wise librarian veneer, she radiated a sunny aura that unsettled Roxane.

'Explain to me how Marc Batailley filled his days.'

'He sometimes went about things slowly,' Valentine conceded. 'When I arrived, six months ago, Marc was still getting over his lung cancer. He was worn out, but always friendly and ready with advice.'

'How long's the Bureau been inactive?'

Delighted to be of service, the student launched into a whistlestop history.

'In the early years, through the seventies and eighties, the BUA spent its time investigating quite a lot of spooky phenomena – hauntings, telekinesis, mind control, what we now call near-death experiences. During that period the unit received hundreds of accounts from all over France.'

Valentine motioned to the boxes around her.

'Ghosts, Women in White, telepathy, you name it . . . It was also the golden age of ufology. If you're interested in looking at any of the case files, you'll see it's like stepping into an episode of *The X-Files*.'

'And now?'

Valentine pulled a face.

'We still get the odd letter – from idiots who think the world's being controlled by reptiles, or that Bill Gates is creating viruses to solve overpopulation and the French government is pumping them out through 5G masts and smart meters.'

Roxane rubbed her eyes. She wanted to be alone, to go to sleep and cut off the current that was surging through her mind.

'You can't stay here, Valentine.'

'Why? The superintendent gave his permission, and . . .'

'Yeah, but I'm in charge now. And a police department isn't a university library.'

'I could make myself useful.'

'I don't see how. You've got until the end of the day to pack up. And don't forget to take your cat with you.'

Valentine shrugged.

'Poutine's not mine. He isn't Marc's either. He was already

here when we arrived. I found a report in the archives saying he turned up at the Bureau in 2002, which makes him absolutely ancient.'

With a stab of frustration Roxane spun on her heels and stomped back up to the top floor. The old cast-iron dials behind the glass of the clockface gave the room a strange, almost otherworldly feel. She had the sensation of being in a cabinet of curiosities. The office equipment, by contrast, was like jumping back thirty years. There was no modern technology to speak of, and the phone reminded her of the one her parents had when she was a teenager.

A little red light was blinking on the handset. Intrigued, Roxane pressed the loudspeaker button to hear the message, which was recorded as having been received at 1.10 p.m. that day.

'Hi Marc, it's Catherine Aumonier again. I really could do with speaking to you about the message I left this morning. Please give me a call back.'

Seeing no further messages, Roxane listened to the previous one that had been left at 7.46 a.m.

'Good morning Marc, it's Catherine Aumonier, Deputy Director of the Prefecture infirmary. I'm calling for your opinion on a rather odd case. Yesterday morning we admitted a young woman in a state of total amnesia, who'd been recovered from the Seine by the River Brigade. She was completely naked when they found her. I don't have your email address, so I've faxed the file over to you. Please call me back to let me know if you recognise her. Thanks.'

Her curiosity piqued, Roxane immediately replayed the message. If Batailley had listened to it – and the light flashing on the machine suggested this was the case – he must have done so only minutes before his fall.

She could feel her stomach tingling. Everything remotely connected with the I3P – the Paris Prefecture's famously opaque psychiatric unit – had always fascinated her. Catherine Aumonier claimed to have sent Batailley a fax. But trawling through the piles of papers, books and magazines on his desk, Roxane found no trace of it. Having clocked the fax machine next to the photocopier earlier, she returned to the first floor. Valentine Diakité was sitting cross-legged in the corner, sulkily sorting through files.

'Have you picked up any faxes today?'

The student shook her head mutely.

There was nothing in the fax tray. Roxane tried to piece together the likely chain of events. Marc had arrived early. He'd listened to Catherine Aumonier's message, gone down to retrieve the fax, then headed back upstairs to his office. That's when he fell. But where could the fax have got to? Roxane looked under the staircase, then under the furniture and filing cabinets. Zilch. On a hunch, she made her way back over to the Christmas tree. The cat had set up camp again on his bed, which was none other than . . . Catherine Aumonier's fax.

She smoothed out the two stapled pages. Poutine had torn part of them, but the content was still easily legible. As the I3P boss had explained, it was the admittance statement for a female patient presenting with memory loss. The report was laconic, but the girl's photograph was tantalising: a delicate face, framed by tumbling shoulder-length hair, and etched with fear.

For a moment she considered ringing Aumonier, before making up her mind to visit the infirmary in person. She'd already got her jacket on when she remembered she no longer had a car. Her standard-issue Peugeot 5008 had stayed in Nanterre, and she wouldn't be reclaiming it any time soon.

On Valentine's desk she spied a motorbike helmet, a brown-and-yellow, open-face model with a chequered band along the bottom.

'Is that moped by the entrance yours?' Roxane asked, already slotting on the rigid headgear. 'Can you chuck me the keys?'

2

THE INFIRMARY

1.

'You've arrived after the horse has bolted,' Catherine Aumonier warned Roxane as she entered her office.

The infirmary's Deputy Director was a huge, formidable-
looking woman with a white coat, half-moon glasses, and
a frazzled demeanour. Without getting up from her small
metal desk, she eyed Roxane suspiciously.

'What do you mean?'

'The Stranger in the Seine is no longer with us,' Aumonier replied.

Behind the snide remarks Roxane detected embarrass-
ment, as if the doctor had been caught napping on the job.

'Take me back to the start,' Roxane requested.

It was the first time in her career she'd stepped foot in
the Paris Police Prefecture infirmary. Nicknamed the I3P,
the medical unit was the only one of its kind in France, and
had acquired a reputation for scandal. It offered emergency
psychiatric treatment to individuals picked up by the police

in the capital who were judged to be suffering from 'clear mental-health issues'. Since its creation a century and a half earlier, the unit regularly came under fire for its lack of transparency – the result of the tight grip the Prefecture kept over its workings.

'Our mystery woman was recovered from the Seine at around 5 a.m. on Sunday morning. She was rescued by the River Brigade just along from the Pont Neuf,' Aumonier began, studying her notes fixedly. 'She was stark naked except for a wristwatch.'

Despite her interest in the case, Roxane felt stifled. Aumonier's office was tiny, barely bigger than a prison cell. Its greenish lighting and pervasive cabbagey smell were making her queasy. Every breath was a struggle.

'She was brought to us at about 10 a.m. the same morning, following a short examination by the forensic medical team at Hôtel-Dieu hospital.'

Aumonier handed Roxane the certificate that had been filled out by the forensic medical team doctor. She scanned it. The guy hadn't put much heart into it, only troubling himself to tick a few boxes and scrawl by way of summary: *The subject is displaying mental-health issues that could pose a risk to her safety and the safety of others.* The Stranger had refused to have her fingerprints taken, and the forensic medical team hadn't been in the mood for a fight. She hadn't committed any crime, with the possible exception of skinny-dipping in the Seine.

'When we fished her out, the girl was disorientated, completely spaced out. Unable to answer even the most basic questions. She more or less behaved herself at Hôtel-Dieu, but when she got here, she totally flipped.'

Aumonier opened a file on her laptop, then turned the screen towards Roxane.

'Everything was caught by the security cameras. We sedated her on arrival, but the effects were limited. She became extremely agitated, clawing at herself and tearing her hair out in clumps.'

Roxane's eyes were glued to the footage. A young woman in a hospital gown, looking utterly lost. Her face gaunt and spectral, like a sylph imprisoned by her own sorrow and madness.

'Impossible to get any sense out of her?'

'I don't think she even understand most of the questions we were asking her,' Aumonier replied.

'Did you reach a diagnosis?'

'In the heat of the moment it's tricky. A combination of delirium and dissociative amnesia.'

'Could she have been faking it?'

'It's always a possibility, but I wouldn't bet on it. She seemed like she'd suffered a profound trauma. Anyway, twenty-four hours later things still hadn't improved, but she did at least manage to string together a sentence that intrigued me. She asked if we could call Marc Batailley.'

'She really said that?'

'Several times, almost as though she was pleading. "*Sie müssen Marc Batailley anrufen!*"'

'In German?'

'Yes.'

'And did you know who she meant?'

'Yes, Marc and I often ran into each other while I was working at Quai de la Rapée.'

'At the Forensic Institute?'

Aumonier nodded.

'I left two messages, but he never called me back.'

On her arrival at the I3P, Roxane had been careful not to let slip that she'd listened to them. Aumonier had assumed she'd been sent by the Prefecture, and Roxane hadn't put her right.

'And then what?'

The Deputy Director dug her pinkie in her ear and began scratching unashamedly. Her face was reminiscent of the Dutch peasants in Van Gogh's preparatory sketches for *The Potato Eaters*: ruddy complexion, coarse features, sunken forehead and a bulbous nose.

'We kept the girl in for a few more hours, but we were under massive pressure to free up rooms.'

'Can I see where she stayed?'

Aumonier hoisted herself from her chair. It was clearly an effort.

'Normally, we get six or seven new arrivals a day. This Monday we had eleven.'

With a sigh she buttoned up her lab coat, revealing the red, white and blue Prefecture crest.

'We don't know what's up at the moment. Between all the druggies, cranks, paranoiacs, down-and-outs and migrants, we can't keep up. We're at breaking point.'

2.

The double doors opened onto a long, yellowish corridor lined with pomegranate-red doors. Staff offices, the kitchen, a break room and the pharmacy were off to the left, while the patient rooms and showers were on the right. There wasn't a window anywhere. It was like the place had been run through a malevolent Instagram filter, with every trace of outside light sucked out to leave only a squalid, deadened glow.

An unsettling murmur of activity pulsed through the walls. Mealtime. Two female nurses were handing out trays to the patients. On the menu: boiled fish, Brussels sprouts, and fromage blanc for afters.

'Legally, our patients can't stay more than forty-eight hours,' Aumonier explained. 'After that time, they're either subject to compulsory hospitalisation elsewhere, released without charge, or handed over to the police as part of a criminal investigation.'

Behind a Perspex window, a toothless man in blue pyjamas was bellowing at the top of his lungs: 'I'm too cold! I'm too hot! I'm turning blue and puce! Gimme a splash of juice so I can drive to Knokke-le-Zoute!'

'By mid-afternoon our hands were tied,' she continued. 'We had to send the girl somewhere else. With the latest arrivals we were up to twenty patients, and our maximum bed capacity across the ten rooms is sixteen.'

'Did you sort somewhere for her?'

'Of course! We pulled out all the stops to get her a place at the Jules-Cotard clinic. It's a smaller unit not too far from here, just down from Montparnasse Cemetery. It was during the transfer that it all turned to shit. We lost her.'

'Lost her? You mean the patient escaped?'

Picking up on Roxane's reproachful tone, Aumonier bristled.

'Normally we operate with four members of security

support staff. One's dropped to part-time, another claims to be sick, and a third's stopped coming in since he requested a move. The rules say there must be two guys per transfer, but this afternoon we only had one.'

The I3P was suffering from that classic French syndrome: the country was overtaxed and overrun with red tape, yet nothing worked as it should. Further away, the toothless man was still ranting away in his room: 'I want a shoot of juice so I can grab a meal en route. I'd rather eat a moose than this stinking fishy sluice!'

'What exactly happened?'

'She gave him the slip in front of the Cotard clinic.'

Aumonier wiped her nose on her sleeve as they drew up outside Room 6.

'This is the one.'

A warder built like a tank came to let them in. The cell was no more than 100 square feet, without a shower or privacy screen. The only furniture was a metal bed bolted to the floor, and a chemical toilet of the kind sometimes used on building sites or campsites. Dated graffiti on the walls gave a flavour of its previous occupants.

'Yurran arsehole with nothin' round it!' the latest incumbent barked at the Deputy Director.

He was sitting cross-legged on the bed, crippled by tics and spouting insults on tap. Roxane observed him uneasily out of the corner of her eye. With his crooked jawline, his lone working eye and the anchor tattoo on his forearm, he reminded her of Popeye the Sailor.

'Get your mum in here so I can redo you!'

Aumonier ignored the tramp's slur and pre-empted Roxane's question.

'The room was disinfected straight after she left, so forensics will have a hard time finding anything.'

Roxane pondered for a moment. She wasn't convinced forensics would swing into action over a case like this. A missing person alert would be put out by the 14th arrondissement force, they'd send a patrol car to prowl around the Cotard clinic, then their guys would twiddle their thumbs until the girl showed up again.

Aumonier knew she'd screwed up, but she still had one ace up her sleeve.

'Farouk, one of our warders, had the brains to collect some of the hair the girl pulled out.'

From her lab coat she retrieved a sealed plastic pouch containing a handful of blonde strands. Roxane examined it sceptically. It was better than nothing, but she wasn't sure there were enough roots to extract any DNA. Not to mention the risk that the sample had been contaminated. As she scanned the room again, her eyes lingered on the seat of the chemical toilet.

'Have you cleaned that too?'

'Obviously. We change the inner container for every new patient – it works a bit like a cat-litter tray.'

'Yeah, I know the script. Try to track down the one she used, then get me as many samples as you can.'

'What are you after, specifically?'

Roxane shrugged.

'Shit, whatever you can find.'

3.

7 p.m.

Roxane was flying along on Valentine Diakité's moped. Her face, arms and legs were numb, her fingers on fire with the cold. Her leather jacket and long-sleeved T-shirt were a flimsy armour against the biting night.

At Place Denfert-Rochereau, she turned down Boulevard Raspail to head back to her new office. The boulevard was thick with traffic as people spilled out of work, the flow partially diverted by the latest in the interminable series of roadworks that were disfiguring the capital. Having lived in Paris all her life, Roxane had never seen her city in such a state. For months the blight had been mushrooming, so that it was impossible to find a street, junction or housing block where the pavement hadn't been gutted. The worst part was that most of the building sites were dormant. Labourers were sent to carve trenches, then for some unknowable reason redeployed to another site. The lethargy of the authorities meant the holes were left gaping for weeks, fenced off by hideous greenish-grey corrugated-iron barriers. The same ones that were used as projectiles at weekends by protestors out to smash some cop skulls.

The 'Stranger in the Seine' affair was rattling around in her mind. The case had a poetic ring that appealed to her, bringing back an episode she'd studied in her foundation-year literature class. The tale of the suicidal young woman whose body was fished from the Seine in the late nineteenth century, after being found near a bridge. Captivated by her beauty, an attendant at the morgue illicitly made a cast of her face. Over the years his death mask was replicated so many times that the Stranger took on iconic status, decorating bohemian Parisian apartments through the early part of the new century. Aragon referenced her in his novel *Aurélien*, where she was likened to 'a suicidal Mona Lisa', Supervielle devoted a poignant short story to her, and Camus kept a replica in his office. Her face had a fascinating serenity, and an unparalleled beauty – high, full cheekbones, flawless skin, closed eyes feathered with fine lashes, and an enigmatic half-smile frozen in bliss as though her journey from this life had plunged her into the sheerest ecstasy.

As she hit Rue de Sèvres, an electric scooter travelling in the wrong direction jolted Roxane from her literary reveries. Narrowly avoiding it, she managed to weave free of the traffic and back onto Rue du Bac, where in her frozen state she navigated the moped through the carriage gates and parked up in the courtyard of 111a. As she opened the tower door, she felt a rush of comfort to be back in her new office: the embracing warmth, the reassuring tinkle of piano music, the Christmas decorations that swept her back to her childhood . . . not forgetting Poutine the Siberian cat, who was already circling her ankles.

There's no place like home . . .

Valentine Diakité was still at her desk on the second floor. Roxane realised she was going to have trouble getting rid of her.

'So?' the student asked, her face lighting up eagerly.

Touched by her spontaneous enthusiasm, and not without an ulterior motive, Roxane gave Valentine the lowdown on her visit to the I3P.

'If you really want to help me,' she announced when she'd finished, 'now's the time!'

She produced two plastic pouches from her inside pockets, one containing the hair samples, the other a tube of the Stranger's urine.

'There's a direct train leaving from the Gare du Nord in half an hour. You can be in Lille by 9 p.m.'

'Lille?'

'That's where the European Genetics Institute is – one of the leading private DNA labs in northern France.'

Valentine was already taking notes on her phone.

'My unit, the BNRF, often works with them as an alternative to the INPS, the National Police forensics lab,' Roxane continued. 'They're good for quick turnaround times, especially in cases where you need results before a suspect's released from custody.'

'But nobody's put you on this case!'

'Who's to know?' Roxane shot back. 'You just need to rock up and hand over the samples to someone called Johan Moers.'

'At 9 in the evening?'

'Don't worry about that. The guy's an oddball, he practically lives there. To make life easier for you, I'll drop him a text so he knows you're coming.'

Roxane had imagined Valentine's willingness would falter at the first hurdle, but not in the slightest.

'I'll get going, then,' she said, sliding on her helmet.

She tucked the samples in her Lady Dior handbag, then handed Roxane a creamy-white business card.

'Can you email me with the tickets and the lab address?'

'Consider it done. You'll be back in Paris by midnight.'

4.

Glad to be alone, Roxane parked herself on the Chesterfield, fired off a message to Johan Moers, bought and forwarded the train tickets, then stared into space for a moment as she replayed the CCTV footage in her mind. The unknown woman they'd pulled from the Seine had an appearance that was at once forgettable and fascinating. She reminded Roxane of the Mazone, Captain Harlock's sworn enemies in the *Space Pirate* series. Plant-based women made of sap and fibre, beautiful and dangerous in equal measure.

In another text, Roxane prodded Catherine Aumonier about her promise to send over the name and address of the officer who'd let the Stranger get away, along with his incident report. Then she phoned the Pompidou hospital for an update on Batailley. After interminable wrangling to get a doctor on the line, the upshot wasn't good: the cop had multiple fractures and a severe head injury. He'd been placed in a medically induced coma so they could operate and bring down the bruising. His condition had stabilised, but it was still touch-and-go.

Roxane rounded off her correspondence with a text exchange with Louise Veyron, the coordinator of the Directorate of Public Order and Traffic — the arm of the Paris Prefecture that oversaw the running of the River Brigade. The two women knew each other vaguely, and agreed on an informal meeting the next day with the frogman who'd recovered the Stranger in the early hours of Sunday morning.

Roxane had a sudden vision of her apartment — the greyness, the cold, the loneliness, the concrete, the call of the void — and balked at the prospect of going home. Despite not having brought a change of clothes, she decided to stay cocooned in the clock tower a little longer.

In the first-floor kitchen, she spotted a small stock of wine next to the fridge. After scanning the selection, she plumped for a bottle of white: a 2011 Pessac-Léognan by Domaine de Chevalier. She poured herself a first glass that she gulped down undiscerningly, purely to have a dose of alcohol in her blood. The second glass was more decadent. It was an exquisite vintage, fruity and woody, with notes of white peach and hazelnut. Batailley had taste.

She carried the bottle to the top floor and fiddled with the old cast-iron radiator to ramp up the temperature. Although she'd never minded the cold, she'd become increasingly sensitive to it lately. Without warning, a paralysing wave would engulf her and chill her to the bone. Wrapping herself in a tartan blanket that was folded on the sofa, she took a moment to rummage through Batailley's CD collection. Once again, he'd chosen well. The guy obviously loved his classical music. There were mounds of discs, some of them still in their blister packs, with a marked predilection for Schubert, Beethoven and Satie performed by star pianists such as Krystian Zimerman, Daniel Barenboim, Martha Argerich, Milena Bergman and Aldo Ciccolini.

The glass walls trembled under successive gusts, reinforcing her sense of being inside a lighthouse. In the clear night, her lofty vantage point afforded an unknown angle over the city. Over in a corner of the room, she suddenly noticed a retractable wooden staircase. Once folded out, it led her up to a sliding panel, and through onto a tiny terrace that was squeezed in next to a New York-style water tank.

The wind was strong, but its effect was revitalising. She'd

taken to the tower from the start. Instantly, she'd felt at home there. Now, sitting on the zinc rooftop, Roxane pictured herself as the guardian of the city, keeping watch from the crow's nest of a ship that was gliding through the Parisian night. The bustle and lights below were hypnotic. There was always something to hold the eye. She pulled the blanket tighter around her shoulders, and a new image formed in her mind – the machicolation of a fortress. Here, she was temporarily out of harm's way. Here, nobody would come looking for her.

And if they did, she'd have time to defend herself.

Tuesday, 22 December

3

MILENA BERGMAN

1.

Roused by the light, Roxane flicked open her eyes without immediately recognising where she was – above the roof-tops, surrounded by sky, floating amid glints of zinc, copper and slate. Swathed in a tartan blanket, with a fat Siberian cat curled around her legs.

She stood up, rubbed her eyelids, and snapped back to her senses. It was steaming hot in the room. Her T-shirt was drenched, the blanket plastered to her legs. She turned down the radiator. After taking a while to get into its stride, it had been running at full pelt all night. On the bright side, the weather was in party mood. For the first time in weeks, the Sun King graced the capital with his presence.

Roxane massaged her neck, shoulders and back, feeling like the heroine of the Princess and the Pea. The Chester-field might have been nice to look at, but it wasn't designed to serve as a bed. Especially when you were knocking on the door of forty.

With Poutine hot on her heels, she headed down to the first floor where she remembered spotting a coffee machine. She filled a plate with cat biscuits and poured a bowl of water to placate the mewling animal, then unearthed a socket on the kitchen counter to plug in her phone charger. She felt mildly hungover, but she'd known worse. While she got the coffee going, she checked her messages. Aumonier had sent her the incident report and the address of the security officer who'd let the Stranger get away – a guy called Anthony Moraes, who lived in the Saint-Philippe-du-Roule area of the city. Most significantly though, she had a missed call from Johan Moers, the Lille biologist Valentine had gone to see with the hair sample. She wasted no time in calling him back.

'I've got your results, Roxane.'

'Already? I was worried the sample might be contaminated, or that there weren't enough follicles.'

'Hair analysis has come on quite a way over the past few years,' Moers replied. 'It wasn't me that did the fiddly bit, but my assistant managed to find a few bulbs to extract the genetic material we needed. I've got the results up on my screen.'

'Brill. Could you email them over to my assistant, Lieutenant Botsaris?'

'I think he's saved in my contacts. Hang on . . . Yep, got him. Did you know the average human being loses between fifty and a hundred hairs a day?'

'I didn't. But thanks to you I'm starting the day with some good news.'

'Talking of good news, I'll be in Paris the first week of January. Fancy meeting for lunch?'

'Sure.'

'You say that every time, and always end up cancelling.'

'You wildly overestimate my conversation skills.'

'To be honest, it's not so much your conversation I'm after . . .'

'Bye, Johan.'

She hung up in satisfaction. On her list of hurdles that morning, the first had been easily cleared. Next step: calling Botsaris.

She was about to punch in his number when she heard the creak of the entrance door. A few seconds later, Valentine Diakité materialised in the kitchen, chicly dressed and made-up, and fizzing with energy.

'Just a flying visit before I leave for the hospital. I didn't know you were planning to sleep here!'

'Me neither,' Roxane mumbled, embarrassed at being caught with her morning face on.

'I've got croissants. Do you want one?'

Roxane thanked her for going to Lille the previous evening, then brought her up to speed on the information she'd gleaned at her end.

Valentine disappeared as quickly as she'd arrived. Roxane sat motionless at the counter for several minutes, wondering if the preceding scene had actually happened. She felt caught out, discombobulated. After fighting off the lingering scent of Valentine's perfume – a heady, cloying mix of honey, white wood and linden – she recomposed herself and dialled her assistant's number.

'Hi, Botsa.'

'Roxane? How are you doing? It's good to hear from you.'

'Do you have a minute?'

'I'm on my way to Nantes with Gibernet and a violent crimes officer from the OCRVP. We've been asked to check on something in the Claret-Tournier case.'

Roxane closed her eyes. In the background she could hear the rumble of traffic and snatches of animated conversation. The rough-and-ready soundtrack to another day on the beat, thrumming with an urgency and adrenaline that were now off limits to her.

'Sorbier told me what happened,' the lieutenant continued. 'I wanted to leave you a message, but . . .'

Roxane cut straight to the point.

'Don't worry about me. Could you do me a favour?'

'Give me the details first. I'm always wary with you.'

'Johan Moers is going to email you a DNA profile. Could you run it through the national database?'

'Roxane! That's totally against procedure!'

'Just slip it in with another case. We've done it a million times before.'

Botsaris was too cautious to admit over the phone that he'd ever played the system.

'Please, don't get me mixed up in your—'

'I just want to check something.'

'Not today.'

'It's important. Please.'

'There's no changing you. It's depressing.'

'Thanks, Botsa.'

2.

After jumping in the shower, she slipped back on her clothes from the day before. As it was decent weather, she decided to go on foot to Quai Saint-Bernard for her meeting with the diver from the team who'd found the Stranger in the early hours of Sunday morning. It was an enjoyable route in the sunshine, winding through Saint-Germain-des-Prés, along Rue de l'Odéon and past the Sorbonne before hitting the quayside. The insidious damp of the previous weeks had given way to a crisp, fresh breeze, and everything was transformed by the good weather.

On the way, she began her hunt for leads with a fruitless phone call with the lethargic administration of the 14th arrondissement force. The case hadn't advanced an inch. They confirmed that a missing person alert had been issued the previous day, and that a car had patrolled the Jules-Cotard clinic without sighting anything of note. It was the same story with the BAC anti-crime squad. None of their guys had reported seeing the Stranger during their nightly rounds. Her final call was to the DOPC coordinator, who confirmed she was expecting Roxane at the River Brigade headquarters.

After crossing the four-lane expressway behind the Jardin des Plantes, where she narrowly avoided being pulped, Roxane wandered for several minutes before finding the path that led down to the quayside. The River Brigade HQ was made up of four unprepossessing geometric buildings, which were moored to the quay amid an assortment of dinghies, inflatable Zodiacs and a patrol boat. Perched on its concrete pontoon, the ensemble reminded her of the

Algeco-style modular buildings used on construction sites. Yet with its backdrop of plane trees, weeping willows and flowering cherries, and the silvery reflections dancing across the Seine, ultimately the view won her over.

In front of the entrance to the main building, Louise Veyron was smoking in the company of a tall, dark-haired guy who was necking coffee straight from his flask. Veyron made the introductions.

'Captain Montchrestien, meet Bruno Jean-Baptiste, our crew commander who oversaw the operation you're interested in.'

Conversation got underway in a slightly strained fashion. For some time the River Brigade had been in crisis. Two years earlier the death of a female diver in a training exercise had sent shockwaves through the force, and its reputation had been left in tatters. In an attempt to draw a line under the incident there had been a change of administration, but the wound was still raw. The Paris fire service's diving section, the River Brigade's main 'competitors', had usurped them in the affections of some media outlets, where they were hailed as the new 'guardian angels of the Seine'.

Roxane tried to defuse the atmosphere by laying her cards out. All she wanted was to identify the unknown woman the crew had fished out two days earlier.

'Do you remember the operation?'

''Course,' the frogman recalled. 'Last Saturday Météo-France put Paris on a yellow weather warning. It was chucking it down and blowing a gale for more than twenty-four hours straight. The conditions were so bad, the city council decided to close all the parks at 5 p.m.'

Jean-Baptiste had to be pushing six-and-a-half foot. With

his bronzed skin, slicked-back hair and solid frame, his reedy voice struck a somewhat bum note.

'We took the call at 4.28 a.m.,' he continued, staring down at a double-page spread that presumably contained the report on the operation. 'A guy said he could see someone drowning near the Pont Neuf from his window.'

'Where did the call come from?'

'Usually they reach us via the central emergency service numbers, but not this time.'

He nodded at the building behind them.

'The guy rang us directly. Must have found the number online. It's happened before, but it's not a regular thing.'

'Did he leave his contact details?'

Jean-Baptiste handed the report to Roxane, who took a mental picture of the details: Jean-Louis Candela, 12 Quai du Louvre.

'We set off immediately with the Cronos – our semi-rigid twin-engine 150 horsepower craft.'

'How many of you?'

'Three. That's standard. A crew leader, a pilot, and a diver.'

'Was it a difficult operation?'

'When you're battling torrential rain, that always makes life harder. Not to mention the 50 mph winds. Even so, we made it within two minutes. When it's winter and you're dealing with alkies or jumpers, you need to shift your arse. With the combination of the currents and the cold, you can go down in less than five minutes.'

'Did you spot the girl straight away?'

'Yes. The guy had been right about her drowning, but Myrielle, our diver, pulled her out without a problem.'

'What was the water temperature that evening?'

'Five or six degrees.'

'What kind of state was the girl in?'

'Pretty much how you'd expect for someone who's spent a good while naked in five- or six-degree water. She was frozen stiff, having mild trouble breathing, and in shock.'

Jean-Baptiste paused and took a long slug of coffee. Roxane shaded her eyes as beads of sunlight ricocheted off the Seine. The sky was uncommonly clear. On the horizon she could see the twin metallic arches of the Pont de Sully, and further out the western tip of Île Saint-Louis and the convalescent towers of Notre-Dame.

'Was it you that took her to hospital?'

'First we stopped to debrief at the Quai de Conti. When we arrived, some guys from the Sainte-Geneviève station in the 5th arrondissement were there already. We'd called them about a drone that was flying over the Senate. Those things are the bane of our lives at the moment. We get at least one alert a day. They hadn't tracked down the culprits, but they did offer to help us. Hôtel-Dieu's just along from there. We unloaded the girl at the Quai aux Fleurs and they took her to A&E.'

'She went through A&E? I thought she'd been taken straight to the forensic medical unit.'

The frogman grimaced.

'Given the risk of infection, it was best to get her checked out.'

'I thought the water was less manky now. Didn't Hidalgo promise we'd be able to swim in there in time for the Olympics?'

'It's been dirtier,' he confirmed. 'But there's still a lot of bacterial pollution. You can catch any number of bugs from it – all sorts of E. coli that'll give you the runs and urinary tract infections. And the piss and dead rats floating in the water can cause serious cases of Leptospira.'

'Even if you're only in there for a few minutes?'

'The issue in the girl's case was her tattoos. They looked very recent, and that significantly increases the risk of skin infection.'

Roxane thought she'd misheard amid the din coming from a group of mechanics who were busying themselves around a tugboat, muffling Jean-Baptiste's words.

'The girl had tattoos?'

'On her ankles, yes.'

The tattoos were a major lead. Catherine Aumonier hadn't said anything about them. The I3P team really had done a shit job.

'As she was naked, it was hard not to notice them. But what struck me is that it looked like they'd been done in a rush.'

'What were they of?'

Jean-Baptiste narrowed his eyes as he summoned the memory.

'The first one's easy – it was ivy leaves winding around her ankle. The other one was more obscure. It made me think of some kind of spotted animal fur, but more like a fawn than a leopard. I can try drawing it for you, if that'd help?'

'Please!'

Louise Veyron, who'd stayed mute throughout the interview, produced a notebook and pen from her bag. While Jean-Baptiste was rendering the tattoo as best he could, Roxane put her final questions to him.

'The girl had a watch on, didn't she?'

'And a bracelet.'

Something else the I3P team had missed.

'How do you reckon she ended up there? Was she pushed or did she jump?'

'How should I know? There were no obvious marks of violence on her, in any case.'

He took the time to finish off his drawings, then spoke in a sneering tone.

'Maybe she appeared there by magic. As if the river had puked her up itself.'

3.

Half an hour later, Roxane was hammering on the door of a small apartment in Rue du Commandant-Rivière, in the Saint-Philippe-du-Roule neighbourhood.

'Police!'

Judging by her buttoned-up parka, scarf-clad neck and the handbag slung over her shoulder, the young woman who opened the door was all set to leave. She was of Slavic appearance, with pale skin and a face that remained deadened in spite of her make-up.

'Captain Montchrestien. I'm looking for Anthony Moraes.'

'Tony's just left,' the woman informed her.

'Who are you?'

'His girlfriend. Well, you could say that.'

'Can I come in?'

'No. Why?'

Roxane stole a glance through the doorway, getting wafts of the still-tepid smells of the night. The apartment consisted of two tiny attic rooms knocked together. By the looks of it, the I3P security officer wasn't there.

'Where is Moraes?'

'In the same bar he's always in.'

'Which is?'

'La Cavalina, on the corner.'

'What's your name?' Roxane demanded.

'"Please" would be nice . . .'

'Cut the crap. Your name?'

'Stella Janacek.'

'Right, listen Stella. If within the next ten minutes you warn your bloke I've been here, your life will become very complicated. Got that?'

The threat seemed to have the desired effect. Or at least, that's what Roxane inferred from the way the girl nodded, as if to say, *You think I'd risk my neck for that waste of space?*

Roxane shot down the stairs three at a time. She wanted to catch the security officer unawares. When she reached Rue du Faubourg Saint-Honoré, it wasn't hard to find the brasserie. It was a trendy-looking place, with black frontage, gold frieze, and patio heaters toasting a small terrace bordered by artificial shrubbery. She scanned outside without locating Anthony Moraes, whose photo she'd tracked down on his social media pages, then ventured inside. She finally spotted him sitting at a table behind the glass partition, glued to his phone screen.

'Hi, Tony,' she said, taking the chair opposite.

The I3P man gave a start and fumbled his phone into his jacket pocket. He was short, with a round face, a sallow complexion and hulking dark eyebrows that converged above the bridge of his nose.

'Who are you?'

'Captain Montchrestien, from the BNRF.'

'What have I done now?'

'I'd like you to fill me in on your mishap yesterday.'

'I already told them everything in my interview.'

'No, you just answered a few questions for an incident report. That's nothing like an interview.'

'Same difference. I told the truth. There's no way I'm taking the rap for this. The I3P's chronically understaffed. Ask anyone! Aumonier should never have let me do the transfer alone.'

'Point taken. No one's blaming you. I just want to know how it happened.'

Moraes sighed and downed his espresso before starting his account, in a tone that implied he couldn't wait to get it over with.

'Cotard's a tiny place, without a courtyard or car park. I had to double-park in Rue Froidevaux, then the girl legged it as soon as I opened the ambulance door. That's it.'

'But the nurses had sedated her.'

'Yeah, a couple of shots of Loxapac. Those should have knocked her out. And she was out of it, on the way there.'

'How did she get away?'

'She went for me like a fucking maniac!'

As he spoke, he pointed to a deep gash to the left of his monobrow.

'How did she do that?'

'Kicked me! The bitch!' His voice rose in anger. 'When we're transferring patients, normally we give them their clothes back. But since she didn't have any, the infirmary sorted her out with some pyjamas, a puffa jacket and a pair of Crocs.'

Roxane left a long silence before chancing her only trump card.

'My theory's that you tried to steal her watch.'

'You what?'

'And she gave you a good clouting to stop you.'

'Total rubbish.'

Moraes made to get up, but Roxane clamped a hand on his shoulder to force him back to his seat.

'When I got here, you were scrolling through Chrono24 – a specialist app for selling second-hand watches.'

'So? That's not illegal!'

'You were trying to offload the watch you stole.'

Moraes gave a dismissive snort.

'Look, let me make this easy for you, Tony. One call from me and your future in the force goes down the pan. If this gets out, you'll land up with a criminal record and zero chance of getting another job in security. You've put yourself in a very sticky situation.'

'Fuck off!'

'Your choice.'

Hunched inside his jacket, the I3P officer crossed his arms and sank into his chair.

'I've not got it anymore – the watch,' he muttered tetchily. 'I left it with a dealer.'

'You don't hang about, do you?'

'I dropped it off last night at a second-hand shop on Rue Marbeuf.'

Roxane knew a few places that could fit the bill.

'Which one? Romain Réa, MMC?'

'No, another a few doors down. Time Regained.'

'Like the Proust title?'

'Huh?'

'Forget it. Nothing else you want to get off your chest, Tony?'

Moraes shook his head like a sullen teenager.

'In that case, skedaddle so I can have a coffee in peace.'

4.

To celebrate her minor victory, Roxane ordered herself a double espresso and a side of biscotti. As she waited for her breakfast to arrive, she checked the opening hours of Time Regained on her phone. It didn't open until 11 a.m., leaving her with half an hour to kill. She couldn't resist tapping Valentine Diakité's name into Google, but apparently the PhD student was one of the few people of her age who didn't have any digital existence. She decided to give her a call. Valentine was still in the hospital lobby, looking out for a doctor who could update her on Marc Batailley's condition.

'I've got a job for you.'

'Always happy to oblige!'

'I'd like you to ring round the main tattoo parlours in Paris to see if any of them have recently worked on a pair of wraparound ankle tattoos – one of an ivy wreath and the other of spotted animal fur.'

'I'm not sure I picture what you mean.'

'I'll ping you a couple of sketches.'

'Perfect!'

As she sipped her coffee, Roxane made a series of calls to

identify the company that managed the 12 Quai du Louvre apartments. When she got through to the right place, she was informed that none of the landlords or tenants in the block went by the name of Jean-Louis Candela. Apparently, the guy who'd called the River Brigade that evening had done so under a false name. That didn't prove much in itself – when people contacted the police out of the blue, it was pretty commonplace for them to use pseudonyms or with-hold their identities. Ordinarily, Roxane could have asked them to trace the number. She'd have made inquiries with the neighbours and studied the footage from all the CCTV around the Pont Neuf. But she had neither the team nor the authorisation to pursue the case. Her investigation didn't exist. That was both her lucky break, and her biggest obstacle.

Just as she was settling the bill her phone vibrated. Botsaris's angular face flashed up on the screen.

'Roxane? I asked Crunchy to run your DNA profile through the national database.'

'And?'

'They found a match with someone called Milena Bergman.'

Butterflies stirred in her stomach. She'd managed to give the Stranger in the Seine a name.

'A German musician,' Botsaris clarified.

Milena Bergman . . .

The name was familiar to her. She'd come across it the previous evening in the clock tower, while nosing through Batailley's music collection. Milena Bergman was one of the pianists he had on CD!

'What's she on file for?'

'Some historic offence. Stole a Bulgari handbag from a

shop in Avenue Montaigne back in 2011. She was a bit of a klepto at the time.'

Holding her assistant on the line, Roxane plugged in her earpiece and loaded Wikipedia on her phone browser. There was an entry on the pianist. Without reading the text, she studied the photo: a young blonde woman with hair like Debussy's Mélisande, who tallied with the forensic medical team's description.

'How did you end up with her DNA?' Botsaris grilled.

From his tone, Roxane could tell he sensed trouble coming. She opted for the truth.

'She was pulled from the Seine two days ago by the River Brigade.'

'What?'

'All the hallmarks of a suicide attempt. She was taken to the I3P, but did a runner while they were transferring her.'

'I'd be flabbergasted if that was her.'

'Why?'

Botsaris paused for a few seconds before replying.

'Because Milena Bergman died a year ago.'

Milena Bergman

Milena Bergman was a German–Swedish pianist, born on 7 July 1989 in Linköping. She was killed in an air accident on 8 November 2019 off the coast of the Portuguese island of Madeira.

Biography

The only child of a German aerospace engineer and a Swedish music teacher, Bergman lived in Sweden until 1996, when the family moved to Hamburg. She began learning the piano under her mother's tuition before going on to study at the Johannes-Brahms-Konservatorium and the Hochschule für Musik und Theater München, where she was taught by Margarita Anke.

As a student she also took part in several masterclasses in Italy, France and the US, working under greats such as Aldo Ciccolini and Regina Noack.

Over the course of her studies she picked up a raft of international accolades, including first prize at the Arthur Rubinstein International Piano Master Competition in Tel Aviv (2002), the Principality of Monaco's Médaille d'Or, and second prize at the International Tchaikovsky Competition (2007).

These propelled her into an international career as a concert pianist, performing alongside the world's foremost conductors in iconic concert venues such as the Moscow Conservatory's Great Hall, the Mariinsky Theatre in St Petersburg, the Berlin Philharmonie, Fondation Louis Vuitton in Paris, London's Royal Festival Hall, Carnegie Hall in

New York and Suntory Hall in Tokyo.

Her performance of Franz Schubert's eight *Impromptus*, released on disc by Deutsche Grammophon, was met with widespread critical and popular acclaim and became an instant benchmark for recordings of the piece.

Though best known for her renditions of Schubert, Milena Bergman was also a prominent performer of Debussy and Ravel, admired for her polished virtuoso technique and poetic, enveloping acoustics. Reputed for being a perfectionist, she made few recordings but gave regular concerts, particularly in Asia where she enjoyed substantial success.

Extremely private and only making rare media appearances, Milena Bergman often commented that her passion for the piano was not her be-all and end-all in life, and took several sabbaticals in her career to pursue studies, reading and equestrian sports.

She was one of the 178 victims of the Buenos Aires-Paris flight that sank off the coast of Madeira on 8 November 2019.

Discography

2007 – Franz Schubert: Impromptus D. 899 & D. 935
2009 – Franz Schubert: Sonatas D. 959 & D. 960
2011 – Johannes Brahms: Piano Concerto No. 2, NHK Symphony Orchestra (Tokyo)
2012 – Claude Debussy: Preludes – Books 1 and 2
2013 – Claude Debussy: Images – Books 1 and 2; Children's Corner
2015 – Maurice Ravel: Sonatas and Trio (with Renaud Capuçon and Yukiko Takahashi)
2016 – Mozart: Piano Concertos Nos. 23 and 26, Seoul

Philharmonic Orchestra, cond. Chung Myung-whun
2018 – Philip Glass: The Complete Piano Etudes
2020 – The Last Recording, Orquesta Filarmónica de Buenos Aires

This article is partially or wholly derived from the Wikipedia article in German entitled 'Milena Bergman' (see list of authors)

4

THE PASSENGER FROM
FLIGHT AF 229

1.

'You're from the police, I take it?'

Time Regained was a warren of a shop, tucked away between the luxury boutiques of Rue Marbeuf. Its décor and ambiance recalled the interior of a high-end saloon car, arranged like a small sitting room with pale leather chairs set around a burl walnut coffee table. The gently purring heating and smell of newness gave it a reassuring feel – an invitation to linger and admire the timepieces from the titans of the watchmaking world. At the back of the room, behind a green marble counter, the owner kept up the tone with his fitted coat, stitched pocket square, tortoiseshell glasses, and paisley waistcoat looped with a fob watch.

'I've been expecting you,' he added, by way of welcome.

'Really?'

'You're from the police, and you've come to see me about the Résonance.'

Roxane placed her tricolour badge on the counter.

'Guilty as charged on the first count. I'd like to ask you a few questions about a watch that someone called Anthony Moraes left with you yesterday evening.'

'That's precisely what I said: the Résonance.'

Roxane scowled. With his frock coat and pompous manner, he reminded her of the White Rabbit from *Alice in Wonderland*. She felt like giving him a good smacking.

'I alerted your colleagues from the 8th arrondissement as soon as the young man left my shop,' he affirmed, producing a small inlaid wooden box in front of her.

Inside was a platinum watch with a case eccentrically shaped like a flatback turtle.

'Why did you call the cops so fast? You were sure it had been stolen?'

'Indeed.'

She threw her arms up in frustration.

'And why was that?'

'Because this watch is one of a kind, and I sold it to its owner personally.'

Roxane nodded. Things were taking an interesting turn.

'Can I get you a coffee, Mademoiselle? Excuse me, I mean a coffee, *Captain*.'

'Please. Black, no sugar.'

While the White Rabbit was busying himself with the coffee machine, Roxane examined the watch up close. She'd never seen anything like it. On a pale-blue mother-of-pearl face, two perfectly symmetrical dials seemed to be gazing at each other in a mirror.

'That's the unique feature of this model,' the watchmaker

explained. 'It has two pendulums that always end up beating in unison.'

'What purpose does that serve?'

'None,' he smiled. 'It's just an astonishing feat of engineering. And above all a magnificent symbol.'

'A symbol of what?'

'Its first owner, the painter John Lorentz, saw two hearts ambling together.'

She liked the turn of phrase. It reminded her of that old Aragon poem: *Between your hands, I've put my heart, / With yours, look how it goes ambling!*

The watchmaker returned carrying two china cups on a silver tray.

'When Lorentz died, the watch was bought by the wife of the writer Romain Ozorski, who wanted it as a gift for him. She's the one that had it engraved on the back.'

Roxane turned the watch over to read the inscription: *You are at once both the quiet and the confusion of my heart.*

'It's from a letter Kafka wrote to Felice Bauer. Lovely, isn't it?'

The words had made something click inside her. Suddenly, she too was struck by the majesty and poetry of the watch, seized by the same desire to wear it and feel the body of the timepiece pulsing against her wrist and electrifying her heart.

'After they divorced Ozorski was keen to get rid of the watch,' the owner continued, 'so I acquired it from him on behalf of one of my clients.'

'Who was that?'

'I'm sworn to professional secrecy.'

Roxane rolled her eyes heavenwards.

'As far as I'm aware, you're not a judge, a doctor or a lawyer.'

The White Rabbit quickly abandoned his resistance.

'My client is an admirer of Ozorski – the novelist Raphaël Batailley.'

Roxane replaced her cup on the tray, wrong-footed.

'Any connection with Superintendent Marc Batailley?'

'Indeed. He's his son. Haven't you read his books?'

She shook her head. What was Batailley's son doing mixed up in all this?

'So the watch belongs to Raphaël Batailley?'

'That's right.' The watchmaker retrieved his phone from his coat pocket. 'I tried to get hold of him yesterday evening, actually. He didn't pick up, but I left a message.'

'And did he call you back?'

'No.'

Roxane motioned with her index finger for him to hand over the iPhone. Making the most of his cooperativeness, she brought up Raphaël Batailley's contact information, which also included the novelist's address: The Glass House, 77a Rue d'Assas, in the 6th arrondissement.

'The Glass House?'

'As it says on the tin. The house was built by an American architect in the sixties, and Mr Batailley acquired it from him. It's a sight to behold, so I believe.'

Roxane returned to the watch, slipping it over her wrist.

'How much is a piece like this worth?'

'A small fortune.'

She took out the Stranger's photo.

'This watch was recovered from the wrist of a young woman who was pulled out of the Seine in the early hours of Sunday morning. Does her face ring any bells?'

'She's a pretty girl. Has a look of Arthur Hughes's *Ophelia*.'

'But you've never seen her before?'

The White Rabbit shook his head and pointed at the watch.

'Don't forget to give that back, before you go.'

'No can do. It's coming with me. And rest assured, I'll see it's restored to its owner!'

2.

From the Pont de l'Alma, Roxane caught an RER train to the Pont du Garigliano stop that serviced Pompidou hospital. She took advantage of the journey to call Johan Moers back.

'There's a major issue with your DNA results.'

'What's that?'

'They've come up as a match for a dead woman, even though the hair came from a girl who was pulled out of the Seine alive two days ago.'

'If there's a mistake, it's nothing to do with me,' objected Moers.

'Run them through again anyway. *Yourself*, not your assistant.'

'Right,' he sighed.

'And see what you can get from the urine sample. I've already asked you once.'

On her phone browser she launched into a quick information-gathering mission on Raphaël Batailley. He was a good-looking guy, forty years old and already with an established writing career behind him. His bibliography was prolific, spanning over twenty titles covering a motley of genres, from crime fiction to horror and children's books. Preferring to keep a low profile, he had a hard core of readers who stayed loyal to him, whatever he was working on. Their devotion and his eclectic output had enabled him to carve out a niche in the French literary landscape, distancing himself from the self-absorbed fatuities of the St Germain-des-Prés clique and the treadmill of the bestseller market. His latest novel was called *The Shyness of Mountaintops*. Taken by the title, Roxane bought the ebook on impulse and resolved to make a start on it later.

The hospital was a sprawling geometric structure on the banks of the Seine, built on Quai André-Citroën and flanked by the Périphérique ring road. It comprised a dozen or so somewhat discordant glass buildings, which were interlinked around a glass-roofed courtyard. Though barely twenty years old, its modern trappings already felt tired and grubby. Just like the city itself.

Roxane spent a long time wandering around the atrium before locating the signs for the ICU. After taking the lift to the first floor, she found a nursing assistant who gave her Marc Batailley's room number, then navigated her way through a maze of corridors congested with metal trolleys until she reached No. 18. She scanned the board on the door, which displayed the patient's name, clinical status, course of treatment and test results to date. Through the glass she spotted Valentine, who waved her over. Roxane tentatively pushed open the door and entered.

Batailley had been lucky enough to get a room to himself – even if, at that precise moment, it was doing him a fat lot of good. He was lying intubated, and had been rolled onto his front to assist his breathing. Through the tangle of transparent tubes, his appearance tallied with how Roxane had imagined him. A huge frame with a shaggy mop of salt-and-pepper hair, deep wrinkles, and a week's worth of stubble. The bed was ringed by an ECG monitor, a flotilla of drips, and a ventilator that was droning oxygen into the patient like an accordion only capable of wheezing out the same dreary note.

From her seat at his bedside, Valentine looked up at Roxane with tear-filled eyes.

'I saw a doctor,' she announced in a quavery voice. 'There's been no improvement in his condition. He has a punctured lung and multiple fractures to his skull, ribs and vertebrae.'

Roxane pulled up a chair from the other side of the bed to join the student. She fumbled for some words of consolation. Finding nothing, she ploughed on with her investigation.

'Are you familiar with Milena Bergman?'

'Yeah, of course,' Valentine replied, dabbing her eyes. 'She was the girlfriend of Marc's son, Raphaël. She died in that plane crash that was all over the news.'

Roxane gulped. Ever since she'd arrived, her throat had been clogged with the mingled hospital fug of disinfectant, meds and lousy food.

'Why are you asking about her?'

'Because the DNA samples you took to Johan Moers . . . are a match for Milena's.'

Valentine almost leapt from her chair. Her face was a picture of incredulity.

'Seriously? How's that possible?'

'Exactly. It *isn't* possible.'

Roxane glanced at 'her' watch before continuing.

'Did you ever see Milena in real life?'

'No. She died before I met Marc, but he often brought her up in conversation. He talked about her with a lot of pride. Raphaël was devastated by her death. Marc said it was a comfort to be living with him, that he'd have been scared what the grief might have driven him to do, otherwise.'

'What about him – *the writer* – have you met?'

'Yeah, he's a great guy. Kind, funny, intelligent. And gorgeous to boot, don't you think?

Roxane made a noncommittal gesture.

'Not really my type.'

The mention of Raphaël Batailley had perked Valentine up no end. Her face was now lit in a starry-eyed smile, like a real groupie.

'This romance with the pianist, when did it start?'

Valentine thought for a moment.

'I'd say about a year before the crash. Last month there was an article about their relationship in *Week'nd* magazine. Raphaël got really upset about it, because the story had never gone public before.'

'Who leaked it?'

'That's the thing. Nobody knows.'

Roxane stood up. She felt suffocated. Hospitals had always had that effect on her. It was as though death was closing in from all sides with its grim cortège of sounds – the beeping of monitors, the metallic jolt of trolleys, the thud of rubber clogs on ageing lino. And the absurd ghostly figures that haunted the place in their faded papery gowns.

'Here's one thing I don't understand,' Roxane continued. 'Why isn't Batailley Junior here? I tried ringing him on my way, but he's not answering.'

'Chances are he doesn't even know what's happened to his dad. When he's writing, he often goes off alone for weeks at a time without telling anyone where he is.'

'The guy really fancies himself as an artist.' Roxane rolled her eyes.

'Have you read his books?'

The cop shook her head.

'I only read dead authors.'

'The height of snobbery.'

'Over time you learn to sift out the chaff. Have *you* read them?'

'Most of them. I love his writing. All his books are dedicated to his sister, who died when she was four.'

Roxane recalled what Sorbier had told her.

'I've heard something about that.'

'Marc was a police legend, you know.'

'Yeah, so I'm told. Headed up the Marseille Major Crime squad back in the nineties, all that jazz about the mythical "Horticulturalist" serial killer.'

Valentine looked at her disapprovingly, like the guardian of the Batailley family legend.

'Marc was married to an ex-dancer from the Marseille National Ballet. They lost their daughter in tragic circumstances.'

'What happened?'

'It was really awful.' She gestured to the motionless body in the bed. 'I'd rather not say in front of him. After the tragedy they separated, and Batailley was given a transfer to Paris.'

'A properly screwed-up family.'

'You're heartless, Captain.'

'I'm not, but I could murder a coffee. Could you get me one? And please, drop the formalities.'

Roxane had come there with one aim in mind, but she needed to be alone to pull it off. Obediently, Valentine got up and retrieved some change for the vending machine from her bag.

'How do you take it?'

'Black, no sugar.'

'I could've bet on it!'

As soon as the student had gone, Roxane made straight for the only cupboard in the room. Inside were Batailley's personal items – a pair of jeans, some boots, a shirt, a V-neck sweater, a black-and-red Seiko UFO watch from the seventies. And, draped on a hanger, a battered leather trench coat containing his wallet, his still-charged iPhone, and a bunch of keys. Roxane slipped all three into the pockets of her jeans.

'Stealing from the sick, eh?'

The voice made her start. An ICU doctor had just entered the room, no doubt to administer the latest round of meds. He was a lanky redhead, with a flaming crew cut and tiny marble-round green eyes.

'I'm just picking up the keys so I can bring him some clean clothes,' she protested.

'Yeah . . . Given the state of him, I doubt he'll be needing his glad rags any time soon.'

'He won't be like this forever, will he?'

The doctor didn't mince his words.

'Your mate's body is in shreds. The ambulance team practically had to spoon him off the floor. With all the bleeding and fractures, there's a strong possibility he won't pull through.'

He checked Batailley's vital signs on the ECG monitor, took his sats, untangled the catheters.

'This afternoon the surgeons are going to try operating on one of his vertebrae,' he announced. 'We'll see how that goes before making any grand plans.'

He left the room smirking like a hard-bitten schoolmaster, just as Valentine reappeared from her trip to the vending machine.

'I just thought of something,' she said as she handed Roxane a paper cup. 'What if Milena had a twin sister? That would explain why the DNA was an exact match, wouldn't it?'

'Nah, forget it. The whole twin thing is just something you see in detective dramas. And not good ones.'

'You could make a few calls anyway, just to rule it out.' Valentine's tone was wounded.

'You just worry about the tattoos for now. It's less fun, but more useful.'

'I've already rung loads of places, but no joy. Ivy wreaths aren't a common request. People prefer laurels, as the symbol of victory. None of them have had people wanting deer or fawn fur either. Stag heads, at a push, to symbolise domination and rebirth.'

'Keep digging,' Roxane instructed as she pushed open the door. 'Meanwhile, I'm off to hunt down Raphaël Batailley.'

3.

The taxi was wedged in traffic in Rue de Vaugirard. On a rampage, the driver was railing against 'middle-class lefties and their bloody cycle lanes', 'fuckwit tree huggers' and the Mayor of Paris, who, so he claimed, had overseen the capital's demise 'from the City of Light into the City of Shite'. The local elections might have been over, but the guy was still hot on the campaign trail.

'Have you heard of Paris Syndrome?' he asked, glancing at Roxane in the rearview mirror.

He didn't wait for her reply before launching into his theory.

'It's a kind of intense psychological shock some foreign tourists experience when they visit Paris. They've been sold Amélie Poulain, *Emily in Paris* and the dreaming spires of Montmartre, and instead they find themselves broken down in skanky RER trains, fending off druggies in Porte de la Chapelle, and wading along the banks of Mother Hidalgo's open-air pissers.'

Roxane couldn't suppress a smile. Plugging in her phone earbuds, she pressed play on *The Last Recording*. The final commercial album to have been released by Milena Bergman's record label, it featured the complete soundtrack from the concert she'd performed at the Teatro Colón in Buenos Aires, accompanied by the city's Orquesta Filarmónica. Two days later, the pianist was to perish in one of the deadliest civilian crashes in the history of French aviation.

Roxane had downloaded several articles from assorted newspapers to jog her memory. Straining over the small screen of her iPhone, she tried to retain as many details as possible.

Air France Flight 229 had gone down in the sea on 8 November 2019, killing all 178 people on board, including ten crew members.

Given the recentness of the accident, multiple court battles were still underway. In France, there had been two major lines of inquiry: the first of these related to the 'legal' charge of manslaughter, and the second to the 'technical' case, headed up by the country's civil aviation accident investigation board, the BEA.

Behind the reams of reports and expert assessments, everyone seemed to agree on a number of facts. When it lost contact, the aircraft was somewhere over the ocean between Tenerife and Madeira. It had left Buenos Aires shortly after lunch, and was due to land in Paris at 7 a.m. local time. The flight had been fraught with difficulty, appalling weather conditions and successive storms provoking turbulence throughout. The vast majority of planes scheduled to fly over the area where the accident occurred had changed path, but this wasn't the decision taken by the captain of Flight 229.

After some outlandish initial hypotheses – the plane had been hijacked by terrorists, a lightning strike had triggered a complete electricity failure, hackers had remotely seized control of the aircraft – the BEA's reports had cast a more rational light on the incident. A storm at high altitude had caused ice crystals to form on the sensors, and this freezing of the measuring instruments had temporarily disrupted the airspeed indicator in the cockpit and shut down the autopilot system.

Euphemistically, the reports described 'inappropriate reactions from the pilots'. In layman's terms, it was obvious the unfolding drama had totally passed them by. The black box recordings were chilling, revealing panic in the cockpit as the situation spiralled out of control. The pilots didn't have the slightest grip on what was happening.

True to form, in a blaze of virtue-signalling one of the tabloids had led a witch-hunt against the cockpit team, trawling through their private lives to expose a 'wretched little pile of secrets'. Under the guise of investigative journalism, nothing was off limits: mistresses, divorces, bouts of therapy, sleeping pill addictions, party lifestyles, visits to strip clubs in La Recoleta. All of them had some shameful skeleton in the closet. However cheap the tactics, there was no denying the facts: none of the three pilots had been able to halt the plane's descent, and they had let it plunge until it smashed into the sea.

In the report's concluding pages, it came almost as a relief to learn that most of the passengers would have had no idea the plane was in trouble. It was night, the blinds were down, and many of them had their seatbelts unfastened.

Everything had happened extremely quickly. Fewer than three minutes had elapsed between the plane starting to lose height and the moment it bombed through the surface of the water. Those on board had died instantly. The debris had sunk, but the area was shallow enough for the black boxes to be located before they stopped emitting their ultrasonic signal. Within a few months, a large part of the wreckage had been recovered. Of the 178 victims, the bodies of 121 had been pulled from the water and returned to their families.

Among them was Milena Bergman.

5

INSIDE THE GLASS HOUSE

1.

From Rue d'Assas, the entrance to Raphaël Batailley's house was easy to miss. The approach was through an iron security gate, which gave access to a narrow passageway that skirted the pharmacy faculty botanical garden for a good sixty feet before leading out onto a leafy shared courtyard. With its assortment of trees and plants, it gave an illusion of rurality rarely found in Paris. From her memories of her grandmother's garden, Roxane recognised an oleander hedge, two tall silver limes, a maple tree and even an unlikely gingko, clinging to the last of its striking topaz leaves. Finally, from behind a high curtain of bare plane trees, the Glass House presented itself before her.

The watchmaker hadn't been lying. Batailley's home was a vast transparent parallelepiped, grafted onto a modest three-storey building in yellow brick. Roxane had read in the taxi that the structure had indeed been built in the sixties by an American architect – William Glass – who had decided to set up home in Paris. A theoretician whose creations mirrored his name, Glass was obsessed with transparency, and had worked on several high-profile projects: the glass theatre in Copenhagen, the Bilbao School of Architecture, the Green Cross company headquarters in New York . . . the list went on.

Roxane walked the perimeter of the building. There seemed to be no one about. The house's tour de force was its simplicity, the purity of its lines. It was a minimalist's dream. A basic matte-grey steel frame supporting a series of windows that took the place of walls. Surprisingly, from the garden it was hard to discern much of the interior, with the sky, sunlight, clouds and branches bouncing off each other in a hypnotic, constantly shifting game of reflections.

As she neared the block of frosted glass that served as a front door, Roxane heard a click and watched in stupefaction as the pane swung back to let her in. One of the keys she'd taken from the hospital must have been fitted with an electronic chip, automatically unlocking the doors when the owner came within range.

She stepped inside to find herself in a kind of loft. She'd never seen a configuration like it. There were no walls anywhere. Instead, the space was portioned off by low, elongated raw-wood units, offering an unbroken view through the rest of the building from wherever you stood. *360-degree living*, she thought as she continued across the red-brick floor. With its herringbone pattern and burnished finish, it was like parquet reimagined in terracotta.

What had she come hoping to find? Even she didn't have the faintest idea. She wanted to sniff out the place, she supposed, since houses often conveyed the characters of those who lived there. And right now, the Batailley family inter-ested her as much as Milena Bergman. Above all, she was keen to cling to the investigation for as long as possible. It had come at her like a lifebuoy from the blue. Just when Sorbier, Botsaris and the rest had thought they could freeze her out, fate – the same bastard fate that had kicked the legs out from under her innumerable times – had launched her on the scent of an exceptional case, intriguing and impene-trable in equal measure.

She imagined herself retracing the Batailleys' steps, saun-tering through the house as if in her own home. Her initial impression was of being in a small private gallery. Like his father, the writer had good taste. The artwork – sculptures and paintings – inhabited the space with disquieting grace. She recognised an immense piece in the typical style of the sculptor Bernar Venet – disfigured patinated steel circles that seemed to coil around each other in an infinite whorl. Then a minotaur sculpted from rusty iron mesh, and a large Hans Hartung lithograph featuring bold swirls and hatching on a backdrop of midnight blue.

The jewel in the crown, however, was the view of outside. The way the building opened onto the surrounding vege-tation made the plants feel like part of the house. Roxane couldn't help wondering why the novelist didn't use such an enchanting setting to write.

Nearly all the walls and bookcases were scattered with photos of him and the pianist. Milena and Raphaël in New York, Milena and Raphaël skiing in Courchevel, Milena and Raphaël basking on the Côte d'Azur. The variations were endless. With the wind in their hair and smiles on their faces, the couple paraded their love, radiating a happiness that was perhaps a little overplayed. The kind of happiness that's more for the benefit of others than oneself. *Come off it*, Roxane told herself. She was just thinking that way out of envy, ashamed by her own descent into mediocrity, resentful that her own romantic history was an unmitigated shitshow. The truth was that Milena Bergman had a rare beauty. Ticking every cliché in the book, with her blonde hair like a halo of stardust, she exuded an aura of ethereal melancholy and consummate gracefulness. The truth, quite simply, was that Roxane was jealous. As she acknowledged this, she felt a pang for the pianist and her gruesome fate.

The room was freezing. The heating must have been buried underfloor, because there were no radiators, no doubt for aesthetic reasons. Instead, a gas fireplace stretched along a low stone wall. She hit the ignition switch, and immediately high orange flames began waltzing over the bed of white pebbles.

The lure of the fire made her loiter. On one of the two lounge chairs that flanked the hearth, under an old waffle-knit cardigan, she discovered a copy of the *Week'nd* issue Valentine had mentioned. A blend of news, lifestyle and celebrity gossip, the magazine fancied itself as a high-end publication, pitching somewhere between *Vanity Fair* and *M*, *Le Monde*'s glossy Sunday supplement. It lay open on the page of the article that, a year on from the Buenos Aires–Paris crash, had revealed Milena and Raphaël's relationship to the world.

For her amusement, as though to summon Raphaël Batailley's presence, she slipped on the cardigan. It had a subtle scent of iodine mingled with bitter orange. Flopping into the chair, she thumbed through the article with a regressive pleasure she never normally allowed herself, even at the hairdressers.

She could see why the article had put Raphaël's back up, reviving his grief by transforming a personal tragedy into gossip fodder. She could also understand why Raphaël Batailley and Milena Bergman had been drawn to each other: both were popular in their respective fields, yet kept themselves to themselves; artists who lived off their craft while practising it in the margins, far from the hallowed spotlight. Milena wasn't as idolised as other stars of her generation – the likes of Hélène Grimaud, Khatia Buniatishvili and Yuja Wang – but nor did she seek to be. She constantly reiterated that her passion for the piano wasn't her be-all and end-all in life.

The article instantly raised two questions in Roxane's mind. Why had it only emerged now? And who'd tipped off the journo, a guy called Corentin Lelièvre, granting him access to private photos along with a raft of personal anecdotes? A thought occurred to her. She fired up a search on her phone and, via the main magazine desk, managed to get Lelièvre on the other end of the line. Obnoxious and cagey, the hack clearly thought he was France's answer to Bob Woodward. After putting Roxane in her place with a lecture about never betraying one's sources, he hung up in her face.

Mustering all her strength to keep calm, she resolved to find another way through at a later juncture. While she had her phone out, she tried the novelist's number again. To her surprise, a muffled ringtone sounded in the room. Following the noise, she found Raphaël's iPhone stashed in the drawer of a walnut desk, alongside his passport, car keys, a cheque book and a magnetic card for André-Honnorat car park. She tried swiping the screen, just in case, but it promptly went dead.

Weird that Batailley left without his phone.

2.

Still swaddled in Batailley's cardigan, Roxane returned to her chair by the fireplace. As she lay back and closed her eyes, scenes from the plane crash filed through her mind. The terror, the screaming, the brutal realisation that death was moments away. She had to go back to the start: the identification of Milena's body. That was the only way she could be sure. She pondered for several minutes how best to play it. She struggled to navigate the web of departments that made up the French police force, which boasted a complexity that was cripplingly counter-productive. Even the most basic inquiry would be met by a wall of Kafkaesque bureaucracy, squabbling between units, and levels of inertia that only the French civil service could achieve.

Refusing to lose heart, she ran a mental inventory of her contacts at the IRCGN, the National Gendarmerie's forensic science unit. As her entry point, she finally settled on Bertrand Passeron – aka 'Nougaro' in a nod to the singer from his home city – a Toulousian who was a veteran of the National Crime Scene Squad, or UNIC for short. She doubted he could feed her any information directly, but he might be able to hook her up with another department. Crucially, she knew she'd been in his good books since their brief stint working together on the fallout from the Dupont de Ligonnès family murder case, one of the biggest cock-ups in the BNRF's history.

'Hellooo, Roxane,' he trilled down the phone.

Passeron could only have been a few months away from retirement, and had worked in Paris for his whole career, but he still spoke with a broad, singsong, south-western accent.

Roxane explained she was looking for details about the identification of the Buenos Aires–Paris victims.

'Ouf, it's the U2I that deals with that kind of thing.'

This was the answer Roxane had been expecting. The Gendarmerie's Investigation and Identification Unit was a response team that had been set up almost thirty years earlier, in the aftermath of the Mont Saint-Odile air disaster. They were dispatched to the scene every time there was a major tragedy – plane crashes, serious road accidents, terrorist attacks abroad – where French victims were involved.

'Do you have a contact there who could give me some intel on one of the bodies they identified?'

'Depends. What exactly are you after?'

'I'd just like to check on a couple of things.'

'I'll see what I can do,' Nougaro promised. 'Bear with me.'

As she hung up, Roxane told herself the subterfuge couldn't last much longer. Over the previous few hours, she'd managed to call in favours only because her interlocutors were under the impression they were collaborating with the BNRF. Sooner or later, though, word of her fall from grace would get round. In the meantime, she still had a few days in which to pursue her inquiries with free rein, without tripping over red tape at every turn. And she was resolved to make the most of them.

A flurry of text notifications jolted her from her musings.

Valentine. The student had called Deutsche Grammophon, then Milena's agent. As Roxane had suspected, the pianist emphatically didn't have a twin sister, or any siblings for that matter. Her father was long dead, and her mother had remarried and now lived in Dresden with a retired teacher.

Call Raphaël Batailley's publishers to see if they know where he is, Roxane instructed.

She closed her eyes again, letting the warmth and silence of the room restore her train of thought. She'd been right to jump straight on the case. Nevertheless, she needed some distance to grasp the ins and outs. There was a lot of context, and without a team to help her, she didn't have the luxury of covering every base. To make headway, she had to re-focus on two priorities: identifying the girl, and tracking her down.

'What are you doing here?'

Roxane snapped her eyes open and shot upright. A woman was standing in front of her, brandishing a steam mop and bucket. She looked to be in her forties, with peroxide-blonde hair and thick-lensed cat-eye glasses. She was kitted out in a yellow T-shirt and denim dungarees that gave her a look of the comedian Coluche, and spoke with a distinctive Gironde twang.

'I'm from the police, Madame,' Roxane explained, pulling out her badge.

'And what right does that give you to be lounging on the furniture? Who gave you permission to enter the property?'

'My investigation.'

'Do you have a search warrant?'

The woman was a tough customer. Roxane attempted to turn the tables.

'Who are you, anyway?'

'Josefa Miglietti, the housekeeper. I come to clean here every Tuesday.'

She swung open a walnut dresser to reveal an assortment of cleaning products.

'I'm trying to find Raphaël Batailley, to let him know that his father suffered a very serious accident yesterday morning.'

'Really?' Josefa sounded genuinely upset.

'Do you know where he is?'

'I haven't seen him for at least a fortnight.'

Roxane showed her the *Week'nd* article.

'What about her? Is she familiar to you?'

'The pianist? Milly something-or-other?'

'That's the one. You haven't seen her around here recently?'

'Recently? She's been dead for a year! Not very quick off the mark, are you?'

'Or someone who looks like her?' Roxane ventured.

The housekeeper shook her head.

'The only time I ever spoke with her was over a year ago. She came to stay here for a few days.'

'When exactly would that have been?'

'Can't remember. Summer, maybe. It was during the time when they thought Mr Marc wasn't going to pull through from his lung cancer.'

'You haven't noticed anything suspicious around the premises these past couple of days?'

'Except you?'

'I'd have thought that was obvious!'

Josefa scratched her head.

'There was a journalist last week. Tried to interview me twice.'

'He came to the house?'

The housekeeper nodded.

'He said his name was Constantin Lelièvre, or something like that.'

'What did he want to know?'

'Pretty much the same as you, actually. He asked me about the pianist.'

Roxane felt her phone vibrate in her pocket. She took it out to discover a new message from Valentine:

R's editor says he's in London, but she doesn't know where he's staying.

'Anyway, you can clear off now. I've work to do!' Josefa wielded her mop handle, intimating that Roxane would be getting the raw end of it if she didn't comply.

The cop didn't need telling twice. Batailley wasn't in London. Since Brexit, you needed a passport to travel to the UK. The writer's was still in his desk. His editor was lying through her teeth, and Roxane was going to pay her a little visit. It was about time she gave that nest of fabulists a firm kicking.

3.

Roxane had tugged down her jumper sleeves in the vain hope of protecting her hands from the glacial temperatures. Blowing on her fingers for warmth, she lengthened her strides as cold-induced tears streamed down her cheeks. Fortunately, Raphaël Batailley didn't have to trek across Paris to reach his publishers. The route was fairly scenic too, taking in the Jardin des Grands-Explorateurs before cutting down Avenue de l'Observatoire onto Boulevard du Montparnasse. The final leg of the journey was along Rue Campagne-Première, one of Roxane's favourite streets in the city. She turned onto its slim pavements with a spring in her step. It was less edifying than the last time she'd been there. Once again, the area hadn't been spared by the scourge of redevelopment, and its colourful, lustrous facades were now jostling for space with soulless, grey structures clad in metal mesh.

Ugliness always triumphs . . .

It was one of the depressing, iron laws of their time. As she made her way up the street, memories rushed back. It was happening to her more and more often lately. Without warning, like a hot flush, a torrent of recollections would descend and invade her mind with fiendish vividness. She suddenly saw herself there, in that very street, one June evening in 1997, celebrating the end of her Baccalaureate exams and happily anticipating the start of her foundation year at Lycée Louis-le-Grand the following autumn.

It was the evening of the Fête de la Musique. The air was balmy. Jospin's Left had just swept to victory in the elections. A teenage rock band were performing a cover of 'Champagne Supernova' in front of Hôtel Istria. Back then, life had felt so full of promise and possibilities. Now it was just a blank wall staring back at her, a series of problems to resolve, a succession of blows to fend off without managing to land any in return. She'd written off any prospect of things getting better or finding personal fulfilment. She knew she was a lost cause. That the world had changed for good, and she could never recover her place in it.

She drew up outside number 13a, the three-storey,

rose-brick building where Éditions Fantine de Vilatte had its headquarters. After pressing the buzzer, she was admitted to a narrow, dimly lit entrance hall that led onto a paved court-yard. Around a central fountain overrun with ivy, a jumble of former artists' studios had been converted into office and living spaces. The publishing house occupied the largest of them – a building that had the feel of a greenhouse, with its glass roof covering the offices below.

'I'd like to speak with Fantine de Vilatte.'

'Without an appointment, I'm afraid that won't be possible.'

The young receptionist had a condescending tone that immediately rubbed Roxane up the wrong way. She took out her badge and slapped it down on the glass counter.

'It's the police asking, *love*. So get your arse off your chair and . . .'

'I'm Fantine de Vilatte,' announced a voice behind her.

The publisher beamed into view. She was a stylish woman in her sixties, draped in a bright shawl. Her ash-blonde hair was twisted into a chic braided chignon that gave her the aura of a medieval heroine.

'Captain Montchrestien from the BNRF. I'm looking for Raphaël Batailley in connection with an investigation.'

'And how can I be of assistance?'

'By telling me where he is, for a start.'

Fantine pulled the square of silk more tightly around her shoulders.

'Raph's in London. Staying in a hotel or holiday let, no doubt, but I have absolutely *no idea* where nor any way of finding out.'

Roxane was prepared for this reply. She thrust out the travel document she'd found at the house.

'He left his passport behind. Which means he's not in London, which means you're taking me for a mug, which means I'm going to get pissed off.'

Fantine de Vilatte flashed back a serene smile, her steely gaze conveying that she wasn't about to be intimidated.

'His father's just suffered a serious accident,' Roxane countered.

'I can't tell you anything, honestly. We have a bond of trust. When he's writing, Raph wishes to be left alone. I'm sure you're familiar with Thomas Mann's definition of a writer as "someone for whom writing is more difficult than it is for other people."'

Roxane changed tack.

'Do you know the pianist Milena Bergman?'

'Erm . . . by name.' The publisher wore a look of mild distaste. 'Not personally.'

'She was his girlfriend. Did dear "Raph" never introduce you?'

'No. Raphaël prefers to talk to me about his characters. For novelists like him, art is more important than life.'

Naw-velists . . . im-paww-tant. With her Parisian accent Fantine de Vilatte was the antithesis of Nougaro, drawling her 'o's and clipping her 't's with anal precision.

'If you say so,' rejoined Roxane. 'But at the end of the day, those are just words.'

'Yes, they are words. And don't underestimate their power, Madame.'

Roxane sighed. These people really were stuck up their own backsides.

'For many artists,' Fantine continued, 'writing is a form of escapism. That's the miracle of fiction – for a brief period it takes you away from reality. But I've no intention of debating that point with you.'

Vilatte had a ruthless sense of her own importance. And the worst thing was that she truly believed the crap she was spouting.

'I don't think you've understood the gravity of the situation. Marc Batailley is fighting for his life in hospital. What justification is there for denying his son the right to know?'

'You're putting me in an uncomfortable position.'

'No, that's the whole point. I'm trying to get you out of one. Mark my words, if Raphaël's father dies without him even being informed about him going into hospital, he'll never publish another book with you.'

This time, the argument seemed to hold. After a long silence, the publisher finally came clean.

'Raphaël is in a psychiatric clinic,' she said in a low voice.

From the outset Roxane had sensed something murky, and she wasn't disappointed.

'Where's he locked up?'

'He isn't *locked up*. He's staying there voluntarily.'

'You think I was born yesterday?'

'It's a place called the Fitzgerald, on the Cap d'Antibes. That's where Raph's taken to writing his books these past few years.'

'Why?'

'He likes the scenery, the feel of the place, being in such close proximity to mental illness. He finds it gives him a sense of dislocation that nourishes his writing.'

'You really do work with some nutters.'

'I wouldn't expect you to understand.'

'No, course not. We coppers are too thick for that.'

Roxane left Fantine de Vilatte and returned to the court-yard. Installing herself on a white stone bench by the fountain, she launched her browser and loaded the Air France website. At this time of day, there were flights to Nice departing from Orly every hour. If she got a shift on, she could make the 14.15. Her investigation was reaching a crossroads. She was now convinced that her quest to find Milena Bergman had to go via Raphaël Batailley. And she was determined to bring him back.

6

A WRITER IN THE MADHOUSE

1.

'Ladies and gentlemen, in preparation for landing please return to your seats, fasten your seatbelts, and ensure that all cabin baggage is safely stowed under the seat in front of you or in the overhead lockers. All doors and emergency exits must be kept clear. The weather in Nice is sunny, with a temperature of 16 degrees.'

With her forehead lolling against the window, Roxane struggled to return to her senses. Despite the adrenaline of the investigation, she'd been hit by a wave of tiredness as soon as the plane had taken off, and had slept for the whole flight. Her back ached. Her skull was throbbing with the beginnings of a migraine. Her clothes, which she hadn't changed since the previous day, were starting to drive her mad. She could feel the sweat leaching from her, like a fusty bedsheet in dire need of an iron.

Before they'd even touched down, she switched her phone back on, to discover a message from Lieutenant Colonel Najib Messaoudi, from the National Gendarmarie's disaster victim identification unit, inviting her to call him back. Nougaro had been as good as his word in playing the go-between. That alone was enough to buck her up. In her eagerness she almost called him back straight away, but resisted the urge. The scramble to exit the plane wasn't conducive to a clear-headed conversation.

On reaching the terminal, she flirted with renting a car before settling for a taxi. The Nice air was springlike, the sky a deep blue. Once the cab was cruising along the coastal road, she asked the driver to turn off the radio and dialled Najib Messaoudi's number. To keep the army man onside, she went in with a softly-softly approach.

'Thank you for taking the time to speak with me, Colonel. I won't keep you long. As part of an investigation I'm interested in finding out more about the Air France 229 crash, and I'd just like to verify a few things with you.'

'I'm listening.'

'I read that you'd recovered almost two thirds of the bodies.'

'That's right: 121, out of 178.'

'Who actually carried out the recovery operation?'

'Myself and my Gendarmerie colleagues, alongside the Portuguese army and the Argentinian interior ministry. The operation was staggered over six months, but most of the bodies were recovered in two phases. The first took place in the days following the crash, and the second once the cabin had been found, with the help of a submarine.'

'What kind of state were they in?'

'Well preserved, for the most part. The low water temperature and the pressure suspend the decomposition process. It's

THE STRANGER IN THE SEINE

only when you get them to the surface that the problems begin.'

'Because of the oxygen?'

'That's right. While the bodies are underwater, there's a saponification effect that blocks the normal putrefaction process. But as soon as the air gets to them, they deteriorate very quickly.'

Roxane lowered the window. The taxi had just passed the hippodrome in Cagnes-sur-Mer. It was a fine afternoon. Where the trunk road would have been logjammed in summer, the traffic was flowing easily, the sea and sky merging in a harmonious swathe of azure blue. The calm reminded her of the Riviera of yesteryear, contrasting with the grim subject matter.

'Then what?' Roxane asked. 'How do you set about identifying the victims?'

'We have two teams working on it. The post-mortem section, who collect DNA samples from the bodies that have been recovered, and the ante-mortem section, who contact the families to gather as much information as they can about the victims – including genetic data.'

'The BEA report said most of the passengers died instantly.'

'Yes,' Messaoudi confirmed. 'The craft was travelling at such a speed, it was smashed to pieces. You can tell that from some of the autopsies – the victims didn't die from drowning, but from multiple trauma.'

'Is there a chance anyone could have survived?'

'No, I can't see it.'

Having prepared the ground, Roxane cut to the chase.

'Look, I won't beat around the bush. I'm after details on one victim in particular: the pianist Milena Bergman.'

'You'll need to go through the official channels for that. I don't think I'll be able to give you that information over the phone.'

'What odds does it make, other than costing me time?'

'Those are the rules. Simple as that. Anything else?'

'Please, I'm begging you. I can't be doing with all the form-filling. It's such a headache. Is there really nothing you can tell me?'

Messaoudi sighed.

'What is it you'd like to know, Captain?'

'The date her body was recovered, for starters.'

She heard a mouse click at the other end of the line, then the tapping of keys.

'The twenty-first of April 2020, a few days after we located the largest section of the cabin. She was one of the victims whose bodies had remained fastened to their seats.'

'Was it easy to identify her?'

'Yes. We were spoilt for choice, to tell you the truth. It was a double identification. Firstly by comparing two DNA samples – the one collected from the body and the one the ante-mortem team had gathered – and then using the dental records her family had provided. We couldn't have asked for better.'

'Do you have photos of her body?'

'We do, but don't count on me sending them to you.'

'Was the body returned to her family?'

Another mouse click.

'Milena Bergman was cremated in Germany, in Dresden, on 18 May last year.'

2.

The taxi was now on the Cap d'Antibes coastal road, coursing towards the headland at Pointe de l'Ilette. With the pictur-esque scenery and the scent of pine trees, Roxane almost felt like she was on holiday. All that was missing was the chirp-ing of cicadas. She was still grappling with what Messaoudi had told her: Milena Bergman was dead. It was certainly possible. She'd been identified by the Gendarmerie's top experts and cremated. But then, why did the Stranger's hair sample match the DNA profile in the national database? She thought back to what Botsaris had said: Milena Bergman's details had ended up in there after she'd been caught stealing from a luxury boutique nine years earlier. Had there been a cock-up with genetic sampling around that time? Had the arrest made it into the papers? She'd have to check.

The driver pulled up in front of a high, soulless fence sur-veyed by two cameras.

'Are you sure this is the place?'

'That's what the satnav says,' he replied, showing his screen as evidence: the Fitzgerald clinic.

'Wait here for me.'

'Meter's running. You're the one paying.'

Roxane rang the buzzer and introduced herself, then waited a good while for the double gates to swing back to grant her access to a wooded park. There, she took a gravel driveway that led down through the grounds for about 500 feet, before giving out onto a large, neoclassical-style build-ing that poked out above the pines and eucalyptuses like a mad relic from the 1920s.

They were into the shortest days of the year. In the space

of minutes, the air had turned crisper. The sun was already sinking in the sky, leaving pinkish streaks in its wake. In the grounds, there were a handful of residents finishing a game of cricket, another group playing skittles, and a further cluster assembled on a bench smoking with vacant looks on their faces. Time seemed to have slowed, with the setting occupying an ageless place somewhere between a retirement home, a kindergarten and a rehab clinic. There weren't really any indicators of modern life. The scene could just as easily have been from a century earlier. Roxane was reminded of the images of luxury hotels that had been commandeered as military hospitals during the Great War.

On instinct, instead of entering the building, she kept following the path until she reached a rocky plateau that dipped towards the sea. That was when she saw him, in the distance, alone in a kind of thatched, bandstand-shaped beach hut. She took a moment to observe him before he spotted her. Sitting at a garden table, his laptop and a bottle of white wine in front of him, Raphaël Batailley was lost in his own world, his gaze fixed on the horizon.

Even as she began to draw nearer, he seemed oblivious to her presence. Over his white shirt he wore a thick marine-blue cardigan, in the same style as the one she'd found in the Glass House earlier that day. Up close, she thought, he had the look of an English aristocrat, a way of holding his head that could have come straight from an E. M. Forster novel. His stormy expression, meanwhile, brought to mind a brooding film actor – the foppishness of Rupert Everett crossed with the moodiness of Montgomery Clift.

'On the aperitif already, are you?' she asked. 'Or is that still the bottle from lunchtime?'

It was all she could come up with to engage him in conversation.

The writer's dark mane whipped around, his pale eyes conveying his displeasure at being disturbed. Roxane might just have administered him with an electric shock. She rolled with the momentum of her wine gambit.

'Aren't you going to offer me a glass?'

With undisguised provocation he proffered her the bottle – the dregs of a Meursault Les Perrières that was now bordering on tepid. To keep her end up, she necked a large slug.

'I'm Roxane Montchrestien,' she announced, taking the free chair opposite him.

'A great name for a fictional heroine,' he decreed after some thought.

'Thanks for the compliment.'

'Are you new here?'

'I'm not a patient.'

'Oh, are you the new nurse everyone's talking about? I pictured you being younger.'

'Try again.'

His expression still impossible to read, he frowned and scratched his incipient beard. His eyes were gleaming as if he were stoned or drunk. Perhaps both.

'Tell me you're not a journalist, at least?' There was a nervy edge to his voice as he scrutinised her. 'No, you don't look like one.'

'Do I look like a copper?'

With all due respect to Valentine, in the flesh Batailley wasn't as 'gorgeous' as all that. He had a sort of run-down handsomeness, tired eyes, a charm undercut by world-weariness.

The writer's face grew even darker on noticing that Roxane was wearing his cardigan.

'What are you doing with my jumper? Have you been sniffing around my house without permission?'

Roxane bit her lip as she realised her blunder.

'I can explain.'

'I hope you have a good pair of oars to paddle yourself back from shit creek, and that the police will cough up for a lawyer.'

Roxane tried to defuse the situation.

'I've come to return something to you.'

She unfastened the watch from her wrist and placed it on the table. Batailley eyed her coolly before turning it over to reveal the inscription.

'Where did you find this?'

'It is yours, I take it?'

'It was, yes. But I gave it to someone as a gift.'

'Who?'

Batailley ran his fingers through his hair.

'Something tells me you already know.'

'Your lover, Milena Bergman. Do you know if she was wearing it at the time of her death?'

'Apparently not. It wouldn't look like this anymore if it had spent six months underwater. Where did you find it?'

'Someone tried to sell it on yesterday, to a watchmaker in Rue Marbeuf.'

'Which someone?'

'A security officer at the Paris Prefecture psychiatric unit.'

'Who did he steal it from?'

'A patient at the I3P. He snatched it from her wrist.'

'And who'd given it to her?'

'That's precisely what I'm trying to establish.'

Roxane sensed Raphaël's interest was waning, that he didn't particularly see what the episode had to do with him.

'Right,' he said, replacing the watch on his own wrist. 'Thanks for bringing it back to me. Do I need to sign anything? Give some kind of statement?'

3.

'Wait, that's not the whole story! Let me explain everything in order.'

'Given where my head is right now, that would be for the best. But make it quick.'

'Last weekend, the River Brigade pulled from the Seine a young woman who was drowning near the Pont Neuf. The girl was naked, disorientated and in a state of amnesia. The only thing she had on was this watch.'

Raphaël rubbed his eyes vigorously, as though convinced he could sober himself up with the force of the action. Roxane pressed on.

'When we analysed the DNA from the girl's hair, we found a match in the national genetic database.'

'Who with?'

'Milena Bergman.'

The writer shook his head.

'I don't see why Milena's DNA would be in there.'

'Because of a conviction for theft in 2011.'

Raphaël shrugged sceptically.

'There must have been an error somewhere.'

Roxane showed him the photocopy of the forensic medical team's admittance report.

Batailley glanced at it. The photo seemed to intrigue him without rousing any emotion.

'A blurry black-and-white mugshot proves nothing.'

Roxane handed him her phone so he could play back the I3P security footage.

This time, Raphaël was transfixed by the videos. He suddenly looked like a different person: wide-eyed, lips pulled taut, jaw clenched.

'Is this some kind of joke?'

'I have no way of explaining it,' Roxane admitted. 'Is it her, do you think?'

'No. That's *impossible*. Milena was on that plane when it crashed. There's never been any doubt about that.'

'I'd like you to help me find this woman.'

'What do you mean, *find* her?'

'She escaped while she was being transferred from the infirmary, and nobody's seen her since.'

At this, Raphaël thrust back the wrought-iron table, stood up and began pacing along the rocks, casting a febrile silhouette against the flaming horizon. The shadowy forms of the cluster pines shivered under the caramel sky.

'There's a taxi waiting at the entrance. Come back with me to Paris,' Roxane urged, joining him close to where the rocks plunged into the Mediterranean.

Batailley spoke more loudly now, wagging his finger in menace.

'No, I'm not coming anywhere near this crazy shit. Milena's dead. That's been hard enough for me to cope with. She was pregnant with our child. It's been . . .'

He faltered.

'I didn't know,' Roxane murmured.

'Get the hell out of here.'

'I'm sorry to come and stir up painful memories, but—'

'FUCK OFF!' he roared.

The writer's shouts had drawn the nurses' attention. Roxane shot a glance behind. Like a scene from *One Flew Over the Cuckoo's Nest*, two men in white uniforms had clocked her presence and were sprinting over. Her window of opportunity was narrowing. Batailley's behaviour was starting to scare her. And the proximity of the cliff edge wasn't helping one bit.

'There's something else I need to tell you, Raphaël. Unfortunately it isn't good news.'

The writer advanced towards her, his arm raised.

For a moment, Roxane thought he was about to grab her by the shoulders and hurl her into the sea, but he settled for a hand gesture to indicate that she should continue.

'Your father suffered a serious accident yesterday morning. He's in hospital.'

'What?'

'He fell on the stairs up to his office. He's in a coma.'

'And you couldn't have told me sooner!'

'Come back to Paris with me,' she pleaded again.

Bringing his hands to his hips, Batailley grimaced and caught his breath like a footballer getting up from a nasty tackle.

'Give me five minutes to pack my things.' As he spoke he motioned reassuringly to the nurses, who were primed to swoop.

While Batailley returned to the clinic building, Roxane

explained herself to the men and was promptly escorted to the gates. She climbed into the back seat of the taxi and asked the driver to hang around a few minutes longer. The writer had a touch of a mad dog about him. It wasn't going to be easy to keep him in check. But to make any progress with her investigation, she needed him there in Paris.

While waiting for Raphaël, she checked her messages. Johan Moers had been trying to get hold of her. She wasted no time in calling him back.

'Listen, Roxane, I've redone the tests myself using different DNA fragments from the hair. The results are the same as this morning. There was no mistake.'

'What about the urine sample?'

Moers didn't hesitate.

'Impossible to get anything from it.'

'Why?'

'For starters, piss contains hardly any DNA, and the little there is deteriorates very quickly. But the biggest issue was that your sample had been contaminated by the disinfectants in the toilet bowl.'

'Shit!'

'Yeah, fitting word choice,' he quipped. 'But I do have one piece of information that might interest you.'

'Go on.'

'I ran a few other tests, just in case. And there was one result that intrigued me.'

'For god's sake, Johan, spit it out!'

'In the urine I found traces of the hormone beta-hCG.'

'Which means . . . ?'

'That the girl's pregnant. Your Stranger in the Seine is in the club.'

As Roxane hung up, a thought flashed across her mind: not only was the Bureau of Unconventional Affairs reopening its doors; it was promising to live up to its original billing.

PART II
DOPPELGÄNGER

7

RAPHAËL BATAILLEY

1.

Paris, after dark

'You can drop me here. I'll walk the rest of the way.'

The taxi left me on the corner of Rue d'Assas and Rue Vavin. Despite the cold, I needed to restore the circulation to my legs and gulp down some fresh air before getting home. Seeing my dad in the Pompidou ICU had been an ordeal. Late that afternoon, they'd operated on his spine. The doc said the procedure had gone well, but there was no question of them waking him up for the time being.

As I stood by his bedside, it was like being back in the darkest days of the previous year, when I'd thought I was going to lose him for good after his lung cancer diagnosis. A token of thanks, for loyal service, imparted on him by the two packets of fags he'd smoked every day since he was fifteen. At the time the chemo had wiped him out, but just when most of the nursing team thought he was a goner, an immunotherapy treatment had spurred him to a miraculous recovery. I now clung to that happy turn of events, telling myself the old lion would bounce back a second time. *Fluctuat nec mergitur*, as the old Paris motto goes. *He is tossed by the waves, but does not sink.*

I checked my watch – the famous Résonance that Roxane Montchrestien had returned to me. 9 p.m. It was perishing. In the rush of last-minute Christmas shopping, the roads were still dense with traffic despite the time of night. After continuing for 650 feet to the Musée Zadkine, I crossed over by the tiny sculpture museum and skirted the pharmacy faculty botanical garden.

Under the full moon, the place looked like one of 'Le Douanier' Rousseau's evening compositions. Behind the railings, a lush tangle of improbable vegetation fanned out in a spectrum of deep blues, the bare branches of the trees spidering through the sky in black webs that ensnared the passing wisps of rice paper-thin cloud.

I pushed open the gate of 77a and headed back up the tarmac path to the Glass House. The clear, exceptionally bright night had given it a milky, greenish sheen, like a giant aquarium. I'd acquired the place on a whim, from a Canadian businessman who'd got himself into a mess after some high-risk investments. On my first visit, I'd been bowled over by the architectural feat and the swish fittings and furniture its previous owner had let me keep en bloc. But the more time I spent there, for all its eye appeal and mod cons, the more it scared the shit out of me. Especially when I was alone. During my first year there, a bird had flown through one of the windows and shattered it to pieces. I'd been so spooked that I'd had all the glazing replaced by unbreakable, industrial-strength laminated glass. But even then, I couldn't shake the uneasy feeling the house gave me, the pervasive sense of being on display and easy prey, like an insect trapped in a vivarium. I knew the threat was all in my mind. The way the façade had been treated meant passers-by could barely see anything that was happening inside. From a very early age, I'd learnt that my defining battle in life – for better or for worse – was precisely that: mastering what was going on in my own head.

2.

I unlocked the door, flicked the main light switch and turned on the heating. Despite my jitteriness, I was relieved to get back to the familiarity of home. After dumping my bag, I went straight to retrieve my phone from my desk drawer. It was switched off, no doubt having died a long time previously.

While it was charging, I called the housekeeper, Mrs Miglietti, from the landline. After asking after my dad and telling me about her encounter with Roxane Montchrestien, she passed on a piece of news that put me on edge: the reporter who'd published the *Week'nd* article about me and Milena had been prowling around the house. He had assailed her with questions, which, she was keen to assure me, she'd refused to answer. The article had enraged me. It had dredged up an episode that I'd buried and never wanted to hear mentioned again. Under the guise of 'narrative journalism' and 'investigative reportage', formerly reputable publications were getting mired in the same muck as the tabloids, while gleefully imagining they were keeping their arses squeaky-clean. When the article had come out, I'd asked myself who could have leaked the photos and so much private information to the journo. After rewinding everything in my mind, I could think of only one explanation: someone on the Salpêtrière hospital staff. When he'd been admitted for cancer treatment the previous year, my dad must have got pally with the nurses and started telling them his life story (and mine). I could just picture him showing off photos on his phone and tossing out anecdotes, without seeing any harm in it. But hospital departments are like sieves. Everyone knows everyone's business. And somebody, taking advantage of his trusting nature and the fact that he was weakened by illness, had decided to cash in on my private life to make themselves 400 or 500 euros.

But why now? And why was the guy still sniffing around my gaff like a truffle dog? I glanced at my phone. The screen had come back to life. With my heart thumping, I scanned through my messages and missed calls. But none of them were remotely connected to Milena Bergman.

Which isn't surprising, a voice in my head whispered, *given that Milena is dead.*

Still beset by the nasty feeling that someone was watching me, I got up to look outside. In a surge of paranoia, I turned on all the outdoor spotlights. The plants and shrubbery immediately surrounding the house were hit by the full effects of the harsh light, while a more troubling layer of wilderness, still steeped in semi-darkness, loomed behind.

I returned to my desk and retrieved from my coat pocket the scanned case documents Roxane Montchrestien had given me.

As I read over them, I tried to assess the emotions running

through me. Front of the pack was fear, tinged with incomprehension. Why was someone going out of their way to make people believe Milena Bergman was alive? I struggled to see what their motive could be. Blackmail? A grab for her inheritance? A hoax to stir up a media storm? Nothing seemed to stack up. Yet the cop who'd travelled out to Antibes to find me was apparently convinced by it. The stuff she'd amassed was perplexing, admittedly – the DNA from the hair, the pregnancy test – but on balance it amounted to little against the hard facts. There was no doubt. Milena Bergman *was* in Buenos Aires two evenings before the crash. The proof was in the Canal 7 recording of the concert, which had been shared on the Argentinian state broadcaster's You-Tube channel. It *was* her that boarded the plane, as attested by the twofold identification – DNA and dental records – the Gendarmerie teams had carried out. I didn't want to hear about the rest. That period of my life was done with. I didn't have the energy to set the jukebox playing again. Especially not now.

I was in one of my bad patches. Since my early teenage years, my life had moved in cycles. Dizzying highs and more gruelling lows. It was common knowledge that my little sister, Vera, had died in seamy circumstances when I was ten years old. But what nobody knew was that I lived with her ghost. Vera would appear to me at different stages of her life – as a toddler, a young girl, a young woman, sometimes much older.

She'd come to chat, to see how I was doing, to share the odd pearl of wisdom. But more than anything, she'd beg me to write for her. To tell her stories like I used to do when we were kids. That's why all my books are dedicated to her.

She's the ground zero of my vocation. Every word I've ever written, I've written for her.

Over time, I'd grown accustomed to her presence. Dependent on it even. I'd wait for her, watch out for her, but her visits always took an emotional toll. Sometimes, months would pass without her making an appearance, but Vera always came back in the end. Usually when I was least expecting her, or when I was just starting to feel better about myself because I'd finally met a girl. No amount of psychotherapy and no medication could stop her. Of course, I'd always been conscious that all this existed solely in my head, but this awareness wasn't a scrap of help.

For years, I'd been 'followed' by a Swiss psychiatrist called Christa Lanzinger – the only person who knew about my troubles. But even with her, I'd spent a long time lying by omission. Right up until the previous month, when, at breaking point from keeping up the lie, I'd unburdened my secret and told her how I came to be responsible for my sister's death.

3.

Aubagne, summer 1990

A Provençal family home in the hills of the town. The school holidays are nearly over. I'm ten years old. My bedroom walls are plastered with posters of Chris Waddle, Eric Cantona and the billboard image from *Big Trouble in Little China*. On the shelves there's an illuminated globe, a *Ghostbusters* figurine, a model of Alain Prost's McLaren, the complete collection of *Tout l'Univers* encyclopaedias, a few *Choose Your*

Own Adventure books, several weeks' worth of *Pif Gadget* comics, and a cardboard box stuffed with the must-have gizmos from the latest issues: invisible-ink pens, glow-in-the-dark squirting glasses, a pocket flip comb, novelty horror sweets, magic powder that turns to jelly when you add water, a prehistoric boomerang, the cutlass and claw necklace worn by the great caveman hunter, Rahan.

I throw on my Olympique de Marseille strip and the Nike Air Pegasus trainers my cousin gave me after he grew out of them. Then I race to the garage, jump on my cyclocross bike and whizz down the hill to the tarmac road at the bottom. Under the burning afternoon sun, to the warbling of the cicadas, I pedal over to my friend Vincent Merlin's house. His dad's promised to drive us to an OM training session at their Luminy ground in the south of the city. When I get there a quarter of an hour later, Vincent's holed up in bed with his parents and a doctor assembled around him. Acute appendicitis. He'll need to be admitted to La Timone. I stay with him for moral support until they leave for the hospital, then turn for home feeling slightly miffed.

From a distance, as I'm reascending the dirt track, I'm surprised to spot a brown Renault 9 that I've never seen before, parked alongside our Audi 80. Immediately I sense a potential threat. I get off my bike and stash it behind some bushes. The heat is stifling. Creeping over to the perimeter of the house, I make a lengthy detour to approach from the back way.

I hear voices coming from the terrace. One belonging to my mother, and a male voice I can't place. My mother, Elise Batailley, is kissing a man who isn't my dad, full on the lips. A lump rises in my throat. I'm shaking all over. I crouch down so they don't see me, then, after a few seconds in which I'm too stupefied to move, I tiptoe down to the basement. I'm still trembling as I install myself under the flue pipe which, by some mysterious force of acoustics, allows me to listen to their conversation as if I were standing a few feet away. I finally identify the man's voice: Joël Esposito, our dentist.

I'm in shock, distraught, but not surprised. My mother has always been like this – she lives and breathes to have men looking at her. It took me a long time to understand it, to grasp the logic that drives it. For her, every conversation, every interaction with a man is a game of seduction – a game that imperils us all, because it threatens to destroy our family unit. My mother fancies herself as an artist. She had a brief stint as a dancer at the Marseille National Ballet, and she tells everyone it was her marriage that stopped her having the career she deserved. Dissatisfaction is the bedrock of her character, and it drives her to unspeakable extremes of selfishness.

I hide out in the basement for hours, waiting for the dentist to leave. Over the days that follow, I'm haunted and consumed by the scenes I witnessed. But I don't know what to do with the information. Who can I confide in? Not my mother. Nor my dad who, in spite of her flakiness, worships the ground she walks on and would go to pieces if they separated. My parents argue a lot, even in front of me, and I can recite by heart the threats my mother hurls at my dad if he dares make the slightest remark: 'take off with the children', 'leave your reputation in tatters', 'get you fired from the police'.

'A bright lad like you.' That's what my dad's always saying to boost my confidence. And a bright lad like me should be capable of finding a way to defuse the situation and save his family. But what can I do? I come up with dozens of hypothetical solutions. Only one of them strikes me as plausible: trying to intimidate the dentist into putting an end to the affair.

I marshal my *Pif* comics and some old issues of *Télé 7 jours* that are loitering in the magazine rack in the living room. I cut out letters, composing them into an anonymous note that I hope won't betray my age:

I KNOW YOU ARE HAVING AN AFFAIR WITH ÉLISE BATAILLEY. IF YOU DON'T END IT, HER HUSBAND AND YOUR WIFE WILL FIND OUT ABOUT IT TOO.

On an envelope, I stencil on the address in block capitals and send it to the dentist's clinic.

It's two days later that everything spins out of control. The fifth of September, the first Wednesday of term. I'm home for lunch after finishing lessons at midday, and I need to leave again at 2 p.m. for handball training ahead of our next inter-school match. My four-year-old sister, Vera, is eating with me in the kitchen. The phone rings halfway through the meal. My mother takes the call and walks away from the table with the receiver. I surmise that it's 'him'. The lover. I prick my ears up and realise he's informing her about the letter he's received. 'I'll drop Vera at nursery, then I'll be straight round,' she tells him.

As I bike over to training, terror courses through me. I know that a chain of events has been set in motion that's more powerful than me. But even in my worst nightmares,

I can't imagine just how devastating it will be.

4.

Four-year-old girl dies after being left in hot car
La Provence, 7 September 1990

Vera Batailley, the daughter of the prominent Marseille Major Crime chief, was left locked inside her mother's car. Unable to escape the overheated vehicle, she suffocated to death.

The tragic incident – the second of its kind to hit the region this summer – occurred two days ago in the upper reaches of Aubagne.

A terrifying furnace

On what starts out as a typical Wednesday afternoon, Élise Batailley, a former dancer at the Marseille National Ballet, drives her daughter to Haut-Caroux drop-in daycare centre. Inexplicably, she forgets to drop her there and continues to her next appointment with the child still in tow. During the journey, the four-year-old girl falls asleep in the back seat. At 2 p.m., apparently having forgotten her daughter is still inside the vehicle, Ms Batailley leaves the Audi 80 parked in full sun in the Val-Claret housing estate car park.

At this point the child becomes trapped in a veritable furnace, and undoubtedly loses consciousness in her sleep. It is only at 5.30 p.m. that the girl's mother realises her mistake. Panic-stricken, Élise Batailley races to the fire station in La Bouilladisse, but the emergency team is unable to do anything. The child has already been dead for a long time.

Forgotten baby syndrome

Every year, particularly during the hottest months, scores of French children lose their lives after being inadvertently left in overheated vehicles by their parents. In the majority of cases, 'Forgotten baby syndrome', as the phenomenon is known, affects otherwise loving and devoted parents, who can only attribute their 'oversight' to stress or fatigue.

'When the temperature outside hits 40 degrees, cars can become veritable ovens, reaching in excess of 70 degrees,' explains Anaïs Traquandi, the head of La Timone hospital's paediatric department. 'The heating effect is compounded by the thermoregulatory systems of young children, whose body temperature rises much more quickly than an adult's due to their extremely low water reserves.'

Mother remanded in custody

The Marseille prosecutor has opened an inquiry into manslaughter.

'For the moment, accidental death seems to be the most likely hypothesis,' a source close to the investigation told us. None of the estate's residents saw or heard anything. 'The girl's autopsy showed she died from dehydration. Her body didn't present any signs of blows, assault, or anything else that would give cause for suspicion,' the prosecutor clarified in a statement.

After being admitted to hospital on Wednesday evening in a concerning psychological state, Ms Batailley was remanded in custody at Thursday lunchtime, but quickly released. She has offered no explanation for the incident other than a terrible moment of absent-mindedness.

The 38-year-old had a brief career as a dancer at the Marseille National Ballet. Her husband, Superintendent Marc Batailley, hit the spotlight earlier this year after his team at the Marseille Major Crime Unit identified and arrested the serial killer Raynald Pfefferkon, dubbed 'The Horticulturalist', whose bloody crimes had ripped terror through the Marseille region for months.

8

THE WORLD AS THE WORLD IS NOT

ROXANE

1.

Paris, 9 p.m.

As she pushed open the clock-tower door, Roxane once again felt the pleasant buzz of 'returning to the fold', a sensation only intensified by the stinging cold outside. It was like being swathed inside a giant heat bubble. With Poutine weaving between her legs, she set down in the hallway the spare clothes she'd bought on the way back from the airport, just before closing time at Bon Marché. The haul – underwear, jeans, long-sleeved T-shirt, jumper, and traditional-style sateen and Calais lace pyjamas – had cost half her salary. To compound the dent in her pocket, she'd also purchased a plump goose-feather pillow to mitigate the assault of the Chesterfield. Bags offloaded, she headed straight for Marc Batailley's old office, which she'd now come to regard as her own. To her surprise, not only was Valentine waiting for her when she got up there, she'd also ordered in a takeaway for two from Luca's, the Italian restaurant across the street. Touched by the sentiment, Roxane polished off her box of truffle coquillettes and washed it down with the remainder of the bottle of white she'd opened the previous evening. It was a hearty and comforting meal.

Roxane began by telling the student about her fraught encounter with Raphaël.

'So . . . what did you think of him?'

'Mad as a box of frogs. Did you know Milena Bergman was pregnant at the time of the crash?'

'Yes, Marc told me. It was a sort of double whammy for him, losing his future daughter-in-law and his future grandchild all in one go.'

'And to make things even weirder, Moers told me the girl they pulled from the Seine was pregnant too.'

'Like time stood still for a year, and Milena re-emerged exactly as she was before the crash.'

'Do you genuinely believe that?'

'Until anyone shows me evidence to the contrary.'

Over dessert, Roxane asked if her sidekick had any update on the tattoos.

'I do, as it happens! I spent all afternoon researching, just following this hunch I had: the ivy and the fawn skin shouldn't be treated separately, but as a symbolic whole.'

'Agreed.'

'Once I'd made the connection, it was like a light went on. I remembered that both elements often crop up in Greek mythology, as symbols of Dionysus and his followers.'

'Just remind me again,' Roxane requested, as the cat

slinked onto her knees and began clawing her thighs through her jeans.

'Dionysus is one of the twelve gods of Olympus. He's often represented as the protector of the vine and wine, which is true, but very reductive. More broadly, he's the god of intoxication, subversion and transgression. The god of excess and madness.'

Roxane thought back to her foundation year at Louis-le-Grand. Images thronged in her mind: the divine lightning bolts of Zeus, the cruel gods with their petty skulduggery, all those hours she'd spent sweating blood and tears over the different versions and themes, the interminable Trojan War, the scheming of Ulysses as he took his sweet time to come home to Penelope . . .

'Dionysus is the *only* god to have been born to a mortal mother,' Valentine continued. 'Zeus had seduced the beautiful Semele. Once she'd become his lover and was carrying their child, she asked him to appear to her in all his divine splendour. But the sight of him with his thunder and lightning burnt her alive. Zeus was just in time to rescue the foetus from Semele's womb and sew it into his own thigh so the baby could reach full term. That's how Dionysus was born, from the union of Earth and Thunder.'

Hence the saying, 'You think you're born from Jupiter's thigh . . .' Roxane mused, recalling the old French put-down for people who thought they were God's gift.

'Beyond the god himself, a lot's been written about the *cult* of Dionysus,' resumed Valentine. 'It's always had a smack of scandal and debauchery about it.'

Roxane's recollections became more vivid. Suddenly she had visions of sylvestral orgies, bacchanals, nymphs thrusting themselves at libidinous satyrs. Or, to put it more crudely, massive sex fests in the forest.

'Dionysus entranced the women who crossed his path, putting them in a state of mystical delirium that made them worship him. Then, once he had them under his spell, he led them into the forest to give themselves over to a kind of orgiastic cult. The women were known as the maenads. They were utterly devoted to Dionysus, and along with the satyrs formed a sort of cortège that accompanied him wherever he went.'

Despite her interest in Valentine's explanation, Roxane refocused the conversation.

'Where's the link with the Stranger's tattoos?'

'I'm getting there. In art and literature, maenads and satyrs are often shown wearing a crown of ivy and a nebris – an animal skin that's worn like a toga or cape. In most cases, the nebris is some kind of deerskin – a buck, a doe, a fawn . . .'

'What's the skin meant to symbolise? The animal's strength?'

'Yes, its energy, its impetuousness. In mythology the nebris traditionally comes from an animal the maenads have hunted down and torn apart while entranced.'

'This is all fascinating, but quite far from our investigation, isn't it?'

Valentine smiled mysteriously.

'Except that I discovered something else.'

The student got up – they had eaten on the Chesterfield, in front of the coffee table – and walked over to the sea of books and folders on Batailley's desk.

'Recently, Marc bought some books on Dionysus.'

'Seriously?'

At the foot of the desk, Valentine pointed to a tote bag with an owl motif.

'The receipt's still in there. Four books purchased from Guillaume Budé bookshop on Saturday, 12 December.'

Roxane joined her by the desk. Laid on the tabletop, the titles of the books spoke for themselves: *The Shadow of Dionysus*, *Dionysus and the Goddess Earth*, *Dionysus and the Maenads*, *Dionysus: The Mad God*.

She opened the covers and began leafing through. From the number of page markers, annotations and highlights, the cop might have been prepping for a university thesis. It couldn't be a coincidence.

'I think you're on to something,' Roxane admitted. 'We need to establish why Marc Batailley was digging into this stuff. Did he never mention anything to you?'

'I've racked my brains, but no. The only thing I'd noticed was that for the past couple of weeks, he'd been spending a lot more time at his desk.'

'Preoccupied by an investigation?'

'Possibly.'

'I'll stop by the bookshop tomorrow to see if Batailley was more talkative there.'

'What about me? Is there anything I can do?'

Roxane thought for a moment.

'I'd like you to do a spot of fieldwork, if you feel up to it.'

She took out her phone and opened Instagram. The app loaded on a profile she'd found during her trip to Nice.

'Meet Corentin Lelièvre, scoop writer at *Week'nd* magazine. He's the one that published the article on Raphaël and Milena.'

Valentine peered at the screen. The scribbler had a head as round as a marble, pinhead eyes, a straggly goatee and a flagrantly receding hairline that he sought to conceal with a cap in half the photos. He also had a penchant for slogan T-shirts: *Less thinky, more drinky*; *You can't please everyone, you're not a waffle*; *There is no planet B*.

'Wow. He's a special case,' Valentine smirked as she scrolled through his posts.

Most of the snaps charted the journo's jaunts to Hipsterland. The guy apparently spent his whole life in bars and restaurants, taking endless shots of the charcuterie boards, burrata small plates and organic beers. The location tags seemed to confine the majority of his outings to two establishments: Les Enfants Terribles, on the Quai de Jemmapes, and The Bootlegger, in Rue du Faubourg-Saint-Denis.

'What would you like me to do?'

'Try to make contact with him.'

'Undercover?'

Roxane smiled.

'The term's a bit strong, but that's the idea.'

'What exactly are we after?'

'Two bits of information: where he got the material for his article, and why he's still prowling around Raphaël.'

'OK. I can do that.'

'Whatever you do, don't put yourself in danger, and don't go playing the heroine. I'm not asking you to sleep with the guy.'

Valentine burst out laughing.

'I think I'd struggle there.'

'It would be good, though, if you could do an initial recce this evening. He hasn't posted anything yet, but that doesn't mean he's not in one of his favourite haunts.'

'I'll keep you posted!' she promised, donning her helmet and parka.

Roxane let her go, forcing her eyes not to follow. The girl moved her in a way that went beyond the bounds of reason. Her spontaneousness and her smile were contagious. Every time she was with Valentine, she felt like someone was giving her a shot of endorphin to the heart. Unfortunately, the jab's effects didn't survive the student's absence. As soon as she was gone, her loss was palpable.

2.

In the small first-floor bathroom Roxane showered, washed her hair, brushed her teeth and slipped on the pyjamas she'd bought earlier. For a second evening, she'd decided not to break the rhythm of the investigation by returning home.

After setting some water to boil for an infusion, she fed her new feline friend and wrestled with the radiators to find the right temperature setting. Before it got too late, she rang the Hôtel-Dieu forensic medical emergency unit and asked to speak to Jacques Bartoletti, the first doctor to have examined 'Milena'. The physician wasn't on duty that evening, but with some cajoling, she managed to procure his personal number. To say he wasn't thrilled to be disturbed at home would be putting it mildly.

'After thirty-six hours on duty, can't I even watch a game of football in peace?'

Roxane pounced on the bluff.

'It's Tuesday evening. There isn't any football on TV.'

'You want to get your facts right. Marseille versus Lens, a replay of the match that was cancelled a couple of months ago.'

'You're brave to back Marseille, with the season they're having.'

'It's the Blood and Gold I'm supporting. What are you hassling me for at ten o'clock at night?'

'I have a couple of questions about the woman you examined on Sunday morning.'

'The blonde I had sent to the I3P?'

'Yes.'

'And can't that wait until tomorrow morning?'

'No. Did you notice her tattoos?'

The Lens man took a moment to think.

'Yeah. If I remember rightly, those are what had the Brig crew so concerned, and with good reason.'

'Why?'

'Because they seemed very fresh, and a bit of a rush job. The design was all shaky and uneven. Hadn't even been done by a professional, by the looks of it, with all the nasty side effects that can lead to.'

'Do you think they could have been done against her will?'

'It's possible. To be honest, that was my gut reaction.'

'Her body didn't show any other marks of violence?'

'No. I examined her for track marks, but I didn't find any. If the girl was a junkie, she wasn't shooting up.'

Roxane had one last question.

'And did you notice whether . . .'

'For fuck's sake, you've made me miss a goal with this bullshit of yours!' The doctor let out a roar of rage. 'Pissing hell!'

He slammed down the phone with such ferocity that Roxane didn't think it wise to try him again.

Instead, she gathered up the Dionysus books and carried them over to the coffee table by the sofa. Sitting cross-legged on the Chesterfield, with Poutine curled behind her and a pad and pen in hand, she immersed herself in the tomes and the notes Batailley had left.

Valentine had hit on something, no doubt about it. It was a nebulous trail, but a compelling one. To begin with, she concentrated on the illustrations. Dionysus, the god of chaos, deviance and frenzy, was often shown riding a panther-drawn chariot. Traditionally he was wearing a goatskin or lynx-fur cape, and brandishing a thyrsus – a staff twined with ivy leaves and topped with a pinecone – that he carried as a sceptre. Behind him processed his fearsome cortège: first the satyrs, the infamous half-man, half-goat devotees of a life of unbridled lust, flashing their repugnant gurns. Then the hypnotic maenads, the god's ecstatic, possessed female worshippers.

Next Roxane got stuck into the words, poring over the many passages Batailley had highlighted. As she pieced them together, a fascinating portrait came into view of a mythological figure of whom she'd previously only scratched the surface. Dionysus was one of a kind in the pantheon, the only god not to live on Mount Olympus. Impossible to pin down, he stole around in a mask, bursting forth in epiphanies, appearing and disappearing without warning, spreading like an epidemic that couldn't be contained.

Wherever he went, Dionysus sowed death and terror among those who refused to join his cult. There was no better demonstration of his vengeful character than *The Bacchae*, the tragedy by the Greek playwright Euripides. On returning to Thebes, the city where he was born, Dionysus vows to punish his aunt, Agave (who has insulted his mother), and her son, his cousin Pentheus (the heir to the throne, who has shunned his cult). Abetted by the maenads, he manages to drive Agave mad, sending her into a wild trance and assailing her with hallucinations that ultimately push her to decapitate her son and parade his head around the city on a pike.

Roxane was now turning the pages in a frenzy. She was particularly engrossed by the sections on the maenads, glimpsing in them a potential door to her investigation. 'Milena' had been branded, tattooed – patently against her will – with an ivy wreath and a nebris, the dual symbols of Dionysus's female worshippers. The god had the power to take possession of these women, to 'seize their reins', as the author had put it in one of the passages highlighted by Batailley, in order to wrest control of their minds and bodies. Once you were in Dionysus's thrall, you inhabited the world of appearances and illusions, beset by hallucinations and delirium. Gripped by a raving madness that could make you commit the most heinous, merciless crimes, to satisfy the demands of his cult. The books described wild animals with their guts ripped out, children butchered, humans sacrificed in cold blood, all for the glory of the one they called 'the eater of raw flesh'.

3.

The buzz of her phone shook Roxane from her books. Corentin Lelièvre, the prematurely balding journalist, had just posted a new photo on Instagram. It was a group shot, taken in a vegan restaurant called Le Potager du Marais. Lelièvre was sporting a black T-shirt emblazoned with a tired spoonerism: *There appears to be a paw in your flan.* He and his chums were posing with broad smiles around a plant-based paella. Seated at the table with them, Roxane recognised Valentine. *Good job,* she thought. The student hadn't wasted any time. She must have spotted Lelièvre in one of his usual haunts in the 10th arrondissement and grafted herself onto his hipster posse.

With a flush of satisfaction, Roxane returned to her reading. The books simmered with a violence that spilled over from the pages – the twofold fury of the god and of the maenads, who, enraptured to the point of madness, wreaked devastation on everything in their path. A fascinating, terrifying brand of femininity, diametrically opposed to the popular ideal of the sweet, self-effacing mother figure who lived only to serve her family.

The aftershocks of the myth had rippled through antiquity. Traditionally, the thiasus, Dionysus's retinue of followers and servants, would pay worship to him in occult, decadent ceremonies typified by alcohol, drugs, and sexual excess.

A loose sheet of folded paper fell from the chapter she was reading and landed on the parquet. Immediately Poutine pounced over, forcing Roxane to sprint down her feline opponent to retrieve it. It was a photocopy – evidently made by Batailley – of a passage from a report by the Interministerial Mission for Monitoring and Combating Cultic Deviances. The cop had highlighted a paragraph that referred to a modern-day resurgence of the cult of Dionysus. The Mission needed to gather more data, but the authors noted the existence – modest, for the time being – of a network of groups operating as thiasi, who were using the myth to justify their drug seshes, benders and orgies. Roxane turned the page over. On the back Batailley had scribbled down a string of sentences, in a sort of private memo:

Remember that the cult of Dionysus is founded on the inversion of values and the subversion of order. Dionysus is the enemy of self-control and moderation. To honour Dionysus is to experience a kind of drunkenness powerful enough to destroy reason and deliver us from the stale confines of reality. The real world alienates us. It weighs us down. Intoxication, in the broadest sense of the word – alcohol, drugs, 'total art' – offers a gateway to a new dimension, a way of plunging into life in its truest form. To worship Dionysus, therefore, is to embrace the power of intoxication and ecstasy, to accept the dizzying sense of being out of our depth, to roll with the excesses and shed all our inhibitions, to abandon our reverence for rules and open ourselves to otherness and difference. Intoxication is what allows human beings, for a few hours, to rub shoulders with the gods.

In spite of her curiosity, Roxane could feel sleep overwhelming her. The influx of new information had set her mind whirring. She needed to conk out so that everything could slot into place. Even if, in concrete terms, she hadn't got much further, she was convinced of being on the brink of something game-changing. The case had stealthily changed its spots. She was no longer just investigating a disappearance. She was locked in a chess game with a cruel and savage opponent. Dionysus, the master of illusions, the son of Zeus. The mad god.

Wednesday, 23 December

9

THE SHADOW OF DIONYSUS

RAPHAËL

1.

The house alarm bored through my eardrums, wrenching me from a deep sleep as though someone had speared a harpoon into my chest. In a state of total disarray, gasping for breath, I lurched upright in bed. In my confusion it took several seconds for the reality to dawn on me: someone had broken into the house. I got up as if in slow motion. Still half-asleep, I groped for the light switch, only to trip over my overnight bag and go sprawling across the floor.

Shit. I staggered to my feet. My head was throbbing like it was caught in a vice, my ears still ringing with the din. It had been an appalling night. Nightmares, a migraine, and insomnia until five-thirty in the morning. Everywhere I turned, I saw Milena Bergman. I'd barely dropped back off for two hours, and now an intruder was tearing me from bed.

As soon as I'd come round again, her image reimprinted

itself. My heart jumped. The switch, at last. Light. The wooden floorboards under my feet. The staircase floating down to the ground floor.

The alarm continued to sound, but the living room was deserted. The glass door, the only way into the house, was firmly locked. *False alarm?* It wouldn't be the first time the security system had misfired. I punched in the code to disable the siren. Outside day was breaking in a pale, almost dreamlike blue. A fine, icy mist bobbed over the garden, which lay immobile in the dawn chill. Naked of their leaves, the dark branches sliced like pinking shears through a sky of fading stars. I rubbed my eyes groggily, then conducted a final inspection of the ground floor.

Although everything was calm, I still felt a gnaw of anxiety. Once again, I had the sense of being imprisoned by the plants and branches that encircled the house, transecting the glass panels with constantly shifting reflections that overlapped to form unsettling images.

A muffled noise rebounded from the glazed wall behind me. It came from the back of the house, where a dense cluster of bay trees led onto the greenhouses of the pharmacy faculty botanical garden. At this time of day, the place had a ghostly feel. With their powdery white coating, the frosted hedges looked like props from a Hammer film, concealing a world of spectral creatures.

All at once, a shadow appeared and a hand struck the glass. I leapt back with a yelp of shock. It took me a moment to admit that it really was *her.* 'Milena.' Panic-stricken, dishevelled, wearing only a nightshirt, and begging me to let her in.

'Raphaël, open the door!'

Her voice, though distorted by the thick glass, was shot through with terror. I'd left the key fob in a tray by the door. I brought it closer to the sensor. The click didn't come, and the door stayed shut.

'Hurry up!'

I tried again, but the smart lock was still unresponsive. *Why?*

'For god's sake, hurry up!'

It was the first time I'd been locked in. The triggering of the alarm must have fucked up the digital system that controlled access to the house.

I held her gaze, doing my utmost to keep calm and avoid scaring her further.

'We're going to find a solu—'

'He's coming, Raphaël! He's coming!'

Who was she talking about? No matter how hard I scanned the garden, I couldn't spot anyone. But I could see the fear in her eyes. Racing back over to the key tray, I grabbed my phone and the card I'd been given the day before. I needed help, and I could only think of one number to call.

ROXANE

2.

Roxane had endured a torrid night. She'd woken up at four-thirty in the morning, drenched in sweat, after a series of

obscure nightmares peopled with satyrs, furies and mad tat-
tooists. Consumed by what she'd read the previous evening,
she'd tossed and turned on the sofa without managing to get
back to sleep. One thought was nagging away at her: she had
to learn more about Marc Batailley's activities in the days
leading up to his accident. He'd clearly been investigating
something to do with mythology. But what was the point of
his research, and how was it connected with Milena Bergman? At that moment, she could only think of one way to
find out.

After striding out into the icy dregs of the night, dressed
in jogging gear, she'd hotfooted it down Rue de Sèvres and
Rue Lecourbe as far as Vaugirard cemetery. The Pompidou buildings were just behind. By the time she entered the
atrium day was breaking, bleeding through the glass roof in
shafts of stark, ashen light that only compounded the gloom
of the place. Unlike the previous day, the hospital was still
slumbering. Taking the lift, she made straight for the ICU.
The stuffy corridors. The stench of food and death. The
bartering with the nursing assistant to gain access to Room
18 – 'five minutes, as part of an investigation'. The white-
coated minion had tried to object. Roxane had carried on
regardless, but it was only a matter of time before the girl
returned with her colleagues or a few security bods in tow.
She had to act fast. She shot a glance at the cop. He was
now lying face-up, with his ragged hair and heavy stubble
barely visible beneath the catheters, ECG cables and ventilator tubes. Opening the cupboard, she rummaged in the
leather trench coat and hit on what she'd come for: Batailley's iPhone. The battery icon was red, almost out of juice.
Fortunately, she'd bargained for that, and retrieved from her

pocket her own charger which she plugged into a socket near the bedside. The phone was a recent model with facial recognition. She tilted the screen towards the cop's frozen face, and the device promptly unlocked. Emboldened by her success, she quickly explored its contents. Emails, texts, browser data, photos . . . Her optimism soon foundered. Marc Batailley didn't bother with the internet, apparently only using his phone for very basic stuff. His recent call history was more encouraging. Roxane took a few screenshots that she texted over to herself, then did the same with the Maps app, showing the last locations Batailley had searched for. Deciding she had enough leads to be getting on with, she returned the phone to its original place and made herself scarce.

Contrary to what she'd feared, she made it through the corridors without incident. The patients were surfacing, and it was all hands on deck for the morning rounds. No sign of the sadistic redhead or the nursing assistant. She took the stairs down, then headed for safety in Relais H, the café she'd spotted in the atrium. For the time being, most of the patrons were hospital staff. After ordering a brace of double expressos for her first caffeine fix of the day, she bagged one of the few unoccupied tables and began investigating the material she'd harvested from the phone.

The Maps app revealed that two days before his accident, Batailley had paid a visit to 14 Boulevard Montmartre, in the 9th arrondissement. Roxane fired off a message to Valentine asking her to check out the lead, then turned her attention to the last numbers Marc had called. Two of them looked of interest. The first was saved in his contacts as belonging to Valérie Janvier. The name immediately rang a bell in

Roxane's mind. Janvier was a copper too, and no small fry. An old-timer from Major Crime who'd climbed the ranks to become Chief Superintendent of the first-district branch of the Paris judicial police. One of the figures systematically wheeled out by the media whenever they reported on 'Women in the Police'. Not only had Batailley spoken with her twice the previous week, but Valérie Janvier had herself attempted to get hold of him in the past forty-eight hours: two missed calls, without voicemails.

Holding out little hope, and in spite of the early hour, Roxane brazenly tried Janvier's number. Counter to all her expectations, the Chief Superintendent picked up.

'Valérie Janvier speaking.'

For a few seconds, Roxane was thrown off guard. In the background, she could hear snatches of domestic breakfast-time activity. The spluttering of the coffee machine, the morning news show on RTL radio, children squabbling before the school run.

'Good morning, Chief Superintendent. I hope you'll forgive me for disturbing you at home. I'm ringing because . . .'

'Who are you?'

'Captain Roxane Montchrestien, from the BNRF. I'm calling you in regard to Marc Batailley.'

'At half-seven in the morning?'

'Marc's in a coma, in hospital.'

'Shit. What happened?'

'He suffered a very serious accident the day before yesterday. A fall that might have been linked to the case he was working on.'

Janvier was silent for a long time before continuing. Her tone was cautious.

'Why have you taken it upon yourself to inform me?'

'Because I know you've been trying to reach him over the past couple of days.'

An even longer silence.

'On what grounds and with what authority did you get hold of his phone?'

'On my own initiative, and outside of all protocol. Nobody else knows.'

Roxane could sense Janvier knew something, but was hesitant to show her cards.

'What exactly do you want from me, Captain?'

What Roxane really wanted was to press Janvier for information, but instead she made a bid to reel her in.

'I'd like to share with you a few things I've discovered.'

Although she was patently no dupe, Janvier took the bait.

'I have a window between one and two. We could meet for a quick lunch at Le Select, if you like?'

With a rush of satisfaction, Roxane accepted the invitation and thanked the chief superintendent before hanging up. There was a second number that cropped up twice in Marc's call history, but which wasn't saved in his contacts. When she dialled it, she landed straight on the answerphone, and rang off without leaving a message. A reverse look-up search yielded nothing either. The caller was clearly ex-directory. As she racked her brains for another way to identify the number without blowing her cover, her phone vibrated and Raphaël Batailley's name flashed up on the screen.

'Raphaël?'

'I need you to come over now, please.'

'Where are you?'

'At home. Rue d'Assas.'

'What's happened?'

'Just get here now, damn it! And bring your colleagues and an ambulance!'

RAPHAËL

3.

In my shock, I'd let my phone drop to the floor.

The scene unfolding before me couldn't be real.

In the foreground, pounding on the glass wall, the willowy body of the young woman. Barefoot, ghostlike and trembling in her pearly nightshirt, her blonde hair rippling over her shoulders.

Set to a soundtrack of screams, howls, and sobs choked by fear.

A little further away, silhouetted against the dawn light, a tall figure was looming into view. A Gothic shadow. I thought instinctively of the vampirish creature in *Nosferatu* – bald-headed, pointy-eared, with talons for fingertips. His gait was slow, unsteady, but his progress was remorseless. The Beast was closing in on Beauty.

I could feel panic spreading through me. What was I meant to do? I resolved to try kicking in the patio door. First with timid nudges, then full-on kung-fu style. The pane tremored in its frame, but refused to shatter.

In the meantime, the monster had continued its advance,

allowing me to appraise it in more detail. I'd been wide of the mark with my vampire reference. A better analogy was something closer to Pan, the god of the wild in Greek mythology. A preposterous hybrid of man and goat. Stooped over on his furry hind legs, the man-beast at hand had a gnarled face, huge bushy eyebrows, and horns that rose like twin corkscrews from his mane of hair.

Draped in a fur cape, the satyr had now swooped on his prey. Right before me, he was pummelling her in the sides, snarling as he went. And I didn't have any weapons to hand. *But wait!* My dad kept his MR-73 stashed in a drawer. I bolted to his bedroom, found the gun . . . but not the cartridges. Nothing that could really help me. In desperation I grabbed one of the decorative pokers from the hearth. With all my might, I began driving the wrought-iron rod against the glass. Utterly indifferent to my efforts, in a frenzied movement the madman hurled out a few more blows, then hauled his victim onto his shoulders. The slab of laminated glass was starting to splinter. Though my fingers were streaming with blood, I kept on hitting until an opening appeared. Using the poker like a crowbar, I forced the glass until the wall gave way.

Free at last, I raced out barefoot into the garden in pursuit of the creature. I caught up with it at the top of the tarmac path. I approached from behind with the poker, but just as I was poised to strike, it whipped around, grabbed the pointed end, and wrenched the implement from my hands. For a split second, my eyes met with its bestial, wild-eyed gaze. I raised my hands to my face to protect myself, but the blow struck me on the neck. It felt like someone had set my skin on fire.

Staggering, I opened my mouth to cry out, but before the sound could leave my throat, I'd already collapsed on the ground.

10

THE NIGHT IN THEIR HEARTS

ROXANE

1.

The tarmac was a swirl of red and blue. At the far end of Rue d'Assas, the soft golden morning glow was drowning under flashing lights. A mob of marked vehicles barricaded access to the pharmacy faculty botanical garden, while triangular signs chicaned the traffic into a single lane by the entrance to 77a.

Roxane slammed the taxi door behind her and presented her badge to the officer manning the gate. *So it's official,* she thought as she made her way along the blind alley to the Glass House, *this isn't MY investigation anymore.*

Straight after receiving Raphaël's frantic call, she'd thought it best to warn both Botsaris and the 6th arrondissement force. From the Pompidou, she risked taking too long to arrive on the scene. The BNRF lieutenant had kept her up to speed on the operation. She knew that Raphaël was safe and sound, but that the cops had been too late to prevent the kidnap of the young woman they believed to be Milena Bergman.

The perimeter of the house was swarming with activity. Caution tape had been plastered around a large area, inside of which an army of forensics officers were bustling around in their astronaut gear. Roxane observed the scene from a distance, sizing up the police units in attendance. All her old team from the BNRF were there, plus the guys from the third-district branch of the Paris judicial police, covering the arrondissements on the Left Bank, who must have shown up at the same time. An antsy-looking Botsaris was deep in conversation with Serge Cabrera, the head honcho of the JP crew, trying to convince him to let the BNRF keep the case. Standing slightly back from them, Sorbier watched on in stony silence. His face was a picture of doom. Further behind, hunched in a garden chair under a foil blanket, a wild-haired Raphaël Batailley was staring into space with the air of someone who'd just been knocked for six.

Roxane sensed her colleagues wouldn't be doing her any favours. If she wanted to escape another roasting, she couldn't hang around there forever. She dialled Valentine Diakité's number.

'Could you pick me up from somewhere on your moped?'

'Where?'

'Rue d'Assas, in front of the entrance to Batailley's house.'

'Has something happened?'

'I'll explain later. When can you get here?'

'Within a quarter of an hour if I leave now. I've even got a car, if you'd prefer?'

'Great. Yes, that would be better.'

Sorbier collared her the moment she hung up.

'You can't just behave, can you, Montchrestien? You can't help it – you're drawn to trouble every shitting time.'

'I'd say this time it's more a case of trouble following me, don't you think?'

'We can get funny about the semantics later. Once we haven't got the press breathing down our necks.'

'What exactly are you talking about, skipper?'

Sorbier handed her the newspaper. The question screamed out from the front page of *Le Parisien*: 'Who is the Stranger in the Seine?' Roxane opened the periodical and scanned through the article. A double-page exclusive described the recovery of an amnesiac young woman from the Seine, her internment at the Paris Police Prefecture infirmary, and her escape. The piece had been dashed off and bulked out with a lot of hot air. The journalist had done a lot of embroidery on the little she knew – presumably obtained straight from the mouth of an I3P employee like that little shit Anthony Moraes. It made no odds. The damage was done. The case had hit the press, and, in light of that morning's developments, it wouldn't be out of the headlines any time soon.

'That's the girl who was abducted this morning, isn't it?' Sorbier demanded.

'Beats me, skipper.'

'Cut the bullshit. Do you realise what this means, having the I3P plastered all over the front page of *Le Parisien*? Why didn't you warn us sooner?'

'But I did—'

Before she could protest any further, Sorbier's phone started ringing and he walked away to answer it. Roxane made the most of the reprieve to wander around the perimeter of the Glass House. One of the wall panels had literally been wiped out, leaving a gaping hole that suddenly made the place look as flimsy as a house of cards. She walked over to Raphaël. The writer was being kept under surveillance by one of the third-district officers while awaiting his next round of questioning.

'Sorry I couldn't get here sooner,' she shrugged. 'Not too much damage, I hope?'

Raphaël grimaced and parted the blanket to show her a bruise that ran from the base of his neck to his nape.

'Was it Milena, the girl?' she asked.

The writer remained silent, still dumbfounded by what he'd experienced.

'And her attacker, did you recognise him? What's this whole monster business? He was dressed as a satyr, right?'

As she had feared, Botsaris sidled over. Both to put the kibosh on her attempted questioning, and to lecture her as if she were twelve again.

'We need to talk, Roxane.'

'What we *need* is for you to watch how you speak to me. That's for sure.'

She didn't like either the tone or the attitude of her former lieutenant. A young guy she had trained, who a week earlier had still been under her command, and was now only filling her shoes because she'd been unfairly shoved to the sidelines.

'Do you get a kick from spending your life landing your colleagues in the shit?' he demanded.

'What are you talking about? I called you multiple times yesterday morning to discuss this case. I didn't get the impression you were that fussed until it hit the front page of *Le Parisien*.'

'That's not true!'

135

She knew he was up against it, but she had no inclination to make things any easier on him. He must have been the one who grassed her up to Sorbier. She eyed her former assistant frostily. He looked livid, and utterly knackered. As well as being a young dad, Botsaris was a self-proclaimed feminist who made a virtue of getting up every night to take care of his four-month-old son's feeds. Roxane knew he'd booked leave over Christmas so that he could spend the break at his in-laws' country pile. The investigation was about to send his festive plans down the Swanee. And he wouldn't be getting a scrap of sympathy from her.

'Are they letting you keep the case?'

'We're hoping we can cling onto it, but it's only going to be a poisoned chalice. That's why—'

'We've found something, Botsa!' a voice exclaimed.

Liêm Hoàng Thông had just materialised behind the laurel bushes.

'Morning, boss,' he called to Roxane.

'Hi, Liêm.'

Hoàng Thông was one of the guys on her sub-team. An easygoing forty-something, and always immaculately turned out, he had the patience of a saint and a gift for getting people talking. He never shirked from conducting neighbourhood inquiries. And once again, he'd come up trumps.

'One of the neighbours caught something mental on his phone.' He jiggled the device in front of him. 'The caretaker at the Musée Zadkine across the street. Said he was woken by the house alarm going off.'

Roxane and Botsaris huddled around the screen. Liêm set the footage rolling. Filmed from the building opposite, the scene was brief, but mind-boggling. Batailley hadn't been making it up. A man dressed as a satyr really had come to snatch Milena Bergman. The video showed him emerging from the tarmac path, no doubt just after socking Batailley, and bursting onto Rue d'Assas with the pianist slung over his shoulder. Despite her best efforts to struggle free, the young woman was powerless against her attacker's vice-like grip. Next, the half-man, half-goat was shown hurling her into the back of a van before tearing off.

'That's insane,' Botsaris declared. 'Play it through again. I think you can see the reg.'

The clip sprang back to life. It was like watching an old found-footage film, Roxane thought, except modern phone cameras were so sleek that the video was teeming with easily retrievable details, like the model of the van – a side-opening Citroën Jumpy – and the vehicle registration plate.

'Yeah, there it is!' Botsaris cried. 'We've got the reg! We're going to catch him!'

The guys began congratulating themselves, a little prematurely for Roxane's taste. Botsaris, glimpsing a chance of saving his holidays, rushed off to tell Sorbier and his JP counterpart.

As she turned back, Roxane realised she had no desire for the case to be resolved. A good investigation was better than drugs, sex, Seroplex and Lexapro rolled into one. A good investigation gave life an electric thrill, a shot of adrenaline. On the flip side, the closure of a case had something depressing about it. Like reaching the end of a good book. It left you with the same empty space, the same sense of despondency, the same pang at being separated from characters you'd started to care about. A hangover that rammed back home the sad reality of your existence.

She pulled away from the house, back up the path to Rue d'Assas. Cameras from the BFM and LCI news channels were stationed around the gateway. As she elbowed her way through the reporters, Roxane was hit by a deep-rooted conviction. This was no normal case, and it was far from over. For a few hours yet, she still had a major head start on the other cops. An advantage she had to seize.

The beep of a horn shook her from her thoughts. Across the street, Valentine Diakité was waiting for her at the wheel of an ice-blue Mini Cooper.

2.

'What's with all the cops?' Valentine asked.

'Get moving and I'll explain.'

'Where are we heading?'

'Turn left onto Rue Vavin, then Boulevard Raspail. I'd like us to stop by Guillaume Budé bookshop.'

During the drive, Roxane filled the student in on the morning's events.

'So we're not the only ones on the case anymore?' Valentine summarised. There was a note of disappointment in her voice.

'It's no bad thing to have the BNRF on board with the hunt to find the girl. Logistics-wise, they're the best guys for the job. But it won't stop us continuing with our line of inquiry: the investigation Marc Batailley was working on before his accident.'

As she opened the window, Roxane caught sight of herself in the wing mirror. She was deathly pale, her hair was a disaster zone, and dark circles and crow's feet splayed from her eyes. A total mess. Valentine, on the other hand, looked as daisy-fresh as ever, with an outfit put together as if she were on her way to a fashion shoot. Tan leather skirt, mohair jumper, glossy tights and high-heeled booties. Life was an unfair bitch.

Guillaume Budé bookshop was a stone's throw away, on the corner of Boulevard Raspail and Rue de Fleurus. Valentine parked up unceremoniously, gaily straddling the central reservation with the hazard lights flashing. It was only half-nine, but as Roxane had hoped, there was already someone inside, arranging the display tables in readiness for the last-minute Christmas rush. She tapped on the window to attract the woman's attention.

'Police, Madame,' Roxane explained, waving her badge.

They entered the bookshop, which was known for specialising in second-hand works on the Ancient World, the Middle Ages and the Renaissance. The sales floor sprawled over 750 square feet, with burnished bookcases and shelf ladders that gave it the feel of an English country library.

'How can I help you?' the owner asked.

She could only be thirty, tops, and her personal style was diametrically opposed to the bookshop's traditional setting: straggly hair, Doc Martens, ripped jeans, a Pearl Jam T-shirt and an oversized, Kurt Cobain-inspired wool cardigan.

'Do you remember serving this customer?' Roxane quizzed, showing her a photo of Batailley that she'd borrowed from Rue d'Assas.

'Of course! He bought a stack of books from us last week. I was the one who advised him.'

'What exactly was he looking for?'

'Books on mythology. The history of Dionysus, the symbolism around him, the meaning of his cult . . .'

'Did he say why?'

'He told me he was a cop and that he was investigating a series of murders.'

Roxane and Valentine exchanged a look of amused scepticism. They could well imagine the old dog dreaming up a cock-and-bull story like that to impress the young woman. The latter brushed some imaginary dust from her shoulder, then appeared to have a revelation.

'In fact, I completely forgot to call him, but his book arrived yesterday!'

'Which book?'

'He wanted a title I didn't have in stock, which I had to order for him. I'll go and get it,' she offered, before vanishing through a mahogany door.

Roxane checked her phone. There was a message from Liêm Hoàng Thông, alerting her that the attempt to trace the van's registration plate had led them to a car which had been stolen a few days earlier near Couronnes metro station. As she'd expected, tracking down the satyr would be harder than it seemed. She showed the message to Valentine, then had a look around the shop. The Budé covers on the shelves brought back her university years. All those hours of slogging late into the night to finish her translations . . . Yellow for the Greek series, red for Latin. The owl of Athena versus the Roman she-wolf. Had anything survived from that, apart from her memories?

She squinted. Beyond the high front windows the sun was climbing in the sky, crowning Valentine with a golden halo and splashing onto the waxed parquet and the mahogany door, which now reopened.

'Here it is.' The owner placed the book down on the counter.

Both women leant in to read the title: *Great Dionysia: The Birth of Classical Theatre in Greece.*

'What's it about?'

'It's an academic work, showing how the earliest forms of theatre were directly descended from the cult of Dionysus.'

'I'm keeping this as evidence.'

'And who'll pay me for it?'

'I'll return it later. Thank you for your help, and Merry Christmas.'

3.

As soon as they were out of the shop, the women raced over to reason with the traffic warden who was poised to slap a ticket on the Mini. After seeing off the threat, Valentine took her place at the wheel again.

'Shall we head for 14 Boulevard Montmartre?'

Valentine had made a note of the address Marc Batailley had apparently visited the day before his accident, which belonged to a café called The Three Unicorns.

'We'll go later. First I'd like to stop by Rue Léon-Maurice-Nordmann in the 13th arrondissement, just along from La Santé prison.'

Valentine swung back onto Boulevard Raspail.

'I'll have to tell you about my evening. I've got news too!'

'I'd completely forgotten about your date with Corentin

Lelièvre! So, how did your secret mission to Hipsterland go in the end?'

'The guy's as thick as a whale omelette,' Valentine began. 'But cagey. He fed me a few anecdotes to begin with, then clammed up when I started to push him. Even so, I did manage to get one juicy titbit from him.'

'Go on.'

'The details in his article and the photos were given to him "ready to roll" by a source, a couple of months back. I did my best to find out who, but that's all he was prepared to say.'

Roxane frowned.

'Raphaël said something during the flight. He thinks it was one of the staff at the hospital where his dad was treated last year.'

'Lelièvre told me his rag got everything *for free*. If the source didn't want paying, that means they had another reason for wanting the article to come out now.'

'Or it just means the guy was spinning you a line.'

'He's invited me for a drink this evening. I'll keep digging.'

'What we need to establish is why he's *still* sniffing around Raphaël.'

'You can be sure I tried. He smelt a scoop, clearly, but he didn't give me much to go on. It will be easier this evening, when it's just the two of us.'

'Don't take any risks, all the same. The guy doesn't inspire me with confidence.'

The Mini continued past Boulevard Montparnasse onto Place Denfert-Rochereau, then sped along Boulevard Saint-Jacques to the junction with Rue de la Santé, where the boulevard was sliced in two by the Glacière overground metro bridge. The prison gave the whole stretch an ominous feel, its fortress-like walls shadowing the pavements and shrouding them in a thick blanket of misery.

The oppressive atmosphere lifted once they hit the next turn-off. Rue Léon-Maurice-Nordmann was a haven of calm and light. Valentine pulled in between the local primary school and an Ethiopian restaurant with an ambery terracotta façade.

'Who have we come to see?'

'Jean-Gérard Azéma, an old paparazzo. I want him to help me track down a lead, without running it through the police database. But I'd rather go alone, to avoid scaring him. Will you wait for me here?'

Valentine nodded, without masking her disappointment. Roxane left the car and walked over to a handsome white art deco-style building set around Square Albin Cachot, which, with its stretched rectangular form, was square in name alone. She rang the intercom, presented herself and asked the photographer to buzz her up. Azéma demurred, but on Roxane's insistence, he conceded to meet her in front of the building.

Roxane tried to rub some warmth into her hands. The air was still icy, but the sun was beaming down. Seeing the Ethiopian restaurant was doing takeaway coffees, she went in to buy herself a double espresso and ordered a second for the pap.

'So, someone's come to see old Jeangégé!'

The slightly rasping voice gave her a start. Azéma had skulked up behind her – clearly a residual tic of the trade. With his tall, still-trim frame, freshly cut salt-and-pepper hair, cashmere coat and dark glasses, the pap had his old-playboy look honed to a tee. Like a Faubourg Saint-Marcel version of Richard Gere.

'Hi, Azéma.'

She'd first met him two years earlier, while interviewing him in connection with a drugs case after his name popped up in the phonebook of the dealer the BNRF were investigating. Nothing had come of the interview, but she hadn't forgotten the guy. After starting out as a photojournalist, Azéma had gone on to become one of the most influential paps of the nineties and early noughties. The golden age when the gossip magazines would pay gigabucks for a shot of Diana with Al Fayed, Mitterrand's daughter emerging from a restaurant, or Kate Moss sniffing a line of coke. He'd made a fortune, but his dope habit, two divorces and the crisis in tabloid journalism had left him in the doldrums. Since then he'd been scraping by, but he still had his contacts.

'*Pig* gravy, is it?' he quipped as he took his paper cup.

Roxane had hoped to linger in the warmth of the restaurant, but the owner made it plain that they should stop blocking the entrance.

'So, what brings you this way, Montchrestien? We're going to freeze our arses off,' he grumbled once they were back on the pavement.

Roxane pulled a Post-it from her pocket.

'I'd like you to identify this number for me,' she explained, handing him the slip of pale-yellow paper. 'It's ex-directory.'

'Are you having me on? You could do that yourself in no time.'

'It's for a private investigation. I don't want the police mixed up in it.'

Jeangégé shook his head.

'Nah, smells dodgy to me.'

'It's a personal thing, I'm telling you. Just a number I found on my bloke's phone. I think he's been playing around.'

'I don't believe you for a second.'

'Please, as a favour. I'm not asking the earth.'

'But what's in it for *me*?'

'I'll owe you one.'

'Too vague. I'll do it for 300 euros.'

'Fuck off.'

The paparazzo adopted an uncompromising look.

'Sorry, sweetheart, but times are hard. Instagram has killed the profession,' he rued. 'The celebs have screwed us over good and proper – now they're all on social media, they can unveil their own private lives to the world. And with these shitty smartphones, everyone's a pap in the making.'

Roxane had already heard this speech many times: the triumph of digital storytelling over real 'journalism'. She rubbed her eyes. It was 23 December, but the school oppos-ite must have been running a holiday club, judging by the clamour of children coming from the playground. One of the most beautiful soundtracks in the world.

'Are you familiar with Milena Bergman?' she asked, to change the subject.

'Never heard of her.'

'A pianist who was on the flight that crashed last year.'

'Ah, yes. Maybe.'

'There's an article about her on the *Week'nd* website. Have a look and let me know if anything jumps out at you.'

'And I'll be doing that for your pretty face, will I?'

'That and the number. Don't forget.'

'Nice try,' he chortled as he walked away. 'Off you trot, you dirty copper.'

4.

The Right Bank

Along the Grands Boulevards, the cult of Christmas was in full swing. People were flocking in their hordes, but without joy. Weary shadows communing in drudgery, victims of the imperative to obey a Christmas spirit that had long since lost its way. The streets were spewed with ugly fairy lights and recycled-plastic trees. Even the department-store window displays, sagging like meringues under their snowy décor, drew only indifferent stares or overplayed whoops.

Roxane and Valentine had left the Mini in a car park, in Rue de la Chaussée-d'Antin. Roxane wasn't expecting the trip to yield much, but experience had taught her that to make a catch in quiet waters, you had to cast all the lines you could.

On pushing open the door to The Three Unicorns, they were assailed by a vibe that screamed cool and contemporary. Potted plants spilled from ceiling to floor, amid an ocean of cerused wood, pastel colours and a spotless white-tiled bar counter that wouldn't have looked adrift in a research lab. The place wasn't a traditional café, but a kind of organic juice bar serving up kale crisps and cold-pressed 'cucumber and wild mint superjuice' at 12 euros a pop. Here, everything was *green, healthy, lactose-free* and overpriced.

Taking out her tricolour badge for reinforcement, Roxane

fought her way to the till and asked to speak to the owner. The manager was just like the furbishings: falsely welcoming. She let the cop say her piece, then checked the staff rota. Magda, the floor supervisor likely to have served Batailley the previous Sunday, wouldn't be clocking on for another quarter of an hour.

'We'll wait,' Roxane declared, taking a seat at one of the tables.

She ordered a coffee, but as the juice bar wasn't offering any, she followed Valentine's lead and settled for an almond milk.

'Can you picture Marc Batailley here?'

'No, I can more see him over the road, nursing a pint of Chouffe and a sausage baguette in one of the little bars in the Passage des Panoramas.'

'If he did come here, then it must have been on someone's suggestion. It wasn't his choosing.'

While waiting for Magda to arrive, they took stock of their progress. What had happened that morning at Raphaël's house – the appearance of the man dressed as a satyr and the kidnapping of the presumed Milena – confirmed their hypothesis about a mythological connection. Was the 'satyr' operating alone, or did he have accomplices? Roxane recalled Batailley's notes about possible sect-like activities linked to the cult of Dionysus. Could a group of cranks, styling themselves as worshippers of Dionysus, have snatched 'Milena' to force her to participate in their ceremonies? Possibly. But that in no way explained how the pianist had survived the plane crash, nor how her body had come to be identified among the victims.

In front of her on the table, Valentine's phone hadn't

stopped vibrating for the past five minutes.

'Reply, if it's important.'

'Nah, it's just some guy I had a thing with last year, and now he won't leave me alone.'

'Do you want me to scare him off?'

'No need, he's more of a pain than a threat.'

'Are you seeing anyone at the moment?'

'I didn't know I was being cross-examined!' Valentine snapped.

Wounded, Roxane shot her a dark look.

'I don't have a boyfriend.' The student's tone was more conciliatory now. 'I've already told you, the guy I really like is . . .'

'Don't say Raphaël Batailley!'

'Yeah! I should feel ashamed admitting this, but I'm not thrilled the pianist is back on the scene.'

'I don't understand. The crash was over a year ago. If you're that keen on Batailley, you could have made your move any time.'

'I'm interested in a serious relationship! I wanted to hang back, give him time to grieve. Not to look like some animal throwing myself at him to exploit the situation.'

Roxane felt a stab of irritation.

'I don't know what you see in the guy anyway. He's all show. A poser who likes to ham it up as a tortured artist and—'

'That's rubbish! You don't know him.'

'Neither do you, not in any meaningful way!'

'At least *I've* read his books.'

'So you think you're in love with the man, just because you've got a thing for the writer!'

'Stop twisting my words.'

'The guy gives me a bad feeling. He's hiding something, I'm telling you. Believe me. I've come across his type before.'

The manager interrupted their argument.

'Madga's arrived,' she said, presenting them with a young woman with huge pale eyes and a shaven head.

Britney Spears, 2007, Roxane mused as she took the situation in hand.

'I won't keep you long, but please think carefully.' She handed Magda the photo of Marc Batailley. 'Do you recognise this man?'

'Yeah, maybe.'

The cop sighed. Question one, and already the girl had her riled.

'"Maybe" means nothing. Do you recognise him or not?'

'I think he came in last week, yeah. Bit of a saddo who kept calling me "poppet", but he left me a five-euro note as a tip.'

'Had you ever seen him before?'

'Nope.'

'Was he alone or with someone?'

'He was meeting a woman. She was ginger, I think. Quite old, with long hair.'

'What age is "old" to you?'

'Older than you. I'd seen her a few times before, anyway.'

'Does she work around here?'

Magda shrugged.

'Dunno, maybe.'

'How long did they stay?'

'A good quarter of an hour.'

'You didn't catch what they were talking about?'

'No, but they were having an argument, I think.'

'A heated one?'

'More a battle of wills. The guy wanted to know something and the old woman was refusing to tell him.'

'What did he want to know?'

'Dunno. Some piece of information. A name, address . . .'

Roxane gathered that she wouldn't glean anything more. She thanked the girl and headed back onto the boulevard. Impervious to the bustle, she ventured out a few feet into the road to keep watch for passing taxis.

'Do you want a lift?' Valentine offered.

'Don't bother yourself, I'll manage.'

'Are you pissed off with me?'

'Yeah, you're doing my head in. I know Raphaël Batailley isn't to be trusted.'

'That's no reason to get worked up.'

'Right. Give me a break, will you?'

'When you're in a mood, you sure don't hide it . . .'

RAPHAËL

5.

The icy outside air gave me the jolt I needed. I turned up my coat collar and took the left-hand pavement down Rue d'Assas. The effects of the painkillers were wearing off, reviving the pain in my neck and my migraine. The cops had interrogated me for over four hours. They were so out of their depth, I hadn't even been obliged to lie. I'd answered obliquely, ducking their questions and asking further questions by way of reply. I'd willingly consented to the DNA sample they requested. In their inability to make head or tail of the situation, they seemed to be throwing everything at technology: CCTV footage, mobile phone data, DNA, GPS tracking. The only one who was slightly more switched on than the rest was Roxane Montchrestien, but contrary to what she'd told me, she didn't have any direct involvement in the investigation.

Things couldn't carry on like this. I had to face up to my responsibilities and get a handle on the situation myself. Only I held part of the truth that the cops would take some time yet to fathom. To find the missing part, I needed to go back to the start. The moment when Milena Bergman had been 'duplicated'. The moment when a double, a malevolent doppelgänger, had swept in, by my doing, to claim her.

I kept replaying the torturer's blows. His vindictiveness, his brutality . . . Who was the man? Why that costume? That ruthless determination? Everything was a blur. I had to get things clear in my head. But where to begin? I was still missing too many links to grasp the logic of the chain.

I snuck across between a gap in the traffic, heading for the underground car park by the Jardin du Luxembourg where I'd left the car. As I glanced behind me, I noticed a figure who'd been following me since I'd left home. A cop? It wasn't inconceivable that those chumps wanted to keep tabs on me. I drew level with the heated terrace of the Liberty Bar, on the corner of Rue d'Assas and Rue Vavin. I paused there, and the guy stopped behind me. To make certain, I headed inside the café. After a moment's hesitation, he came in after me. That's the point at which I grabbed him by the scruff of the neck and bundled him onto the pavement.

'Who the hell are you?'

He didn't look like a cop. Scrawny build, hipster goatee, anti-capitalist T-shirt proclaiming *#EatTheRich*. He was swamped by his biker jacket, and wore a stripy woolly hat over his thinning pate.

'Get your hands off me! I'm a journalist.'

'I don't give a fuck. Beat it.'

The guy was nervy, obsessively fiddling with his goatee as if he were intent on yanking it off. In a defensive move, he took out his phone and started filming me. I finally twigged. This must be Corentin Lelièvre, the hack who'd been skulking around me for days. He was a pathetic sight, wielding his iPhone at me as if it were a shield and a semi-automatic rolled into one. He pressed on in a menacing tone.

'I'm on your case, and I have some questions to ask.'

After the cops I didn't fancy a fresh round of interrogation, especially not with some journo hell-bent on making the case for the prosecution.

The sudden screech of tyres made me look up. Sixty feet ahead of me, the lights had just turned green. A Mercedes Coupé had roared into gear, slicing in front of the car to the right. On instinct, I flung myself sideways.

Like a rocket, the speedster was hurtling straight for me.

11

THE PALACE OF ILLUSIONS

ROXANE

1.

'François Hollande wasn't a bad president', 'the French healthcare system is still the best in the world', 'France is an ultraliberal country', 'Macron is a genuine dictator'.

Roxane glanced up at the two men on the next table. In the race to see who could spout the most bullshit per minute, these were a pair of serious contenders.

It was 12.45 p.m. The cop was sitting in Le Select, rereading her notes on her phone as she waited for Valérie Janvier. The Boulevard de Montparnasse's legendary brasserie was far from full. Usually thronged with publishers and journalists, the dining room of the capital's 'people of letters' had seen most of its faithful decamp to their second homes in Brittany and the Luberon for the holidays. With its glass roof, wicker seats, lashings of stucco and ornate mouldings, the place oozed the France of the twenties and kept the tourists reassured. Suddenly a familiar figure appeared in the doorway. Jean-Gérard Azéma. The pap scanned the room for Roxane, then strode over with a wide smile.

'We can't keep away from each other!'

'How did you track me down?'

'That's my job!' Jeangégé replied as he took the chair opposite.

Hailing down a waiter, he ordered himself a pastis with crème de menthe.

'Since when did coppers lunch at Le Select? You don't stint yourself, do you?'

'Got any news for me?'

'I might have. What do I get in return?'

'Zilch. I told you this morning.'

She'd hoped the pap would come crawling back. In these lean times, the Milena Bergman story was tantalising bait.

'OK,' he ploughed on, 'as proof of my good intentions, I'll give you the details of the ex-directory caller on the house.'

He handed her back the Post-it she'd left with him a few hours earlier. Azéma had added a name to it.

'Gaétan Yordanoff?'

'A colleague of yours, apparently.'

'A cop?'

'Yes, the Financial Brigade's finest. I love it when you piggies start going after each other. It gets me all choked up.'

Roxane found the tip-off intriguing. Further evidence, if any were needed, that Batailley had pulled on all the strings he could, and that the case had complex ramifications.

The waiter returned with the cocktail. Jeangégé drained it in one, luxuriant mouthful, as if he'd just traversed the Sahara without a water bottle.

'Aaah, that's the stuff! The real deal! You can't beat a good pastis. Reminds me of holidays in the South – pétanque, Saint-Paul-de-Vence, La Colombe d'Or . . .'

'I'm expecting someone, so if you've nothing more to tell me, you can go and finish your drink at the bar.'

'Hold your horses. I had a look at your article. Pretty interesting . . .'

Azéma wasn't stupid. After all these years, he still had the same eagle eye and ability to sniff out the sordid, scandal-filled recesses of the soul. All while dressing up his dirty dealings as the 'quest for truth'.

'Explain to me why the cops are interested in this story.'

'That's the million-dollar question, Jeangégé. But if I need any information putting out there, you'll be the first to know.'

'Promise?'

'Cross my heart and hope to die. Now get out of here. My lunch date will be arriving any minute. And ask them to put your pastis on my bill at the bar.'

12.55 p.m. Roxane made a quick call to confirm what the pap had told her. He almost had everything right. Gaétan Yordanoff was a cop, but rather than being on the Financial Brigade proper, he worked for the BRIF, the judicial police's brigade for financial research and investigation. She rang the unit, stated who she was and asked to be put through to Yordanoff, although she kept her expectations modest, given the date and time of day. A woman answered, one of his colleagues, who informed her that Yordanoff was on leave until 3 January. As she seemed friendly, Roxane tried to wangle the cop's number, to no avail.

'It's been a hellish end to the year. Gaétan wouldn't take

it well. He's been talking to me about his festive plans for months.'

The French and their holidays. An indissoluble love story.

'Text him with my contact details at least, explaining I'd like to speak with him about Marc Batailley.'

She hung up without much hope that the cop would bite.

2.

'I was third-in-command on Marc Batailley's Major Crime squad in the early two-thousands. He taught me everything I know.'

With her trouser suit, bob cut and designer trainers, Valérie Janvier had nailed the art of stylish power dressing. Duty-bound by the school holidays, she'd come with her daughter in tow, a girl of seven or eight with a slightly spaced-out look and her nose buried in a fat Geronimo Stilton book.

Contrary to Roxane's fears, she and Janvier had hit it off immediately. Not only was the senior officer approachable, but she had a relaxed, almost detached demeanour, as if nothing in the profession could faze her anymore. Having been given the latest on Batailley's condition, she was now recalling her formative years under the old dog's stewardship.

'At the time,' she resumed, 'Marc was still traumatised by his daughter's death. He had his ups and downs, but he was a good team leader despite what senior management thought. They saw to it that we weren't given first refusal on cases, so we didn't notch up many spectacular triumphs, but we did our job without having anything to be ashamed of.'

Roxane let the Chief Superintendent take a few more

mouthfuls of her ceviche before prompting her to continue.

'Did you keep in touch once you'd moved on?'

'Yes, you could say he accompanied me from afar as I climbed the ladder. He's good with advice, and even after he was put out to grass, he was always happy to do me a favour.'

'When was the last time you heard from him?'

'About ten days ago. I'd never known him like that – excited, but anxious too. He told me he was working on an investigation alone, outside of procedure.'

'He didn't tell you what it was about?'

'Let's say he was very vague at the start. His way of trying not to scare me, of protecting me if things took a nasty turn.'

Valérie Janvier filched a few chips from her daughter's plate. Roxane pursued her line of questioning.

'What did Marc want from you?'

'The first thing he asked was if I could hook him up with a trusted contact at the DSC.'

Formerly housed in the old fort of Rosny-sous-Bois, and now based in Cergy, the DSC department of behavioural science was a small team of specialist officers, comprising a mixture of lab analysts and field researchers. They were drafted in to work with local investigation units wherever a crime involved a violent MO that strayed outside the norm.

'Do you know what he was looking for?'

'From what I could gather, he was after information on any historic murder cases where the crime scene hinted at a mythological connection. He wanted to run a search of the DSC database to see if it was possible to establish any common MOs.'

'Did he mention Dionysus?'

'You're very well informed! Yes, he did come on to that

later. His trip to Cergy was a fruitful one. Their Violent Crime Linkage Analysis System – the ViCLAS – threw up two cases of particular interest, one in France and another in England.'

Roxane retrieved a pen from her pocket to take notes. Janvier concentrated for a moment, choosing her words carefully.

'I'm sure you'll have heard of the first case – it got some media attention at the time. In 2017, the body of a soldier was found in a container in Avignon, near the Palais des Papes.'

Roxane was scribbling on her forearm like a sixth-former. 'And the second case?'

'It happened a year later. The murder of a judge in Stratford. I'll leave you to search out the details online.'

'And how were the two cases linked?'

'On both occasions, the bodies were covered with a goatskin that had been sewn directly to the skin.'

The little girl looked up from her book, on hearing the details of the murders. Janvier gave her a reassuring smile.

'Did Batailley think he was on the trail of a serial killer?'

'Not necessarily, but maybe a series of murders. Something juicy, in any case. The kind of thing that made us all choose this job in the first place.'

So Batailley hadn't been bullshitting the bookshop owner after all.

'You were taking a risk in helping him, weren't you?'

'Marc's an excellent cop. He wasn't pursuing this investigation for the fun of it, or just to mix things up. I could tell he was on to something big. And when someone of his calibre comes and offers you a potential serial killings case on a plate, you'd be pretty stupid not to help him out.'

'So what was the agreement you came to?'

Janvier shrugged.

'That he'd pass on the case to me once it was ripe.'

'Why are you telling me all this?'

Rather than replying, Janvier finished off her sea bass.

'I've been finding out a bit more about you, Montchrestien. Why has Sorbier given you the cold shoulder?'

Roxane remained impassive, as if the question didn't concern her.

'I'll be straight with you,' the Chief Superintendent continued. 'I'm leaving the police next spring. I've had an offer to head up security at a big luxury brand.'

Roxane was unable to conceal her surprise.

'Nowadays, all you get in this job is constant abuse and shitty salaries.' Janvier's tone was defensive. 'In the end, there'll be nobody decent left.'

'But you wouldn't be against ending your career in a blaze of glory.'

The Chief Superintendent's face hardened, her voice taking on an edge of menace.

'I've put you on Batailley's trail. In return, I'd expect you to—'

Roxane's phone began vibrating on the table. Liêm Hoàng Thông. She gestured with her hand to indicate that she was obliged to take the call.

'Hi, Liêm.'

'I've got news for you, boss. You're free to do what you like with it.'

'Go on.'

'Someone's just tried to kill Raphaël Batailley.'

3.

As luck would have it, Roxane wasn't far from the site of the incident. After settling the bill, she made straight for the Liberty Bar via Rue Vavin. In front of the café, a swarm of police cars and fire engines were blocking the traffic and drawing a herd of onlookers.

It was a striking scene. A car – a Mercedes Coupé – had ploughed into the front of the bar, smashing all the windows. Roxane hung back for a moment with the bystanders behind the police cordon, listening out for an initial salvo of details. Apparently there had been one victim, but it wasn't the driver, who'd just been rushed to hospital by ambulance after a lengthy struggle by the firefighters to rescue her from the vehicle. The airbag had saved her life. Roxane spied Botsaris deep in conversation with Major Gallonde, the head of the daytime branch of the STJA, the Prefecture's judicial accident processing service charged with investigating RTAs that had resulted in serious injury. Her former lieutenant's face was drained of colour, his features contorted in an uneasy fixed grin.

Roxane flashed her badge to get past the roadblock. The 6th arrondissement force might have been first on the scene, but Gallonde's team and the forensics bods were now running the show, converging on the area to take photos, assess distances, collect prints from the steering wheel and interview witnesses. Inching as close as she could to the wreckage of the vehicle, Roxane was chilled by the vision that met her. The pavement was soaked in blood. Thick smears of deep red flecked with black, like the killing floor of a slaughterhouse.

'It's not a pretty sight, boss.'

Roxane recognised Liêm Hoàng Thông's voice behind her.

'Fill me in, Liêm. What exactly do we know?'

'The driver lost control of her Merc, then went haring over the kerb and barrelled through the terrace and front window of the bar. It's a miracle there weren't more victims.'

'What was the damage, in the end?'

'A young woman who was having a coffee on the terrace, with her baby in a pram next to her, was hit head-on and sent flying to the other end of the café. She was already dead when the ambulance got here.'

'Shit . . . And the kid?'

'Completely unscathed, thank God.'

Roxane couldn't take her eyes from the pavement. The car had flattened all the bollards that were meant to act as crash barriers. To have ended up there, the driver must either have jumped the lights or accelerated like a lunatic. She recalled a similar incident a couple of years earlier, when an old codger had confused the brake and accelerator pedals.

'Did you see the driver?'

'Yes, after the firefighters pulled her out.'

'How old?'

'Somewhere between thirty and forty. Asian. Nice looking.'

'Was it just her in the car?'

'Everything seems to suggest so.'

'What about Raphaël Batailley?'

'He's got some nasty cuts from the glass, but he'll be OK. He's already been taken to Cochin for treatment.'

Botsaris made his way over to them, rubbing his bloodshot eyes. He looked like he hadn't slept for days. He gesticulated at the pavement in rage.

'This wasn't an accident, for fuck's sake! There are no skid marks.'

'Maybe the girl had a funny turn,' Roxane ventured.

'She's barely thirty! I'm not buying it for a second. It's your mate she was targeting.'

'Batailley isn't my "mate". Have you identified the driver yet?'

Botsaris nodded towards the two officers and the forensics technician who were congregated around the car.

'Gallonde's gone in search of news. I've left him to it. I don't want to step on any toes.'

'Talking of news, I take it the satyr's van still hasn't been found?'

'It has actually, and it's shit news. A pensioner found it dumped in a forest near Chartres. The guy must have fled from there in another vehicle.'

'Did he set the van on fire?'

'No, which surprised me. He mustn't be on file, because there'll be no shortage of prints.'

'What about this morning at Batailley's place? Did forensics pick up anything usable?'

'We're still waiting on the results. But with it being so close to Christmas, everything's moving in slow motion. You know how it is.'

Gallonde, who had been crouched by the car, got up and beckoned them over. His face was grim.

'We've found the driver's passport,' he announced, holding out to them a dark-blue booklet with gold lettering.

Yukiko Takahashi. American foreign national, born in Japan in 1989. Tucked inside the document were a boarding pass and a car rental contract, together with a hotel key card. The young woman had arrived in Paris the previous evening, on a flight from Berlin. She'd rented the Mercedes from Roissy airport and had spent the night in Hotel Lenox, in the nearby Rue Delambre.

'We found this in the glove box,' Gallonde continued, unfurling a scanned copy of the *Week'nd* article on Raphaël and Milena.

'In case we were in any doubt about the link with Batailley,' Botsaris muttered.

Roxane stared at the passport. The photo showed an attractive young woman with high chiselled cheekbones and long, swept-back dark hair. Yukiko Takahashi. She was sure she'd already come across the name in the investigation. But where?

A quick Google on her phone. The upshot: Takahashi was a violinist, who had regularly played in duos and trios with Milena Bergman. She'd even partnered with her on chamber music recordings. Not a leading light in her field, more of a luxury second fiddle. And clearly a friend of Milena's. The women had spent years performing together in concerts around the world, which pointed to a truly close connection. But what did she have against Batailley – enough to want to kill him?

'We need to interview Batailley as soon as possible,' Roxane declared as she put her phone away. 'Botsa, let's go to see him in Cochin together.'

The lieutenant shook his head.

'We can't flout procedure like that, Roxane. You don't work for the BNRF anymore, and you've no business being here.'

'Don't be a dick, Botsa. You haven't got it in you to solve a case like this.'

'Oh really? Why not?'

'You lack the experience, the instinct, the composure, the brains, the balls. You're just a thirty-five-hour-a-week light-weight who only cares about his poxy holidays.'

'Right, that'll do nicely. Liêm, you head back to Nanterre to keep an eye on the base. Roxane, I won't keep you any longer.'

'You're going to lose this case, Botsa. We've got a dead mother on our hands, an orphaned baby, a kidnapping, the involvement of an American national, a woman who's come back from the dead, and a media storm brewing. Yours will be the first head to roll.'

Botsaris had already turned on his heels, giving her a parting finger.

'It's all going to blow up in your face. Mark my words. And it will damn well serve you right.'

4.

'Come on, boss, calm down. It's not worth it.'

As usual, Liêm attempted to play the mediator.

'What a jerk! You know I'm right, don't you?'

'You have to put yourself in his place . . .'

'In the place of that wanker? No thanks!'

'Do you want me to drop you anywhere?'

He nodded to the Peugeot service vehicle he'd left straddling the pavement a little further up the road.

'No, I'll walk. That imbecile's got me all in a tizz.'

'Please, boss. I'd like to speak with you about something.'

She grudgingly followed him to the car.

Liêm took the wheel and swung back onto Rue d'Assas.

'Where shall I leave you?'

'Keep driving. I'll let you know when to turn. What did you want to discuss with me?'

'I'd better explain first,' he began cryptically.

Roxane exhaled deeply.

'For god's sake, Liêm, spit it out. I'm not in the mood.'

'This morning at Raphaël Batailley's place, while forensics were all over the garden and the perimeter of the house, I did a quick tour of the living room.'

Roxane opened her window as though struggling for oxygen. Liêm pressed on.

'Everyone was obsessed with the crime scene, but nobody was rushing to search inside the house – even though in a blatant case like that, there's no need for a warrant.'

'So you thought you'd take the initiative, if I follow?'

'It was a stroke of luck, really. I was just having a look through the bookcase when I spotted this.'

He rummaged in his shirt pocket and handed Roxane a small black cube, barely half an inch wide.

'What is it? A mic?'

'An ultra-compact spy camera. This one was clipped onto a shelf, but there were five more scattered around the living room. Enough to cover every angle.'

'Seriously?'

Liêm nodded.

Roxane gauged the weight of the device: a couple of ounces, tops.

'This is pro gear, isn't it?'

'Nowadays anybody can order it online, but it's pricey stuff, yes.'

'So Batailley was being watched from every direction, twenty-four seven?'

'Yes and no.'

'How's that?'

'The cameras work using a battery that doesn't have a great charge capacity. I'd say two hours at best.'

'There's no memory card inside?'

'No.'

Roxane was straining to understand.

'But who has access to the footage?'

'Whoever installed the cameras had them connected up to Batailley's home Wi-Fi network, which frankly isn't secure.'

'Meaning . . . ?'

'Meaning they can get real-time access on their phone, from anywhere.'

'Even from the other side of Paris?'

'Even from the other side of the world.'

'How's the camera controlled?'

'It's motion-activated, but it can also be switched on and off remotely.'

Once they hit Boulevard Raspail, she signalled to Liêm to indicate onto Rue de Grenelle.

'That's not all, boss. When I found them, the cameras were still live. I reckon they'll have captured everything:

the moment the girl showed up, the satyr's attack, the police arriving . . .'

Roxane was speechless. Yet another lead that plunged the already baffling investigation even deeper into the unknown.

'What should I do with the information?' Liêm asked as he turned down Rue du Bac.

'Get it on file. Tell Botsaris you went back to Batailley's later, and that's when you noticed them.'

She motioned to him to pull in by the Square des Missions-Etrangères.

'And be sure to keep me posted on anything you find. Ping me every new development over Telegram.'

She unstrapped her seatbelt, gave her teammate a final wave, and headed back up the pavement to the carriage gates. She was just punching in the code when the prolonged blare of a horn made her look up. Liêm was flashing his headlights, beckoning her back to the car. He wound down the window.

'You have to see this!' he shouted.

Roxane got back into the passenger seat. Liêm's phone was open on his message screen.

'I'd left my number with the Musée Zadkine caretaker.'

'The guy who filmed the kidnap?'

'That's right. And turns out he wasn't the only one. His wife also caught some footage, from the floor above and from a different angle.'

Roxane set the video rolling. The frame was wider, offering more of a bird's-eye view.

'Nothing that bothers you?' pressed Liêm.

She frowned. The footage was as brutal as before, but she couldn't see anything fundamentally new. Then, suddenly, something caught her eye. She dragged her fingers over the screen to pan closer.

'What's that?' She pointed to a large, moving orange dot.

'It's a drone,' Liêm replied. 'And I'm willing to bet that whoever installed the cameras in the house was *also* recording the scene from outside.'

5.

It wasn't yet 4 p.m., but the sun had already packed its bags. Since late morning the sky had been greyish white. Even from up in her crow's nest, all Roxane could see on the horizon was a dense, pearly curtain waiting to usher in the dusk. After jumping in the shower, she'd changed into her pyjamas and bundled on the old waffle-knit cardigan she'd found at Batailley's. Despite her hankering for a glass of wine, she'd resolved to hold off until a more reasonable hour and had brewed herself a mug of scalding tea – a bitterly black, Jeju tangerine blend from South Korea – that she'd propped against her leg as a stand-in hot-water bottle. She was now lying on the sofa, hibernating under two blankets with her head resting on her new pillow, the lights dimmed, and the cat purring sleepily next to her.

She was ready. Not for bed, but to continue with her investigation, iPhone in hand. First port of call: the internet, to unearth more details about the two cases Valérie Janvier had talked about.

She began with the simpler of the two, the one that had taken place in France. When it came to miscellaneous news items, local newspapers were often more clued up than the nationals, so she began with the *La Provence* website. After typing in a few keywords, she worked her way down the list of articles on the Avignon murder. On 18 October 2017, the body of an ex-soldier, 62-year-old Jean-Louis Crémieux, had been found in a refuse container in Rue Banasterie, just along from the Palais des Papes. In the post-terror attack climate in France, the murder of the military man was initially feared to be another terrorist incident, but it seemed this theory had been quickly dismissed. Crémieux had served as a captain in the 21st marine infantry regiment in Fréjus, but he'd long since left the army. The cause of death was evident: the ex-soldier's throat had been slit. His body was discovered half-naked, dressed and made-up as if he'd been a drag queen: stiletto heels, basque, suspenders, and a fur stole stitched to his skin.

The case had dragged on interminably. Roxane only had access to a fraction of the details – a few press articles didn't come close to an investigation file – but she inferred between the lines that nobody had ever got a proper handle on the case. For the first couple of weeks, *La Provence* had published articles on it almost daily, probing into the ex-soldier's character, the drag scene, the theory of a settling of scores, and so on. Behind the headlines, however, the genuine news was scant. Over time the coverage had thinned out, and it was now over a year since the paper had last updated its readers on the case. To find out more, Roxane's best hope would have been to try calling one of the cops who'd worked on the investigation at the time. But with only twenty-four hours until Christmas Eve festivities got underway, and without any official referral, it was a non-starter. Hours of being passed from pillar to post that would end up nowhere.

She switched her attention to the other case. The judge who'd been killed in the county of Warwickshire, in central England. Again she started with the local press, flipping between the sites of the *Harborough Mail* and the *Warwick Courier*, but she soon realised that the case had sparked national interest too. Stratford-upon-Avon was the birthplace of Shakespeare. A murder in a tourist hotspot like that couldn't fail to make headlines. So what was the deal? Terence Bowman, a Commercial Court judge, had been found with his head smashed in and pockets turned out in the grounds of Holy Trinity Church. The investigation had been swift. His watch, phone and wallet had been recovered from the outbuildings used by the parish gardeners. Several arrests had followed, leading to a confession in custody by twenty-one-year-old James Deller, a well-known drug addict who'd spent multiple stints in rehab.

As she rounded off her press review, Roxane felt a mixture of excitement and frustration. Excitement to be working, albeit indirectly, on a series of murders, coupled with frustration at not having access to the investigation file. Contrary to what Janvier had told her, there was no mention of a goatskin in the second murder case. Had the Chief Superintendent got her wires crossed? Or had that detail not made it into the press? Whatever the explanation, it wasn't easy to see why Batailley had been so fascinated by the murders or to draw any direct link with the cult of Dionysus.

The buzz of her phone woke the slumbering cat on her leg. A call from a private number.

'Gaétan Yordanoff speaking.'

The guy from the financial research brigade!

Roxane sat up against her pillow.

'Roxane Montchrestien, from the BNRF.'

'I'm on holiday,' Yordanoff began in a reproachful tone.

'That's what I gathered. Thanks for calling me back.'

'What's all this about Marc Batailley?'

'Have you had contact with him recently?'

'No. I haven't heard from him in five or six years.'

'Really? Your personal number appears in his call history from the past few days.'

'What exactly are you investigating?'

'Batailley's in a coma. I'm picking up one of his cases.'

There was a long pause at Yordanoff's end.

'A coma? Is it serious?'

'It's touch-and-go, yes.'

'He . . . he phoned me last week. Wanted me to help him trace a transfer of funds.'

'For what?'

'No idea. I told him to do one. I don't make a habit of working under the table.'

'Come off it. Batailley didn't ring you by chance. If he called, it's because he knew you'd help him.'

'That's all there was to it, I'm telling you!'

'We can play it like that if you want, Yordanoff, and wait until you're called in for official questioning. Or we can clear things up this evening, and your name stays off the record.'

'Nice try, but that's not how it works. I reckon *you're* the one digging around outside of procedure. *Adios.*'

He hung up before she could say another word.

With a sigh, she closed her eyes and surrendered to the warmth of her makeshift bed, listening as the rain battered the windows of the belfry. It wasn't even 6 p.m. It was the night before Christmas Eve, she'd been sacked from her job, her love life was non-existent, she was rubbing up everyone the wrong way, and everyone was doing the same to her. She'd had it with this city, this country, these people, this day and age with its torrent of crap the moment you turned on the radio, looked at the headlines or checked social media. The great triumph of mediocrity. All the time. Everywhere. *I am sad, and want my light put out. [. . .] Do not write. Let us learn to die, as best we may.* Marceline Desbordes-Valmore's words crept into her head. That was it, in a nutshell. She wanted to be *put out*. The flame that had once driven her had faltered, growing weaker by the day. No part of her was able to shine anymore, to emanate light and warmth. Her flame was just waiting for the breath that would snuff it out for good.

She'd never be a great cop. In people's minds, the greats were those who'd cracked extraordinary cases, captured notorious criminals. Broussard and Mesrine. Borniche and Émile Buisson. Monteil and Guy Georges. Batailley and The Horticulturalist . . . She drifted into sleep, lulled by Poutine's purrs. When she opened her eyes again, it was 11 p.m. Liêm's face flashed up on her phone.

'Evening, Liêm.'

'Did I wake you, boss?'

'Are you kidding? I was still hard at it. And you?'

'I'm heading home now.'

Liêm was in his car, with his phone suckered to the dashboard.

'Do you have news?'

'I've just come off a long call with Botsa. He was on his way out of Cochin.'

'Did he manage to see Raphaël Batailley? How's he doing?'

'He's got cuts all over him, but nothing too serious.'

'Did Botsa question him?'

'Yes, but Batailley wasn't giving anything away. He confirmed the car ploughed straight at him, but claims he doesn't know the driver.'

'And the Japanese woman? Yukiko Takahashi?'

'In shock, as you can imagine. When they told her she'd killed a young mother, she had a meltdown and became uncontrollable. The docs had to sedate her up to the eyeballs to calm her down.'

'Has she said anything or not?'

'It was pretty disjointed, but basically, she's insisting it was the *Week'nd* article that made her flip.'

'I'm not with you.'

'She's saying Raphaël Batailley stole her story. That he's an impostor.'

'Make an effort, Liêm. You've totally lost me.'

The lieutenant cleared his throat.

'What she's claiming . . . is that Milena Bergman has always preferred women. Well, you don't need me to spell it out for you.'

'Milena was a lesbian . . .'

'. . . and Takahashi's adamant that she and Milena were a couple.'

'So she was jealous of Milena and Raphaël's relationship?'

'No, not jealous. As far as she's concerned, the relationship simply never existed.'

Thursday, 24 December

12
THE HIDDEN REASON

1.

Roxane was advancing through a snowy landscape that stretched out into infinity. An immaculate, noiseless, eerie expanse of nothingness. A frozen prison without walls or guards. Every step she took echoed out with a piercing crunch, swollen by the silence into a harrowing pall of sound. Crunches that became wails, moans, and choked sobs. To stifle them, she'd stopped dead on the snow. But the threnody had continued its march, pounding through her skull until she could take no more. And pressing her hands to her ears did nothing. Suddenly, she heard a crack underfoot. Looking down, she spotted a dark shape poking through the powdery ground. She crouched to brush off the snow, to reveal a phone, pealing out its carillon call.

The ringtone wrenched her from sleep.

Fuck . . .

During the night, her iPhone had slipped off the sofa.

Retrieving it from under the Chesterfield, she answered without even checking the number.

'Hello?'

'It's Gaétan Yordanoff. Did I wake you?'

Roxane checked the time: 9.10 a.m.

'Are you joking? I've been at my desk for an hour.'

'I've thought about it. I'm willing to tell you what Batailley wanted.'

'So a good night's sleep has knocked sense into you.'

'I've nothing to hide, that's all.'

'I'm listening.'

'Marc wanted to trace a payment that was made on 14 December to a shop in Paris.'

'Which shop?'

'Memorabilia. An antiques store in the Passage des Panoramas, from what I could gather.'

Roxane got up from the sofa. The mention of the location had jolted her wide awake. The Passage des Panoramas was just across the road from 14 Boulevard Montmartre, the address of The Three Unicorns!

'Who did the payment come from?'

'That's one of the things Marc wanted to know.'

'And?'

'I couldn't find any trace of it. There was no transfer. If a transaction was made, it must have been in cash.'

'What was the payment for?'

'Marc didn't tell me. And that's everything I know. So Merry Christmas and all the best to you and yours.'

It was the second time he'd hung up in her face. But that didn't matter. This Christmas Eve, against all odds, Father Yordanoff had delivered her a juicy present. She got dressed at full tilt, fed the cat, then flew down the stairs with her eyes glued to her phone. Memorabilia didn't have a website, just a sparse Facebook page which nevertheless confirmed the shop would be open from 9 a.m. to 7 p.m. that day.

When she reached the street, the arctic conditions pitched her back to the previous night's dream. She glanced up at the sky. It was snowing! Fat, pillowy flakes were dusting the pavements with a white film that was starting to stick. The rush of cold air intensified her stirrings of hunger. She'd noticed that in the fervour of an investigation, some of her colleagues lost their appetites altogether. That had never been true of her. The thrill of the case always came with an underbelly of stress that made her want to devour anything she could lay hands on. Preferably dripping with fat and sugar. She dived into the open-air shopping passage that linked up Rue de Grenelle, Rue du Bac and Boulevard Raspail, where she'd clocked a bakery that did croissants and coffee to go. As she was making for the taxi rank in Boulevard Saint-Germain, three toots of a horn pulled her up short. She whipped around. On the corner of the boulevard, Valentine Diakité's little ice-blue car blinked back at her.

2.

Bare make-up, hair in an unruly tangle, Goth T-shirt, hastily thrown-on parka. For once Valentine didn't look like she'd stepped out of a fashion magazine. But her face was glowing in triumph.

'I've discovered something! A real bombshell!'

'Turn right here,' Roxane instructed, cutting out the radio mid-song. 'We want to head back onto Boulevard Montmartre – Passage des Panoramas, to be precise.'

While they waited at the lights, the student grabbed her iPad from the dashboard. The screen was open on a pdf of the *Week'nd* article on Raphaël and Milena.

'How did it go, your little dinner date with Corentin Lelièvre?'

'I managed to get it out of him! I know why he's so interested in Batailley!'

'Go on.'

'Because Milena isn't Milena!' Valentine's eyes were gleaming.

'Meaning . . . ?'

As the lights turned green, she handed the tablet to Roxane.

'Look at the photo in the article.'

'Which one?'

'The one of Milena and Raphaël in Courchevel. It was taken in front of Les Airelles, one of the swankiest hotels in the resort.'

'Yeah, and?'

'Have a look at the decorations by the entrance.'

Roxane narrowed her eyes and zoomed in on the image.

'Russian dolls.'

'Exactly. Have you ever been to Courchevel?'

'Do you know what cop wages are like?'

'You've hit the nail on the head. Over the years Courchevel's become one of the top holiday spots for rich Slavs. Every year it has them flocking to the Savoie – especially around Orthodox Christmas in early January, when they account for almost three-quarters of the tourists. The resort puts on all kinds of events to mark it. The monitors from the École de Ski Français do a special torchlight descent, and the hotels go all out with their decorations.'

'Right. Where are you going with this?'

'At Les Airelles, the Orthodox Christmas decorations stay up from 2 January to 23 January.'

'So?'

'So this photo was taken in January 2019.'

'Patently.'

'But the problem is . . . that's not possible. Milena Bergman spent the whole of January 2019 giving back-to-back concerts in Japan.'

'A month of concerts?' Roxane's tone was incredulous.

Valentine nodded.

'I read up on it. Japan's perhaps the only country on earth where the public still goes mad for classical music. There's a really deep-rooted musical culture. From infancy, the Japanese receive hours of music lessons a week. Most universities have their own orchestras, and there are loads of concert halls renowned for their acoustics. Some Western performers are seen as idols over there, which is what happened to Milena. Her first album was a massive hit, and after that they couldn't get enough of her.'

'And how does your journo pal explain it?'

'That's just it. He can't. Milena Bergman couldn't have been in two places at once. That's why he's been snooping around Raph, to get to the bottom of the mystery.'

Roxane frisbeed the iPad across the dashboard in frustration. She knew she should have insisted on interviewing Raphaël and Takahashi herself after the accident.

179

'Hey, careful with that!' Valentine protested.

Roxane lost no time in calling Liêm. Before he could get a word in edgeways, she laid into him for not chasing up the forensics results.

'Call the lab and make them get a fucking move on! Batailley told us the girl was hammering on the window. Forensics must have collected dozens of prints. We need the results THIS MORNING, PRONTO! I don't want any more bullshit about Christmas delays. We need to know if—'

'Calm down, boss,' Liêm interrupted, as cool as ever. 'We've had some partial results back from the prints. I sent them over to you twenty minutes ago.'

Shit. She'd checked her texts and emails, but she'd forgotten about Telegram.

'Spoiler alert,' her lieutenant continued. 'The girl that was abducted outside Batailley's house isn't Milena Bergman.'

3.

Ten o'clock, Passage des Panoramas

Roxane elbowed her way through the crowds in search of the shop Yordanoff had mentioned, unceremoniously fending aside every obstacle that rose in her path.

The Passage was one of the city's oldest covered arcades. Snaking from Boulevard Montmartre in the north to Rue Saint-Marc in the south, it was famously the first public building in Paris to have been fitted with gas lighting. At this time of morning, the place was already a hive of activity, crammed with festive drudges and tourists making for the bistros, restaurants and old-fashioned boutiques – stamp emporiums, vintage postcard shops, coin dealers, craft stores – that studded its narrow alleyways. The Americans and the Japanese couldn't get enough of its olde-worlde charm. At last, it offered them a vision of Paris that lived up to the one in their imagination. Everything was present and correct to paint the Belle Époque vibe to perfection: gilded finishes, sculpted wood, mosaic floor tiles, daylight streaming triumphally through the glass roof, mirrors reflecting off each other into infinity.

The arcade was a veritable labyrinth. The central walkway branched into multiple offshoots, each housing yet more philatelists, bookshops and cafés. Finally, Roxane caught sight of an enamelled, azulejo-style sign proclaiming *Memorabilia – Est. 1956*. With Valentine at her heels, she headed inside the tiny boutique and was met by a noseful of wax and dust.

The first image that came to her mind was a cabinet of curiosities. Rows of aged walnut shelves were stacked with a hotchpotch of oddities, ranging from stuffed and fossilised animals to autographs, letters and manuscripts. The unifying thread: all of them had once belonged to celebrities.

Presiding over the miniature kingdom was a woman of indeterminate age, with a mummified face and a scaly dress like a giant fish costume. Wisps of faded bottle-red hair trailed from her turquoise turban.

'Captain Montchrestien,' Roxane announced.

'The police again? You lot won't leave me alone!'

Clearly, she'd come to the right place.

'I already told your colleague. I don't share information about my clients.'

'Things have moved on since then, Madame. The

individual you're trying to protect is suspected of murder and attempted kidnap.'

The woman held an ivory cigarette holder to her lips, as if channelling Alice Sapritch, and took an imaginary drag.

'That's not my problem.'

'It soon will be if I slap you in custody for 48 hours. That'll mean a hefty day's profits down the pan, goodbye to your Christmas Eve celebrations, and—'

'But what exactly do you want to know?'

Roxane groped for inspiration.

'What you should have told my colleague.'

'The client in question bought a strand of hair belonging to a German pianist.'

A strand of hair . . . Roxane felt a surge of excitement.

'Take me through everything from the beginning, please.'

The owner sighed, fiddling with the tangle of necklaces that draped down to her waist.

'If I must, but please take a seat. It's tiring me out watching you standing there.' The order was barked in a gruff smoker's rasp.

Roxane and Valentine sat down in a pair of gilt bronze armchairs with backrests shaped like painfully contorted crocodiles.

'About four months ago,' the woman began, 'a man turned up here. He'd clearly done his research, and knew exactly what he wanted: a long strand of hair belonging to Milena Bergman.'

Roxane trembled. She was closing in on the truth. It had taken her four days, but she was on the cusp of exposing the sham. She'd never swallowed the story about Milena Bergman's resurrection, the idea of her doppelgänger exploding onto the scene. The real Milena was dead. Everything else was nothing but smoke and mirrors.

'Do you *genuinely* sell hair?' asked Valentine.

The shop was oppressively warm. Sapritch flourished a carved-bone fan in front of her face.

'Absolutely. It might be niche, but the market for the hair of celebrities and historical figures is thriving – and very profitable.'

'But who's buying it?' cut in Roxane.

'There are two sorts of collectors,' the owner explained. 'The obsessives who go around amassing valuable items like children with their Panini stickers, and the superfans who want to establish a special connection with their idol.'

'A connection?'

The owner gave another impatient flick of her fan.

'Hair gives you a degree of intimacy that's on a whole different level to autographs, letters or even clothes. It's something intensely personal, natural. It allows you to own a little piece of the person, in some small way making them yours.'

To support her exposition, she stood up and retrieved a selection of glass-fronted display frames.

'I have a few fine examples. Look, here's David Bowie, Charles Trenet, Nathan Fawles . . . Over the years, I've had the privilege of participating in auctions of some of the most sought-after hair samples around: the Beatles, Elvis, Marilyn Monroe, Napoleon, JFK, Churchill . . .'

'But where do they come from?'

'There are all kinds of possible sources. Personal hairdressers, domestic staff, stylists from photoshoots and film sets . . .'

'What about the Milena Bergman piece?'

'From a charity auction organised by the Swiss Red Cross just over three years ago. Several big names were invited to donate personal items. Yannick Noah gave one of his rackets, Soulages contributed a lithograph, Le Clézio a pen, and so on. The pianist decided on a signed score and a strand of her hair. I bought the lot for 200 dollars. The items were fairly run-of-the-mill at the time, because Bergman wasn't that famous in Europe. It was primarily after her death that she became more talked about.'

'And so a man bought the hair strand off you?'

'Yes, and he also wanted me to plait it into a bracelet. That's why the process took a while.'

'Into a bracelet?'

Roxane froze. *The girl was wearing a watch and a bracelet.* Her conversation with Bruno Jean-Baptiste, the frogman from the River Brigade rescue mission, came back at her like a boomerang. Why hadn't she probed deeper into that lead? She had hoped to broach the question with the doctor from the Hôtel-Dieu forensic medical unit, but he'd hung up before she got the chance. The Stranger in the Seine case hadn't kicked off the previous Saturday. It was a plot that had its origins months earlier. A plot in which she'd starred as both a pawn and an active cog. She'd thought she was being clever in gathering the hair samples from the I3P. But they hadn't fallen there in such abundance by accident. They were put there expressly *so she would find them.*

'We might struggle to comprehend it nowadays,' Sapritch continued, 'but before the invention of photography, hair was a very potent symbol of attachment. People would cut off locks of the deceased's hair before burying them, and carry around the hair of their lovers, mistresses and children. Mostly they kept it in lockets, but it was also common to have the hair set into other types of jewellery.'

'What did he look like, the guy who made the request?'

'Forties, brown hair, unremarkable.'

Roxane pressed on more forcefully.

'Try, Madame. This is a criminal investigation.'

'I can't make it up! Neither short nor tall, fat nor thin, ugly nor attractive. Commonplace, invisible. Like Mister Cellophane in the musical.'

Roxane had a stroke of inspiration. On her phone, she brought up a photo of Raphaël Batailley and showed it to the woman.

'Was it this man?'

The woman shrugged dismissively.

'Certainly not. I'd have remembered him.'

Roxane was struck dumb for a moment. She felt suddenly floored. Ashamed to have been duped by a ploy that, however inventive, was fundamentally homespun. Blindsided by her faith that DNA was king. Confounded by a simple hair strand.

Her phone ringtone interrupted her ruminations. Liêm. *Again.*

'Yes?'

'I can only talk for ten seconds, boss. I'm just leaving Cochin with Botsa. Batailley's done a runner!'

'What? When?'

'Within the past few minutes, according to the nurses. He got out through the window.'

'I knew it!'

What a band of amateurs.

'We're off to try and track him down,' Liêm continued. 'I'll keep you posted.'

4.

'Put your foot down and take the bus lane!'

'But where are we going?' Valentine asked.

'I don't know yet. For now, just head towards the Louvre and Rue de Rivoli.'

It was one of those occasions when blues and twos would have been seriously useful. Roxane closed her eyes, taking her head in her hands as she tried to block out the commotion around her. What was Batailley's role in all this? Victim or culprit? What was going through his mind right now? And most pressingly, where was he? In her head she pictured the Cochin complex. She was familiar with the site from having frequented their fertility clinic for a time. It wasn't very far from Rue d'Assas, but the writer wouldn't risk returning home. *Where, then?* Maybe he'd simply taken a taxi from the Port-Royal rank on his way out of the hospital. Or, more likely, perhaps he was aiming to recover *his own car.* She remembered the card she'd found at his house. Batailley had a permit for the André-Honnorat underground car park, just along from the Jardin du Luxembourg.

'Cross the Seine and take Rue Saint-Jacques.'

She still had her eyes closed. How long was it since Batailley had left the hospital? Twenty minutes? Half an hour? Even on foot, he must have reached the Jardin already. They were going to lose him.

'Turn right, it'll be quicker down Boul' Michel. Fuck the red light, we don't care!'

Hôtel de Vendôme, the École des Mines building, then, further on, Lycée Montaigne. The vehicle entrance to the car park was on Rue August-Comte, and pedestrian access was on either side of the Jardin. As they rounded the corner of the Rue, she spotted one of the BNRF's unmarked Peugeot 308s. Botsaris and Liêm had clearly had the same idea as her! But without reinforcements to storm each floor, they'd decided to wait for the bird to fly the cage.

'The ramp, quick!' Roxane urged. 'Grab a ticket and head inside.'

The Mini descended the first four storeys. Access to the fifth was guarded by an automatic barrier that required a permit card.

'Wait for me here,' Roxane instructed as she left the car.

Striding over the barrier, she inched along the wall to the level below, then wove in between the concrete columns, bumpers and bodywork. Bathed in a yellowish light, at that level the car park was silent and deserted. She scanned the surrounding vehicles. There wasn't a trace of engine or tyre noise. Batailley wasn't here, or else she'd already missed him. Suddenly the timer lights cut out. For a moment Roxane stayed motionless in the darkness. Screwing up her eyes, she conjured back the memory. The parking card she'd discovered in the writer's desk had been in a drawer with his passport, phone and car keys. *The keyring.* She could vaguely recall it. *A shiny white-and-blue disc. A letter 'A' shot through with an arrow . . .* The Alpine logo!

She flicked the lights back on and continued up the aisleway, scanning once more along the rows of cars. The blue A110 she was hunting for was right at the end, parked between two chunky SUVs. As she drew closer, a shape came into view on the front seat. Raphaël was crumpled over the steering wheel, his head buried in his arms. For a second she thought he was dead, but when she pressed her face up to the window, she realised he was crying.

She tapped on the glass. The writer gave a start. After taking a moment to recognise her, he unlocked the door.

'You and I need to have a very serious chat, Raphaël,' she said, sliding into the passenger seat.

Looking utterly defeated, he wiped his eyes.

'It's all my fault. The woman who died in the accident yesterday. It's *my fault* . . .'

'If you want my help, you have to tell me everything.'

'It was a mistake, a lie that spiralled out of control. And now someone's dead because of it.'

'I know that the young woman I've been chasing after since the start of the week isn't Milena.'

'No,' he confirmed. 'Her name's Garance de Karadec.'

'Why didn't you tell me sooner, for god's sake?'

'I thought I could make everything OK. It's a long story.'

She sighed, then shook him on the shoulder.

'You have to tell me EVERYTHING,' she repeated. 'From the beginning. NOW.'

13
BÉBEL'S SON

RAPHAËL

1.

It's easy to pinpoint when it all started. The day everything began to go off course. It was a Saturday morning in October, just over two years ago. At the time my dad was still living at his house in the suburbs of Moret-sur-Loing, an hour outside Paris. It was 10 a.m. I'd carried on ringing the buzzer, but nobody had answered. Seeing his car in the drive, I'd climbed over the gate and entered the house through the garage.

My father, Marc Batailley, was lying blind drunk in the middle of the kitchen. It was a familiar scene. Since I was ten years old – ever since my little sister Vera's death – it had replayed itself countless times, always following pretty much the same script. At more or less regular intervals, my dad would exhume the family albums and my sister's teddies that he'd clung onto. To ramp up the sense of tragedy, he'd then sit himself opposite the highchair where she used to eat and get off his face talking to her ghost, begging for her forgiveness and rerunning the film of our lives together. Finally, at a certain point, he'd remove his Manurhin MR-73 from its holster and toy with the idea of blasting a bullet through his head to join her.

As always, I'd swung into my tried-and-tested protocol: undressing him, dragging him under the shower – hot water first, then a jet of cold – and putting him to bed with a steaming mug of pu-erh tea and a big glass of lemon and ginger on the nightstand next to him.

I'd never resented him for it. Quite the reverse. I knew these dives into the well of despair were safety valves. Decompression chambers that had kept him going this long. And anyway, I'd had my own bouts of hopelessness, my less glorious moments, my familiar demons. Through thick and thin my dad had been there, never once lecturing me. On many occasions he'd picked me up from the police station after I'd got into fights. He'd twice helped me through stays on the psych ward, after the call of the void had got the better of me too. We'd always stuck by each other, always supported each other in our darkest days. My dad was the main man in my life, and I was the main man in his.

After tucking him in, I'd gone back down to the living room to restore some order. I'd tidied away the highchair and the toys, including the famous 'Babywabbit' Vera carried with her everywhere, and who'd witnessed her dying hours in my mother's car. Her final companion. The last image she must have taken with her. Make no mistake, every time I see the animal, I bawl my eyes out and feel like topping myself too. At that point, I'd taken my own turn at stroking the barrel of the MR-73 and entertaining the idea of blasting my brains out to join her in the sky. I knew it was very likely that one day things would end that way. Part of me had spent a long time preparing for it. But not today, and not like that.

In the end I'd stashed the gun back in its case. My dad and I had that much in common: we were reasonable in our unreasonableness, moderate in our immoderation. We flirted with madness and chaos without succumbing to them entirely. A lingering hunger for life always brought us back to the light.

I'd finished my clean-up by slotting the photos back in the albums, unsurprised by my own resultant outbreak of goose-pimples. I wish my mother weren't in nearly all of them. In her obsession with her own image, she always found a way to hijack the shot. The opposite of my dad, who was left to officiate as photographer. As I was flipping the pages, I only came across four where my sister and I appeared with him alone. Four photos that reminded me I'd enjoyed a happy childhood until I was ten. My innocence was short-lived, but that decade at least gave me a framework and foundations to fall back on – a baseline that, when push comes to shove, protects me from a lot of things. But not from everything.

2.

In one of the albums, I'd read back over some old press cuttings I hadn't seen in years. Articles from *La Provence* and *La Marseillaise* published in the days following the arrest of Raynald Pfefferkorn. It had been the pinnacle of my dad's career. Just a few months before Vera's death, the Marseille Major Crime unit he headed up had identified and arrested one of the first French serial killers of modern times. Nicknamed 'The Horticulturalist', Pfefferkorn was a perverse psychopath who'd abducted and assassinated eight people – six women and two men – in the Marseille metropolitan area between 1987 and 1989. In February 1990, knowing the game was almost up, he'd tried to board a train to Belgium. My dad and two of his guys, Nucerra and Albertini, had collared him 'old-school' style on the grand staircase of Saint-Charles station. A bit like Belmondo in his *Fear Over the City* heyday.

The reference to old Bébel was there in the *La Provence* article. Thirty years on, it still gave me a flush of pride. That was the image I'd conserved of my dad. Indestructible. The image that had got me through all the others I'd witnessed. After his moment in the sun and his transfer to Paris, his career had been marred by downs and deeper downs in line with his fluctuating psychological state and successive redeployments. On multiple occasions he'd faced disciplinary action from the board. I'd feared for him every time they tried to bring him down, but the knocks always seemed to give him a fresh dose of motivation. Three years earlier, he'd come perilously close to dismissal after turning a blind eye to two soap bars of cannabis in return for a tip-off. Thankfully, the big-shot lawyer I'd hired for him managed to get the case dropped in time.

He was now approaching retirement, although I knew that he'd long since been put out to grass. He'd been palmed off from one unit to another like a dead horse, and had lost nearly all of his allies. The whole situation made me ache. I thought about it a lot, fuelled with a mixture of rage and pain that even he couldn't have suspected.

The prime target of this rage was Élise Batailley. After

my sister's death, when both parents were vying for sole custody of me, a family court judge had somehow found in my mother's favour! Our living arrangement had only survived two months. I refused to speak to her other than to hound her with abuse, running away time and again to my dad's house. As the final stain on her reputation, I went around telling my classmates that she kept me locked naked in the basement while she invited random men over to sleep in her bed. Then, one morning, I learnt that her lover, Joël Esposito, destroyed by the scandal that had followed my sister's death, had committed suicide by hanging himself on a tree in his garden. Esposito's death accelerated my mother's decline. Initially she agreed to shared custody, but when my dad got his posting to Paris shortly afterwards, she didn't stand in the way of my joining him.

For years Élise kept phoning and writing to me, but I never answered her calls or opened her letters. Once I turned fifteen, she tired of trying, and I stopped hearing from her. After my first book was released, she made a renewed effort to contact me through my publishers, but I asked them to return her letters. Her last attempt had been around ten years earlier, at a book signing I was doing in the Virgin Megastore on the Champs-Elysées. I'd spotted her from a distance and given her the finger, which had dissuaded her from coming any closer.

On that fateful Saturday, I'd put the albums back on the bookcase, next to the hundreds of classical CDs. Although he'd had no formal training, my dad had always nursed a passion for the piano. I'd picked a CD more or less at random, purely because I liked the sleeve – Erik Satie's *Gymnopédies*, performed by Milena Bergman – and stuck it on while I washed up and swept the floor. Once I'd finished, I made myself a coffee and went out to drink it on the terrace. On the teak patio table, my dad had left a packet of fags and his Zippo engraved with the head of a fiery-maned lion. Even though I'd never smoked in my life, I'd taken one and lit it. A pathetic attempt to stay close to him. Killing myself one puff at a time so that I could follow him to the grave. So that he wouldn't feel so alone. Because for days now, the hour of reckoning had been closing in. Earlier that week, a lung scan and biopsy had revealed that an already well-advanced cancer was storming through the old lion's lungs.

I'd gone along with my dad for the tests. At the hospital, a doctor had recommended he get started straight away on a course of chemo – the only way of containing the spread. After thanking him, my dad had replied that he didn't wish to go down that route. With that, he'd risen from his chair and, more in derision than defiance, had sparked up before exiting the doctor's office.

3.

'All right, champ?'

My dad had re-emerged just before 1 p.m., not looking too much the worse for wear, all things considered. He'd ruffled my hair as he had done since I was a kid. He was freshly shaven, and had slipped on a white shirt, jeans and a Kenzo blazer that he must have owned for at least fifteen years, but which always boded well.

'Shall we head out for a bite to eat?' He mooted the plan as though nothing had happened.

'OK.'

'La Belle Équipe?'

'Why not.'

La Belle Équipe was an open-air restaurant on the riverside and his usual haunt. Despite the amount of alcohol that must still have been in his system, he'd insisted on driving us there in his Caterham. I'd bought him the British roadster as a present five years earlier, in homage to the model driven by Belmondo in *Cop or Hood*. When we arrived at the restaurant, he'd given the manager his spiel to wangle us a table with unbroken 'sea views'.

We'd ordered oysters and fried whitebait. I was drinking Pessac-Léognan and he was on the Coke Zero. It was the weekend. The décor was kitsch, but it was a picture-postcard setting: red-and-white gingham tablecloths, blooming planters, a guy in a boater playing the accordion . . . All around us, people seemed to be enjoying themselves. It wasn't really my cup of tea, but the place had its charm if you were into moules frites at €19.90 a pop and white wine that tasted of summer evenings under the arbours.

'I've been thinking. It would make sense if you came to live with me, in Rue d'Assas, while you're having the chemo. You'd have less to-ing and fro-ing that way.'

'I've already told you, Raph. I'm not having the chemo.'

'Come on, that's crazy talk. You can't let yourself die without even trying!'

'I can. I'm exhausted, I've had enough.'

'I thought you had more fight in you.'

'Listen, all this talk about "battling the illness", "staying strong", "thinking positive", it's meaningless crap. It has no bearing on the spread of the cancer cells.'

'And you're not scared of dying?'

'Not really.' He looked straight at me. 'We both know part of me has been dead for a long time.'

'"Part of me has been dead for a long time"? Now that's meaningless crap too.'

He couldn't suppress a half-smile.

'Fair point. Even if it is the truth.'

'So you're just going to let yourself die?'

He scratched his chin with a grimace.

'It should all be over quite quickly.'

'And me?'

'What about you?'

'You're not arsed about leaving me on my own?'

'I've nothing left to give you, Raph.'

He hadn't tried to look away, and what I saw in his eyes broke me. The proof that he'd given up the fight.

'I'm emptied out.' His words confirmed it.

Then he'd stood up, muttering something along the lines of, 'Need to piss again. Ruddy prostate. Damned useless.'

I'd remained where I was. Distraught. Lost. Throughout the exchange I'd forced myself not to look over my shoulder, but I knew *she* was there listening. Vera, my sister. Or rather, her ghost. Or rather, the mental image I'd created of her ghost. I turned around, resolved to take her to task. Today, she was around seven or eight. She was wearing heart-shaped sunglasses, with her hair in long bunches, sucking on a mint-flavoured Mr Freeze.

'This time it's for good,' she affirmed. 'Daddy's going to come and see me soon.'

'No, I don't think so.'

'He made it clear, didn't he?'

'I won't let him go.'

She pushed her sunglasses down her snubby nose.

'Why don't you come too? We'll be happy up there, the three of us.'

'No. That's not how it works.'

'There's a giant trampoline and horses. It'll be fun!'

'Off you go. That's enough.'

She stuck her tongue out, but made herself scarce before my dad returned. His face still inscrutable, he ordered himself a glass of rosé and lit a cigarillo.

'Anyway, how are things with you? Life, your books, the ladies . . .'

That's when the scenario had taken shape. Like the seed of a novel, a flash of inspiration exploding into a blaze of ideas, fusing into a coherent plotline. Where did the spark come from? No doubt from my guilt at not giving my dad the one thing that would have made him happy again. A daughter-in-law and grandchildren to recreate the family unit my mother had ripped apart. He'd been telling me for years how he dreamed of becoming a granddad, but I'd never pictured myself having children. It would have meant living in the constant fear of losing them, just like we'd lost Vera.

'Things are going well, actually. I've met a great girl!'

'In Paris?'

'No, in Switzerland. Last month. We were staying in the same hotel in Lausanne.'

'What the hell were you doing there? Research for a book?'

'No. My Swiss publishers invited me there for a signing.'

'So who's this girl? A banker?'

The CD sleeve I'd seen at his house flashed into my mind.

'A German pianist. You might have heard of her, come to think of it. Milena Bergman.'

Just as I'd hoped, his face lit up.

'Of course I've heard of her! I have nearly all her recordings. Schubert, Debussy, Satie . . .'

I liked the mixture of incredulity, curiosity and amusement I could read in his eyes.

'But, the two of you . . . are you a proper item?'

'We have been for a month now, yes.'

'That's fantastic news. Tell me everything! What's she like in real life?'

And that's how the bomb was launched. A throwaway remark over a riverside lunch to catch my dad's attention. To put a few drops of fuel back in his tank. And now the machine was on its way. We'd ordered a round of coffees, then another, and talked for a good hour. I was doing what I do best: inventing, bluffing, lying. And I was on a roll. His smile fed my profligacy with the details. Bit by bit, I got swept up in the game. My account became more vivid, more involved. I sculpted the character of Milena Bergman just as I knew my dad would want her to be: a Scandinavian blonde with Mediterranean warmth. Discreet, maternal, generous and loyal to a fault. The antithesis of my mother. The more I talked, the more I saw him transform. I capitalised on my advantage. I dangled the possibility of marriage and the perhaps not-so-distant prospect of a family. And by the time the hour was up, I'd brought him round. After the meal, as we got back in his car, the deal was sealed: he would sell his house, move in with me, and start chemo as soon as possible.

4.

In 1971, the tiny commune of Illiers, in Eure-et-Loir, submitted a request to change its name to Combray, the toponym under which Proust had famously described it in *In Search of Lost Time*. I like this anecdote. It's a testimony to the power of fiction: the ability to create a world that sometimes displaces reality.

I'd invented for myself a relationship with Milena Bergman. Now I had to bring it alive. There was just one sizeable stumbling block: my dad was a copper. I couldn't pull the wool over his eyes for long if I didn't firm up my lie.

In choosing Milena Bergman – about whom I knew hardly anything – I'd had a serious stroke of luck. The pianist was fiercely guarded about her private life. She had an Instagram page, of course, but it was very sparsely populated, and all the posts were clearly put out by her record label. From the few interviews I was able to find with her, I gleaned a handful of extra titbits that I used to flesh out my conversations with my dad.

Acutely aware that I needed more ammunition, I went to see Julien Hoarau, the freelance graphic designer who did the covers for my books. Hoarau was obsessed with all things visual, and had run the gamut in his time: after starting in advertising, he'd branched out into web design, short film production and book trailers. Without going into any detail, I asked him to rig up a few montages of me and Milena, using photos of her I'd found online. The results were pretty mind-blowing, and invaluable for buying me a few weeks' more grace with my dad. By that point though, he only wanted one thing: to meet the pianist in person.

I searched desperately for a solution to escape the consequences of my lies. I came up with nothing. I was all set to come clean, tell my dad everything, but once I was in front of him, I bottled it. The chemo was really taking it out of him. I felt like confessing the truth would be the final nail in his coffin. The only person I'd ever loved, and whose opinion mattered to me, would go to his grave with the image of his son as a stinking traitor. I had to do whatever it took to save face. In the end it was Hoarau, after I told him the whole sorry story, who set in motion the masterplan. He'd tossed it out as a joke: 'You just need to hire an actress to play Milena for your old man!' But in the days that followed, the absurd scenario kept ticking over in my mind. I had an agent who looked after the audiovisual rights to my books. I contacted him asking if he could introduce me to a casting director. He suggested Adrienne Koterski, in his view one of the best in Paris.

'I have just the person,' Koterski assured me over the phone.

She set me up a date with someone called Garance de Karadec, who I met early one evening on the terrace of Le Zimmer brasserie, just down from the Théâtre du Châtelet. Having arrived late, I spent a good five minutes looking for her, such was her lack of resemblance to Milena. Neither fair nor dark, Garance de Karadec faded into the crowd. Average height, angular face, indistinct features, pale yet bleary eyes, dull mid-length hair that was matted in knots. Clothes-wise, she looked like a mash-up of your caricatural sociology student, the leftie primary-school teacher of my childhood, and a squatter from the anti-airport commune in Notre-Dame-des-Landes. Crumpled harem pants, Palestinian keffiyeh,

'Made in the Larzac' sheepskin waistcoat, khaki Pataugas trainers. Anything went.

I had trouble hiding my disappointment, but out of politeness, I forced myself to engage her in conversation. She gave me a brief overview of her credentials: she taught improvisation in schools, did the odd walk-on part, had worked as a costume designer on some amateur productions, and performed as part of a theatre troupe. Within three minutes I felt like walking out. With her knitted messenger bag I could easily picture Garance de Karadec outside the lecture halls on the Nanterre campus, handing out pamphlets for the French National Union of Students and La France Insoumise calling for the 'convergence of struggles'. But never in a million years could I see her incarnating Milena Bergman.

'I won't waste your time,' I told her, motioning to the waiter to bring over the bill. 'I don't think Adrienne Koterski quite understood what I was after.'

'We could at least give it a try!'

'Honestly, there's no point. Don't take this the wrong way, but I think this one's beyond you.'

With that low blow, I put the money on the table and left. Over the days that followed, I forgot all about the whole mad plan. My dad's health had taken another turn for the worse. The chemo wasn't working, and death was mercilessly gaining ground. Then, a week later, I arrived home one evening to find my dad beaming from ear to ear, having a drink on the terrace with the woman he believed to be . . . Milena Bergman. This was no impersonation. It was a living embodiment. Garance de Karadec's metamorphosis was almost scary. She had every detail to a tee: the faint accent, the intonation patterns, the head posture, the sleek blonde hair, the self-assurance of the high-born coupled with attentiveness to the other person. Even the outfit was pitch-perfect: enamel bangle, Loro Piana cashmere, subtle perfume, Heritage trench coat. How could a second-rate actress have pulled off a transformation like that? And where had she got the money for the clothes? I was so stunned – and so made-up to see my dad on cloud nine – that I brushed these questions under the carpet.

After my arrival, my dad offered to cook dinner for the three of us. We had a great evening together that cheered him up no end. This scenario was replayed several times over the following weeks. Garance took her role seriously. By then we'd reached a financial agreement, but the actress remained an enigma to me. In the September, my dad was taken into hospital. He was ravaged by his cancer, and a doctor coolly informed me that it would 'all be over within ten days'. So, to make the end less painful, I sank deeper into the lie. And I told him Milena and I were expecting a child.

5.

My dad didn't die within the ten days. Two months after that macabre prediction, he was back home, revitalised by a new immunotherapy treatment to which he was responding well.

'The old lion's still roaring,' he declared. 'I'm going to be lucky enough to meet my granddaughter.'

He'd got it into his head that 'Milena' was expecting a girl, and was waiting on the 20-week scan for confirmation. Once again, I was torn. Blessedly relieved to see my dad clinging to life, yet terrified when I contemplated the repercussions of my deception. I couldn't sleep. I was backed into a corner with a knife to my throat. Not only did I know there was no possible solution to the mess I'd got myself into, but the mythical pregnancy lent an unbearable cut-off point to my lies.

Then, yet again, something saved me. A tragic twist of fate. One of the worst disasters in the history of modern aviation. On 8 November 2019, Flight AF 229 crash-landed in the Atlantic, killing all passengers on board, including the pianist Milena Bergman. In a few short hours, thanks to this horrific accident, my predicament was resolved.

I gave Garance de Karadec her marching orders. In spite of myself, I reprised the role of the son my dad needed to protect. The inconsolable, tortured widower. Buoyed by his immunotherapy, my old man refused to give up the fight. He reclaimed his position at the head of the family, watching over me like I was ten again. His remission was spectacular. As the months went by, gradually I was able to cast off my mourning garb. Our relationship had never been stronger. Life was moving on. My dad went back to work and I launched into a new novel.

I never heard from Garance de Karadec again. I'd almost forgotten she existed. Until a cop tracked me down in my secret hideout to return the watch Garance had taken with her.

PART III
DIONYSUS'S TROUPERS

14

THE FOUR TRUTHS

ROXANE

1

Adrienne Koterski's offices were located in Rue Lincoln, in
the 8th arrondissement, on the third floor of a building that
gave both onto the street and onto a small courtyard dusted
with melting snow. The sun had made a rather impromptu
return to see off dreams of a white Christmas. Roxane had
been about to ring the buzzer when a modelesque young
woman, with dark glasses and headphones grafted to her
ears, pushed open the door to the agency. While the girl
gave the person at the other end of the line a blow-by-blow
account of her casting audition in a blend of Hebrew and
English, the cop pounced on the opening to dive inside the
building.

At lunchtime on 24 December, the reception desk was
empty. Winding through the deserted floor, Roxane followed
a corridor with pale parquet and walls lined with arthouse
film posters from the likes of Leos Carax, Philippe Garrel,

Bruno Dumont and other darlings of the French highbrow media. At the end of the maze she reached a photo studio, from which animated voices were drifting. She nudged the door ajar. It was a cavernous space, flanked by light-grey partitions that housed projectors, reflectors and a mixing desk. A skeleton team was casting for a female role. Perched on a stool in the middle of the room, recognisable by her shock of long blonde hair, Adrienne Koterski was feeding lines to one of the hopefuls. Two male technicians were assisting, one controlling the camera and the other behind the console.

'Police! Let's call it a break, guys!' Roxane shouted to the men.

With a tilt of the chin, she intimated to the actress to leave too. To lift the oppressive atmosphere, she raised the electric blind to let some daylight in, then took the seat the auditionee had vacated opposite the casting director. The latter had watched her without uttering a word.

'Are you here for an audition?' she finally asked.

'No. Today it's your turn in the hotseat,' Roxane replied, flashing her badge. 'I'd like you to tell me about Garance de Karadec.'

'Oh, Garance, of course . . .' the casting director murmured, with a faraway look in her eyes. 'She hasn't got into any bother, I hope?'

Adrienne Koterski was a bottle blonde with a fair complexion and skin that was peeling as if she'd just stepped out of a baking August bank holiday. Her gaze was hidden behind octagonal blue-tinted glasses, while a figure-hugging skirt and denim jacket teamed with wedge sandals accentuated her slender frame.

'Have you known her a long time?'

'Four or five years. You still haven't answered my question: has something happened to her?'

There was genuine concern on her face.

'You answer my questions first.'

'The police . . .' Koterski whispered.

Roxane got into the spirit of the game.

'You know, I reckon my job isn't all that different to yours.'

'What do you mean?'

'Sniffing out talent is a bit like hunting down criminals, wouldn't you say? There's a touch of the chase about it. Prowling the ground to get closer to our prey.'

'If you say so. In any case, I was the one who discovered Garance. That much is certain.'

'Tell me more. Where was it?'

'In a pretty seedy theatre – on the old factory site around the Grandes-Serres de Pantin.'

Koterski lit a cigarette while she summoned the memory.

'Nowadays a lot of things have shifted online, but I'm of the old school. I'm not scared to trek out to amateur performances in the suburbs, even the shittiest ones, in the hope of unearthing a gem. The first time I saw Garance, she was performing with an improv troupe – a totally wacko Living Theatre-inspired production.'

'That means nothing to me,' Roxane admitted, sitting up on the unyielding stool.

'The original Living Theatre company was founded in New York by a couple of anarchists. It had its heyday in the sixties. Their ethos was making the audience part of the scenography. Dissolving the barrier between performers and spectators.'

'What does that actually involve? The audience

playing along and getting in on the performance through improvisation?'

'That's the idea. With endless variations on the theme, following the libertarian politics of the time. Sometimes the actors would have sex on stage and invite the audience to join in. They'd bring along drugs to incorporate into the action. You get the picture. It was all pretty radical and squalid . . .'

Roxane was fixed on her investigation, vainly trying to link up what the casting director was telling her with the facts she already possessed.

'What was the aim?'

'Questioning the relationship between reality and fiction. Using theatre as an outlet for desires that society repressed.'

Koterski took a couple of nervous drags, then steered the conversation back to Garance.

'Anyway, even from such a dire production, I sensed immediately that this girl had something. A presence, a vibrancy, a magnetic appeal. I went to see her to suggest she come in for some auditions and offered to become her agent. She said, "Why not?", then never showed up!'

Koterski got up to commandeer a paper cup as an ashtray. Opening the window a crack, she continued puffing away in the weak winter sunlight.

'It was me that did all the running. Gradually, I got to know her work and I realised I'd been way off the mark. Garance didn't just have "something". She was a truly exceptional actress.'

Roxane sighed. She was struggling to conceptualise what 'being an exceptional actress' meant. As far as she was concerned, it was just empty talk. Pretentious bullshit. But now wasn't the time to rub Koterski up the wrong way.

'What's so special about her?' she quizzed. 'What is it that sets her apart, in your eyes?'

'For one thing, she has an incredibly rare talent: the ability to play any role. Garance is the ultimate actress. Think Meryl Streep or Dustin Hoffman back in the eighties. Just as believable playing the sex symbol as the everyman or woman. Actors like that resist typecasting. They're utterly malleable.'

Roxane pulled a sceptical face.

'I'm finding it hard to grasp what that means *in practice*, once you strip back all the clichés.'

'That's understandable,' Koterski replied, stubbing out her cigarette. 'Come and see this.'

She made her way over to a laptop on the mixing desk.

'For a long time, hopefuls had to lug a physical portfolio around with them. Nowadays, they all have their demo reels on video hosting sites.'

A few seconds later, a montage of clips from short films and theatre performances began flashing across the screen. The footage was indeed a testament to Garance de Karadec's impressive acting range. Most striking of all was the variety of identities she assumed in the clips, to the extent that, from one to another, it was hard to believe it was the same woman.

'She makes it look effortless because she's so accomplished, but it's very difficult to be that convincing when playing such different roles,' Koterski stressed. 'There's an element of natural instinct, but it also takes a lot of blood, sweat and tears to truly get inside a character. The camera loves her. The stage loves her. As soon as she appears, something happens.'

'I get all that,' Roxane agreed. 'But there's one thing nagging at me: if Garance is so talented, why hasn't she found any film or theatre roles at the level she's capable of?'

The casting director gave a long sigh.

'You've put your finger on the second thing that's special about this girl, and which sets her apart from all the other young actresses I've met: Garance isn't really interested in getting the roles.'

2.

'Do you know how many part-time entertainment industry workers there are in France?' Adrienne Koterski asked.

Not wanting to be caught out, Roxane plucked a figure from the air.

'Thirty thousand?'

The two women had migrated to a small kitchen that adjoined the studio. The casting director poured hot water into the two cups on the table: tea for herself; instant coffee for Roxane.

'Three hundred thousand,' Koterski announced, 'including over fifty thousand actors. And that's not counting all the Instagram princesses, the slew of reality TV candidates, the models of every kind who'll do whatever it takes to get their big break. Basically, in France, everybody thinks they're an actor in the making.'

Roxane saw where the casting director was heading. She threw out the olive branch Koterski was after.

'So the number of roles available is necessarily limited . . .'

Koterski nodded.

'My agency only works with the best. I have between 150 and 200 roles a year to fill, max. So my job is to say no. To crush the hopes of deluded and fragile egos. Nobody refuses when I offer them a role. Even for a walk-on part in a France 2 series, I'll have fifty actresses battling it out. NOBODY turns me down . . . except Garance de Karadec.'

Roxane detected in Koterski a sentiment akin to that of a spurned lover. Wistfully, the casting director emptied a sachet of sweetener into her tea. On the mug Roxane could make out a quote from Marlon Brando: *An actor is a guy who, if you ain't talking about him, he ain't listening!*

'Three years ago, Garance stood up Jacques Audiard,' Koterski continued bitterly. 'Then last year, I oversaw the casting for the French parts in the latest David Fincher film. We must have shown him over a hundred girls, and guess who was the only one he wanted? Garance, obviously! Except that Little Miss de Karadec wasn't interested. She'd done the audition for fun, but that was the end of it. It's criminal to have a talent like that and let it go to waste!'

Her admiration had now morphed beyond irritation into full-on anger.

'But what *is* her motivation, then?' Roxane quizzed.

'What she cares about is the experience and the challenge of acting. The act itself. Not fame. Not becoming the next big thing. Garance is passionate about theatre. She's trained in classical literature and is well versed in all the key texts, but for her, acting is the ultimate form of performance. Time and again, she'll tell you that she only feels alive when she's on stage. That theatre has an inherent magic, because everything is consumed in the moment. She's a real visionary.'

Roxane changed the subject.

'The name "de Karadec", what's its origin? I'm guessing it's from Brittany.'

'Yes. Garance comes from an old aristocratic family there. Her father, Abel Toussaint de Karadec, was quite an illustrious diplomat, who was a key player at the foreign ministry during the Mitterrand years. Her mother, Tiphaine de Karadec, was a Maoist shrink. The pair of them were opium addicts and ended up sliding into heroin. After that they went on a downward spiral from manic fits to psychiatric internment, and both died with their brains completely fried in their mansion on an island off Finistère.'

'How old was Garance at the time?'

'Seventeen or eighteen, I reckon. After finishing her studies, she went to work as an au pair in England. While she was over there she met a crackpot called Amyas Langford, a British actor who'd set up his own acting troupe. A really twisted character, totally barking.'

An alarm bell sounded in Roxane's mind.

'Tell me more about him.'

Koterski lit a fresh cigarette, as if she needed the shot of nicotine to jog her memory.

'Amyas trained at RADA, the Royal Academy of Dramatic Arts, the oldest and most prestigious drama school in England. He could undoubtedly have had a glittering career too. He's been in a number of BBC productions. There's a legend about him, which I'm inclined to believe. A few years ago, while playing a Second World War Resistance fighter for a TV film, he got so into the role that he had a fake tooth implanted that contained a genuine cyanide pill! You get the measure of the guy . . .'

'So he's into the same shebang – art for art's sake?'

'More radical than that, even. Amyas Langford is a man of excess, influenced by the anti-capitalist and anarchist schools of thought. He advocates for a total theatre built on conflict and revolution.'

'In practice, what does that equate to?'

'A load of crap. It's all dressed up in lofty words – defying the limits of the stage, inscribing theatre in real experience, blurring the boundaries between art and life – but basically it's just provocative guff. I remember the performance I saw at the Grandes-Serres de Pantin. Amyas wanted to recreate one of Peter Brook's "happenings". So at the end of the play, he had the cast release live butterflies into the audience with their wings set alight. That's what they're all about: putting the spectator ill at ease so that their discomfort becomes part of the performance.'

Roxane had kept her phone on the table. It was in silent mode, but she'd been glancing at the screen every time a new message came through. After the fiasco of Batailley's escape, Botsaris had been relieved of his duties and invited to take his holidays. It was Sorbier himself who'd taken over the investigation. Although unable to reinstate Roxane officially, he'd admitted that he couldn't do without her on the case. So Liêm was still keeping her up to speed, this time with the big boss's blessing. The BNRF had run Garance de Karadec's details through various databases, but so far they hadn't picked up much. Her last declared address had been rented out twice since she'd left, she wasn't known to the tax authorities, and there was very little action on her bank account. While she listened to Koterski, Roxane did a Google Image search for Amyas Langford. Finding only one result, she texted it over to Valentine with the instruction: Ask your neanderthal mate if this is the man who gave him the material for his article.

'Do you think Garance is in thrall to Langford?'

'He isn't a positive influence, that's for sure. Amyas encourages her in a radical mindset that rejects all forms of commercial theatre and cinema and opposes the established order. I was born in Poland in the seventies. My family experienced the yoke of communism, and I've absolutely no sympathy for these tossers who want to start a revolution by tweeting about it on their latest-model iPhone.'

Roxane couldn't stifle a smile.

'Do you think he could become violent towards her?'

'It's possible. There's something you should know about Garance. Men go crazy around her. Like they've been put under a spell. And Amyas is a possessive type. It wouldn't surprise me if he flipped.'

She waited a few seconds before rounding off the psychiatric portrait of her protégée.

'Garance is a complicated young woman. A bit bonkers, but extremely endearing. A romantic in search of the absolute. She has a kind of darkness inside her, a deep-rooted melancholy. I don't think she'll ever be happy. But now, I'd like the truth: are you asking me about her because she's a suspect in a case, or has something happened to her?'

'We think she's been kidnapped.'

'Who by? Amyas?'

'Possibly. Have you ever heard Garance talk about the cult of Dionysus?'

'No. But the company she and Amyas set up . . .'

'Yes . . . ?'

'They call themselves "Dionysus's Troupers".'

Roxane felt her body surge with adrenaline. As sure as night follows day, she was closing in on the puppet-master who was pulling the strings of the whole murky affair.

'You're not the first to ask me these questions either,' Koterski continued. 'One of your colleagues came to see me a couple of weeks ago.'

'Really?'

'He shared a name with the wine.'

'Which wine?'

'Château Batailley.'

Roxane nodded. Of course a cop like Marc Batailley wouldn't have swallowed his son's charade. When he'd fallen into his coma, Batailley had been investigating the Troupers and was no doubt already hot on their trail.

A fresh flurry of texts from Liêm, punctuated by a string of exclamation marks. A cleaner at a hotel in Orléans had alerted the management after finding a bloodstained animal skin and a horned goat mask in one of the bathrooms. The CCTV cameras had captured images from the corridor and hotel lobby.

The screenshots of the footage flashed up on her phone. It was Amyas Langford!

She was about to fire off a reply to Liêm when her phone vibrated. Sorbier himself.

'Boss!' she blurted down the line. 'I know who he is, the guy from the hotel CCTV!'

'So do I,' the BNRF skipper replied calmy. 'Amyas Langford. We've just identified him.'

Roxane struggled to hide her disappointment.

'What are you calling about?'

'I wanted to know if you're ready.'

'Ready for what?'

'A little excursion. I'll meet you on the corner.'

'The corner of where?'

'Rue Lincoln.'

Roxane opened the window and scanned the street outside. Sorbier's Peugeot was parked at the intersection with Rue François Ier.

'Where are we heading?'

'Villacoublay Air Base. I'll fill you in on the way.'

MARC

3.

My name is Marc Batailley. Sixty-two years old, with my body in shreds and my soul drowning in sorrow. Ribcage smashed in, collarbone shattered, spinal cord shot, lungs punctured. My fugged-up mind drifting in the sham limbo of a drug-induced coma. And don't even get me started on the face. I've had my fair share of knocks in life, have taken more blows than I've dealt out, but I've always managed to pick myself up again. A bit of grit and a lot of luck. Thick skin and a bleeding heart. This time, though, I'm scared. Not for myself, but for those left behind. My son Raphaël leading the pack. I'm going mad stuck in this hospital bed, unable to lift a finger or say a word, even though I know the spiral of danger that's brewing.

As is often the way in life, it was a good intention that raised the curtain on the tragedy. A kid's lie . . . It makes me cold thinking back to it. And angry. I wanted to believe Raphaël's story, of course I did, but I still can't fathom how I could have been *that* blind, for over a year! It was the article in *Week'nd* that brought me to my senses. The Orthodox Christmas in Courchevel, despite the fact Milena Bergman was performing in Japan at the time. I blamed my own gullibility, but Raphaël's lie cut me up inside. Because I knew I was in large part responsible. And because it was a real act of love.

But from a copper's perspective, something fascinated me. THE GIRL. How had she pulled the wool over my eyes? How had she played her score so convincingly, without the slightest bum note? To spare his blushes, I resisted the temptation to say anything to Raph. But for my own peace of mind, I decided to do some digging by myself. Who was she? What was her background, her motive? How had she pulled off a performance that demanded so much effort and commitment?

I discovered her name from a stub in Raphaël's cheque book: Garance de Karadec. But that didn't answer my questions. There wasn't much about her online, although enough for me to sketch an initial picture. A part-time, small-fry actress who was part of an obscure theatre troupe. I needed to know more. Going old school with graphite powder, a brush and a strip of Sellotape, I tried to collect any prints she might have left on the cases of the Milena Bergman CDs she'd given me. I managed to get a couple that could be useable. Something told me there was a chance the girl was on record. And my copper's instinct advised me to tread carefully.

To stay under the radar, I gave the prints to Vincent Tircelin, a less-than-squeaky-clean cop I'd had a few dealings with at the regional judicial police base in Versailles. He agreed to run them through the central database for €400. When he delivered the results, he had the look of someone who'd thought he was laughing his way to the bank, only to find himself knee-deep in shit.

'What the hell have you dragged us into, Batailley?' he demanded.

The print, although unidentified, was on record – in connection with a murder case from 2017! It had been recovered in Avignon, from an industrial waste bin that had been found containing the body of an ex-soldier. I urged Tircelin to forget all about it and resumed my investigations alone.

It transpired that Garance de Karadec was subletting a poky room over a sushi restaurant in Rue Monsieur-le-Prince, with a guy called Amyas Langford. He was a Brit, also an actor. To probe deeper, I started tailing her. At the same time, I amassed all the information I could find about the Avignon murder.

It was a nebulous case. In the autumn of 2017, a retired soldier called Jean-Louis Crémieux had been found with his throat cut in a container bin in Rue Banasterie, not far from the Palais des Papes. Crémieux had served in the 21st marine infantry regiment in Fréjus, and he wasn't remembered with universal affection. Dubbed 'Sergeant Hartman' by his colleagues, in reference to Kubrick's sadistic drill instructor, he was said to have an 'intransigent' character which had led the investigators to suspect a revenge killing. Where could Garance de Karadec slot into all this? I decided to take a day trip down to the papal city to meet with Gabriel Cathala, the superintendent who'd headed up the case.

I didn't have any trouble securing a meeting. Cathala had since taken retirement and, from what I could gather over the phone, he had a lot to say about the case. On the day, I arrived to find him tending his olive trees on the terrace of a plot of land near Gordes, where he'd built himself a dry-stone cottage. He was a copper of my generation. He already knew my backstory and the 'legend' of The Horticulturalist. Conversation flowed easily, and he didn't need asking twice to start recounting his investigation over a glass of peach RinQuinQuin.

'The ex-officer's body was found half-naked,' he recalled, 'dolled up in sexy underwear, stiletto heels, and a long fawn-fur muffler that had been attached directly to his skin.'

I felt shivers as the image flashed through my mind. Thrill and revulsion, emotions that often go hand in hand in the job.

'But the weirdest thing,' Cathala continued, 'is that there were live snakes in the bin.'

That detail hadn't made the papers.

'Poisonous ones?'

'No, just ordinary Montpellier grass snakes. We never got to the bottom of why they'd been put there.'

Cathala had pursued each line of inquiry meticulously, and each time had hit a brick wall. At an impasse, the investigation had ultimately been handed over to a differ-ent examining magistrate, who'd ordered further inquiries under a new team. Meanwhile, a humiliated Cathala had slid into depression while he waited it out until retirement. He'd left the force by the back door, his career end ruined by the case that could have immortalised him in the pantheon of great coppers. Three months later, he'd suffered a stroke that had aged him by a decade overnight. Now he was a sort of Pagnolesque Papet, withdrawn from the field of play with no hope of return.

'Why have you come to see me, Batailley?' he asked as he refilled our glasses. 'For you to be here today, you must have discovered something new.'

'I know who left one of the prints they found on the bin.'

'Fuck . . . who?'

'A second-rate actress – Garance de Karadec. Ring any bells?'

'No, absolutely none. That name never came up in the investigation.'

'She's part of a company called Dionysus's Troupers.'

'We've no shortage of theatre companies passing through Avignon.'

'I'm going to do more digging. I'll keep you posted, but I need you to give me a way of accessing the investigation file.'

'The most interesting part isn't in the file,' Cathala smirked. 'This case is dynamite. I'm convinced it goes way beyond Crémieux's murder.'

'What makes you say that?'

'Do you know who found the body?'

'A homeless guy, at six in the morning. That's what I've read everywhere.'

'Spot on. My team arrived on the scene ten minutes later. The body was swimming in plonk, with the three snakes for company. After the snakes, that's what intrigued me the most: the wine, when there was no other rubbish.'

'Maybe the homeless guy dumped it there?'

'No, it had been there a while. Properly steeped. That's what made me have it analysed.'

'Seriously? The wine? What were you looking for? Traces of drugs? Poison?'

'What I wanted to know was *where* the stuff had come from. It became an obsession. I even sent off samples to oenologists for blind testing – without mentioning the provenance, obviously.'

'And it turned out to be cheap plonk, I'm guessing?'

'Nope. A top-notch Pauillac. A couple of them even thought they could pinpoint the vintage: a 1973 Château Mouton Rothschild.'

'It doesn't stack up. Why would someone chuck away a priceless wine?'

'That's the proof Crémieux's murder was a ritual killing. The staging was all painstakingly planned. The antithesis of your crime of passion. And given that we didn't catch the perp . . .'

'. . . You reckon there must be others.'

4.
6 p.m.

As the train sped me back to Paris, I racked my brains for the link between what Cathala had told me and Garance de Karadec.

'Could I borrow your tablet for five minutes?'

The student sitting next to me had an honest face. He held out his iPad with a faint air of mistrust, which evaporated when I showed him my badge. After tapping in a few search terms, I stumbled on an article that caught my attention:

Le Parisien exclusive
Criminals steal top vintages from luxury wine merchant

The story has echoes of *The Sewers of Paradise*, the film dramatising bank robber Albert Spaggiari's heist of the Societé Générale in Nice. Not for the nature of the swag, but for the manner of the plunder. According to our sources the incident was the work of one or several thieves, who targeted Les Caves de Monceau, a premium wine merchant in Rue de Courcelles, in the 17th arrondissement, during the Easter weekend.

The robbers took advantage of the festivities to gain entry to the adjoining building, a small clothing alteration workshop without an alarm system.

Once inside the premises they bored a foot-wide hole in the party wall, through which they fed a rod to reach the bottles.

While the scope of the theft was modest, the owner did report the removal of five bottles of Château Mouton Rothschild: *'All the bottles were from 1973, which thankfully isn't the best vintage for that wine,'* he told our source.

The scene was caught on CCTV, but from the footage it isn't possible to ascertain the number of thieves or identify their faces.

An investigation is underway by the first-district branch of the Paris judicial police.

Continuing with my search, I discovered that the wine Cathala had mentioned had a special quirk: every year since 1945, the Château Mouton Rothschild estate had invited a top artist to illustrate the label for its Premier Cru Classé bottle. Most of the iconic painters of the twentieth century had featured: Miró, Chagall, Warhol, Bacon, Hockney . . .

The 1973 design, which was by Picasso, had the additional idiosyncrasy of having come out in the year of the Spanish artist's death. In tribute to him, Baron Philippe de Rothschild, the estate's owner, had hand-picked a Picasso canvas from his private collection to be reproduced on the label.

I scrolled down the page and clicked to enlarge the image. The painting was titled *Bacchanal*. The composition harked back to Ancient Greece, depicting one of the typical drunken dances performed by female worshippers of Dionysus, the god of wine and theatre.

Dionysus?

Garance de Karadec's theatre company was called Dionysus's Troupers! There's no such thing as a coincidence in an investigation. Each discovery is like a brushstroke on an Impressionist canvas. I brought up Wikipedia to jog my memory. A quick skim was enough to confirm I'd found the link I was after. Snakes and fawn skin were indeed among the many symbols of Dionysus. The maenads, the god's female worshippers, were often decked with crowns of ivy. They followed him through the forests and hillsides with snakes around their necks, in a frenzied armed convoy that blazed a savage trail of death and destruction.

As I closed the tablet, my whole body was tingling. It was a sensation I hadn't felt for years. In that moment, I vowed I wouldn't pass up my chance. Thirty years on from The Horticulturalist, fate had thrown a new foe in my path.

And what could be more exhilarating than taking on an Olympian god in my final battle?

RAPHAËL

5.

'Your green tea, sir.'

Warmth flooded my hands as I took the scalding cup. The snowy interlude hadn't lasted, and the Jardin du Luxembourg was bathed in pale low winter sunlight. It was 4 p.m. I'd come for some air in the park to avoid brooding alone at home. I'd phoned the hospital for an update on my dad. His condition hadn't stabilised, and the outlook was bleak. They'd abandoned their plan to gradually wake him after finding inflammation in his veins. As for me, my heart was in bits, my brain in overdrive, and my morale close to rock bottom.

The scenes from the accident refused to leave me. I was a MURDERER. For real. It was all down to *my* lies that Yukiko Takahashi had flipped, and, in trying to kill me, had stolen the life of a twenty-eight-year-old mother whose only crime was finding herself in the wrong place at the wrong time. And what about Garance de Karadec? Where was she now? And who was the predator into whose claws that strange girl had fallen?

Still holding my cup, I grabbed one of the sea-green metal chairs and moved it into a shaft of sunlight that was filtering through the branches. I collapsed onto the seat and closed my eyes. Rocked by the familiar sounds of the gardens – the shouts of children playing by the Medici Fountain, the wind rustling through the trees, the flutter of pigeons taking flight – I tried to gather my thoughts.

My path hadn't led me here by accident. This was where I'd seen Garance de Karadec for the last time, just over a year earlier. We'd arranged to meet at the Pavillon de la Fontaine, the Jardin's historic refreshment area. Our collaboration had run its course. Milena Bergman's death had freed me from my lie, and she was now surplus to requirements. I'd promised her a final settlement to call things quits. We'd sat at a table and ordered two mulled wines. Everywhere was ablaze with autumn colours, tinting the sky caramel. A school brass band was playing in the music kiosk. I can still picture vividly how she looked that afternoon. Gradually she was shedding the persona of the pianist. Her hair was becoming wavier and darker. Her features had softened. Her gaze was bright, her posture less Germanic, her smile more spontaneous.

I was there without really being there. As usual my head was elsewhere, preoccupied by my dad's illness, by my sister who was sitting there with us, scrutinising me over her mug of hot chocolate. By the irrepressible urge to make my mother pay for the decades of pain she'd caused us. By the sense I'd always had that my adult life had never begun, and that all the light inside me had died with Vera.

Garance was in a buoyant and talkative mood. She'd admitted that the role was the one she'd most taken to heart in her life, and that she'd be sad to stop seeing me. She told me she'd read my books and that we resembled each other in our madness. That only the mad could save the mad. That we shared the same compulsion to flee reality.

It was one of those moments when life can swing in either direction. She'd thrown me line after line that I hadn't grasped. There were too many dark places inside me. My baggage was too heavy. I was sick and tired of it all. Of lugging around my demons everywhere I went.

More than anything, as I looked into her eyes, watching them flicker from green to chestnut in the sunlight, something told me I mustn't grow attached to this girl. Despite the clear attraction she exuded, an alarm bell had sounded in my mind – insisting that if I carried on seeing her, Garance de Karadec would make me suffer, dragging me into her own black holes, and endangering those around me.

She'd asked me if she could keep the watch as a 'break-up present', and I'd agreed in spite of its value.

I kept watching her as she laughed, straining to resist the appeal of this unknowable, novelesque woman with the ability to burn away her personality and conjure another from the flames. I wondered how this power could be channelled, what criteria decided the causes it serviced. But I didn't vocalise either of these questions. Garance de Karadec scared me. I imagined her with a past like Milady de Winter. A succession of roles and identities. A life of manipulation and false appearances.

As I was remembering that doomed encounter, the trill of my phone shot me back to the present. Even though I never took calls from unknown numbers, this time, on some instinct, I did.

'. . . phaël? Raphaël, is that you?'

The voice made me tremble. A familiar inflection amplified by the echoey line. I sprang from my chair in panic.

'Garance? Where are you?'

'In . . . boot of a car! . . . locked me in.'

'Who? Who locked you in?'

'Amyas.'

The signal was bad, interference splintering the

conversation. But I could distinctly make out the engine growling in the background.

'Do you know where you are? The nearest town?'

'No . . . I grabbed his phone from . . . motorway . . . but he's going to notice! You have to do something!'

I rubbed my eyes, desperately trying to think.

'Tell me . . . what . . . what kind of car is it?'

'. . . sort of 4-by-4 . . . metallic blue-gree . . . boot . . . says Q7.'

'An Audi Q7. OK.'

'Help me, Raphaël . . . begging you!'

'Calm down. I'll call the police. They'll find you, don't worry. Do you know where he's taking you?'

'I think . . . border . . . to . . .'

The interference was getting worse. Her voice became more muffled, then faltered to nothing.

'I can't hear you anymore.'

There was a long tunnel of silence and static. Then the unmistakeable tick of the indicator. In turn the engine noise cut out, to be replaced, a few seconds later, by the sound of the boot clicking open.

'*Fucking bitch, you stole my phone!*' Amyas roared in English, then again, even more ferociously, in French.

Garance let out a long cry.

Then the line went dead.

15

THE POINT OF MADNESS

ROXANE

1.

Yvelines

Sorbier's Peugeot 5008 nosed deeper into Villacoublay Air Base. In the passenger seat, Roxane was in communication with a representative from the Gendarmerie air division, who was explaining how to reach the safety area. A helicopter was waiting for them in front of one of the hangars, along with the crew — Colonel Stéphane Jardel, the captain, and Gendarmerie officers Audrey Hugon, the pilot, and Alain Le Brusque, the flight engineer.

After the introductions, Jardel nodded them aboard the H160 and Hugon set the turbine whirring. Roxane slid on her helmet, then took her place at the back of the craft. Orienting the heli windward, Hugon pulled on the collective lever for take-off. Roxane had previously flown in the old Squirrels used for Gendarmerie intervention missions, but this was her first time in one of the new Airbuses. With its boomerang-shaped blades, the craft was considerably quieter. She listened for a minute to the engineer's rapturous description of his latest toy – cruising speed of 178 mph, 550-mile range, 8-person capacity – before zoning out to take mental stock of her investigation.

As was often the way, after an initial dry spell the revelations and discoveries had flowed in thick and fast, barely leaving her time to process them. Following Garance de Karadec's call to Raphaël, the phone had been traced to a location between Vienne and Condrieu. The number was from a UK provider, registered in Amyas Langford's name. After his stopover in Orléans, the Brit had evidently carried on towards Lyon. By the looks of it he'd taken the A6 motorway, and it was just after passing the ancient capital of Gaul that he'd realised Garance had stolen his phone. The device was no longer traceable, but a motorbike from the BRI – the National Police's specialist Research and Intervention Brigade – had spotted the Audi near Tournon-sur-Rhône and had kept it in sight since then. The SUV was heading south along the classic holiday trail: Valence, Montélimar, Carpentras. To make sure it didn't escape into Italy, the examining magistrate had approved the deployment of a BRI search unit tasked with arresting the fugitive and freeing his captive.

It was a risky operation. With Christmas Eve celebrations beginning in a few hours' time, and the school holidays in full swing, the motorway was rammed in both directions. Langford was almost certainly armed. The possibility that he had accomplices couldn't be ruled out, and it was odds on that sooner or later he'd clock that he was in danger of arrest. Still with her eyes shut, Roxane let herself rock to the sway of the helicopter. It seemed the case was nearing its conclusion, yet the motives of its chief actors still eluded her. What was driving each of them? A simple crime of passion on Amyas Langford's part? She didn't buy it for a second. The staging of the 'Stranger in the Seine' episode was far too elaborate, requiring the complicity of Garance de Karadec herself. Something else was bothering her as well. The fact of Garance's pregnancy. Even if she admitted having been royally stitched up by the hair samples, Roxane found it a stretch to believe the pregnancy was a sham too.

She rooted in her bag for the pack of Petit Écolier biscuits she'd snaffled from the casting director's kitchen, then reached for the book she'd picked up from Guillaume Budé. The one Batailley had ordered, but, by dint of circumstance, had never collected. *Great Dionysia: The Birth of Classical Theatre in Greece.*

Pen at the ready, she plunged inside. The introduction and conclusion were dense with detail, giving the reader a summarised, academic-style overview of the author's line of argument.

The book set out to show how classical theatre was directly descended from the cult of Dionysus. Its focus began in Athens in the late sixth century BC, with the authorities struggling to contain the sexual debauchery and violence sparked by the cult, which had reached such a level that they were threatening to destroy the city. To maintain social order, the city's leaders sought to reclaim the cult for their own benefit by institutionalising it as a city-wide festival centred on theatrical performances. Over time, the religious dimension of the cult was supplanted by a civic push to educate citizens through playwriting competitions, with theatre emerging as an instrument of social control.

Roxane thumbed the pages with interest, underlining any passages that could have a distant resonance with the case. Once a year, Great Dionysia pitted the talents of Athens's most famous the Great Dionysia festival – the likes of Aeschylus, Sophocles, Euripides and other big names of the age – and had them battle it out on stage, in the hallowed arena of the theatre. At the end of the performances, a jury of ten judges would choose the best play and crown the winner with an ivy wreath.

The festival was a unique event in the Athenian calendar, unfolding over five days in front of over twenty thousand spectators. Nobody was excluded. Men, women, the rich, the poor, even slaves – everyone was allowed and duty-bound to attend. Because theatre was a way of purging emotions and passions. For the duration of the show, the onstage drama blurred the boundaries with reality. By vicariously stepping into the shoes of characters ruled by their passions, the audience witnessed the devastating effects of such behaviour. A salutary scaring, at minimal cost.

Roxane dug her hand back into her bag, hoping without much faith to unearth another packet of biscuits. Why was she so hungry? The feeling was insatiable. And she wasn't hankering for some detox cucumber salad or steamed fish with green beans. She wanted an explosion of calories. Fat, carbs, grease. The kind of stuff that clogs your arteries and sends your bad cholesterol levels rocketing off the chart. Closing her eyes once more, she tried to refocus on the case, but all she could see was food. The juicy kebab gulped down on the hoof in the street. The Burger King Steakhouse with its still-warm fries in their bag, devoured in the back of a surveillance van during an interminable stakeout. The apricot pastry she sometimes bought from Paul in the morning, a slab of steak with pepper sauce, a hunk of apple tart, a raspberry doughnut, chicken wings, a hot dog with fried onions, a . . .

2.

'ROXANE!'

She opened her eyes to find Sorbier shaking her shoulder. *Shit!* She'd nodded off. She checked her watch. She'd been out for the count for over two hours! It was now pitch-black outside. Against the driving wind and rain, the heli was preparing for landing.

'Have there been any developments?' she asked, a touch sheepishly.

Sorbier proffered her the tablet on which he'd been tracking Amyas Langford's progress. The Audi had continued its advance south: Salon-de-Provence, Aix-en-Provence, Brignoles, Fréjus, Cannes, Nice . . . It was now near Cap-d'Ail, not far from Monaco, only 20 miles or so from the Italian border.

'The BRI are going in!' Sorbier shouted over the whir of the turbine.

On the map he pointed to the interchange in La Turbie where the heli was headed. Roxane pressed her face to the window. Through the fog, a long amber stream of car headlights was snaking through what must be the maquis.

'Where are we touching down?'

Overhearing her question, the pilot tilted her chin towards what appeared to be a car park, just beyond the toll lanes.

When they dived out of the craft a few minutes later, Roxane could barely see anything through the storm that had erupted in the Mediterranean sky. She followed Sorbier into the night, holding her jacket over her head to shelter from the rain. Judging by the sea of flashing lights, they'd rocked up late to the party. A young Gendarmerie officer in an orange bib came to meet them by the automatic booths.

'Squadron Leader Luigi Muratore,' he introduced himself.

He invited them through a series of barriers that were blocking their view. Once they were on the other side, the situation became clear. Traffic had been stopped in the direction of the Italian border, and a dozen police and Gendarmerie vehicles had shot up the hard shoulder to assist their BRI colleagues.

'Has the suspect been arrested?'

'Affirmative,' Muratore confirmed. 'The BRI team created a false bottleneck on the motorway so they could surround the vehicle.'

Roxane shielded her eyes to peer through the rain. Just over 150 feet away she could make out the Audi Q7, its metallic-blue bodywork glinting in the searchlights.

'Did he surrender without resistance?' Sorbier asked.

'No. He tried to run away after an exchange of gunfire,' the Gendarmerie officer explained, 'but we immediately caught him in the long grass by the roadside.'

'No casualties?'

'One of the bullets grazed the suspect's shoulder. He's been transferred to L'Archet hospital as a precaution.'

'And the girl?' Roxane pressed.

'Which girl?'

Leaving the two men sheltering under a canopy, Roxane

pelted through the rain towards the SUV. She checked the vehicle from all sides. The boot was wide open. Empty.

A small group of BRI officers were huddled a few yards away, lightening the mood with some banter.

'Captain Montchrestien,' she announced as she drew level with them. 'Were you the ones that caught the suspect?'

'Yes, Captain.'

'And . . . in the boot, there was nobody?'

'No. But a lot of blood stains.'

MARC

3.

I needed help to get any further with my investigation, but I was scraping the barrel for allies. The only person that could lend me a hand without asking too many questions was Valérie Janvier, one of my old trainees who'd since risen through the ranks. She hooked me up with an invaluable contact, Pierre-Yves Le Hénaff, one of the top guys at the Gendarmerie's Criminal Intelligence Information Service, or the SCRC for short. I spent three days with him at the department of behavioural science in Cergy-Pontoise, combing their criminal database. The Avignon prosecutor had also referred the case to the DSC three years earlier, but the new evidence I brought along spurred Le Hénaff to get back on the job.

Our aim? To see if there'd been any other murders that

displayed an MO similar to the Avignon case. Murders bearing the hallmark of the cult of Dionysus. In theory, you'd think it would be an easy thing to check, but detecting serial murders is riddled with obstacles. Territorial jurisdiction, trouble accessing foreign databases, the slapdash approach that investigators – often up against the clock – take to filling out the forms the IT system relies on.

Every time we found a potential lead, Le Hénaff and I were straight on the blower to check it out. We drew a blank when it came to France, but there was a case in the UK that caught our eye. Terence Bowman, a young judge from Warwickshire, had been found with his face bones smashed in and his skull shattered in the grounds of Holy Trinity Church in Stratford-upon-Avon.

From an outbuilding used by the gardeners, they had recovered the judge's watch and wallet along with the murder weapon, a wooden stick. This wasn't any old stick though. On further inspection, it turned out to be a dogwood lance, carved with ivy leaves and topped with a pinecone. A thyrsus! The name given to Dionysus's sceptre. The investigators hadn't dwelt on this link. As soon as they'd nailed a potential suspect – a twenty-something junkie up to his eyeballs on drugs – they'd gratefully closed the case. But, at the exact moment of the incident – as a blog post and the official event website testified – Amyas Langford and Garance de Karadec were in Stratford for a theatre festival. At that point, I knew I'd unmasked the ex-soldier's and the judge's killers.

I decided to keep the finding to myself for a few days, and resumed my tailing of Dionysus's Troupers. In parallel, I trawled through books and websites to brush up on that chunk of Greek mythology. What was driving this demonic couple? What could their motive be? Observers of cultic practices cited a modern-day resurgence of the cult of Dionysus. Some groups, styling themselves as 'thiasi', openly identified themselves as his followers. Dionysus fascinated them because he represented the inversion of values, the subversion of order. That line seemed to square with the murders of a solider and a judge, both synonymous with a rule-bound society.

While I waited for the lightbulb moment, I didn't let the pair out of my sight. Amyas had bought some drones from a model aircraft shop and was spending a lot of time teaching himself to fly and programme them. He'd also gone to collect something from an antiques store in the Passage des Panoramas, but the old crone who owned the place refused to tell me what. When they weren't in Paris, Garance and Amyas squatted on a farm near Vitry-le-François, in the Marne. On 15 December, Amyas had taken a trip to the Swiss Alps to poach an ibex, then brought it back there. After butchering it in the farmyard, he'd tried to tan the skin using the beast's own brain. I'd followed the ceremony through my binoculars. The stench was so appalling it made me gag, even at over 150 feet away. The pair of them were plotting something, I was sure of it. Another ritual murder? But who would be the victim this time?

On Monday, 21 December, I arrived at the office early. Further reflection over the weekend had convinced me it was only a matter of time until they struck again, and I resolved to call Valérie Janvier to warn her. I was about to dial her number when I noticed a light flashing on the phone cradle. I clicked to play the message and was met by a voice from the past:

'Good morning Marc, it's Catherine Aumonier, Deputy Director of the Prefecture infirmary. I'm calling for your opinion on a rather odd case. Yesterday morning we admitted a young woman in a state of total amnesia, who'd been recovered from the Seine by the River Brigade. She was completely naked when they found her. I don't have your email address, so I've faxed the file over to you. Please call me back to let me know if you recognise her. Thanks.'

Intrigued, I couldn't resist going for a look on the first floor.

'No!'

When I saw the file Aumonier had sent over, I realised the danger was even more imminent than I'd imagined.

I have to warn Janvier now! I thought, just before I smashed my face on the stairs and everything went black . . .

ROXANE

4.

Nice, 24 December, 11 p.m.

Behind her unruffled appearance, Roxane was spitting feathers. She was livid with Sorbier. After Amyas Langford's arrest, her skipper had taken advantage of the helicopter to hightail it from La Turbie and join his big-shot mates at the investigation HQ that had been set up in Nice police station. Finding herself abandoned at the toll road, she'd had to wait an age for Muratore to finish his duties there before he could drive her back to the city centre.

The Gendarmerie officer's Megane had turned off the Promenade des Anglais a few minutes earlier, but instead of heading north to the usual departmental police headquarters, it was weaving deeper into the Old Town.

'Aren't we going to the station in Auvare?' Roxane asked in bemusement.

'Did nobody tell you?' Muratore exclaimed. 'Langford's been transferred to the *new* police HQ in the Carabacel quarter, on the old Saint-Roch hospital site.'

He launched into a lengthy explanation. For years, the authorities of the self-proclaimed 'safest city in France' had been trying to bring to life an ambitious project to move all the city's security services – national police, local police, and its dedicated video surveillance centre – into a single, one-stop hub. 'A police HQ designed for the twenty-first century', as the city's mayor touted it.

'The move's meant to be getting underway after Christmas, at the very start of January. In the end, there'll be two thousand officers based there.'

'And why have they brought Langford there?'

'Auvare's full to the rafters. And understaffed.'

The car drew up in Rue de l'Hôtel des Postes, in front of a colossal ochre building. The façade, with its pediments, symmetry and bas-reliefs, was typical of the neoclassical style found across the city, from Place Garibaldi down to Cours Saleya.

Again using her jacket as an umbrella, Roxane followed Muratore to the main steps. The Nice night had a foreboding feel to it. The sky was a wash of charcoal grey, with icy gusts lashing the few passers-by and ferrying in bursts of lightning and growls of thunder. Côte d'Azur, Finistère style.

The inside of the building was equally imposing, not remotely resembling a police station. On entering, the visitor was immediately greeted by a huge plant-filled courtyard, surrounded by galleries with columns and arches that recalled the cloisters found in monasteries and certain Spanish paradors.

Throughout the building, the only illumination came from torches and construction-site spotlights.

'Is there an issue with the electrics?'

'The storm tripped part of the system. It's also taken down the heating, so it's bloody freezing . . .'

Roxane craned her neck towards the constellation of skylights above. The immense scale and emptiness of the place gave the acoustics a crystalline quality that amplified every word and reverberated it into a legion of echoes.

'It's right at the top,' Muratore directed.

They climbed the central staircase to the first floor, where a series of long corridors veered off to service the four wings of the building.

'This way,' the Gendarmerie officer indicated. 'Langford's been taken to the old psychiatric wing.'

Even through the gloom, it was obvious that the renovation work wasn't finished. Doors without handles, bare wires dangling from the ceiling, tarpaulin sheets covering the areas that were still in chaos. Twice, Muratore himself was wrong-footed by the maze of corridors, before finally guiding them to a line of adjoining offices from which animated voices could be heard. The chief of the third-district force had clearly got all hands to the pump. By the looks of it, his guys were the ones leading on Amyas Langford's interrogation. Roxane recognised a few faces among them, including that of Serge Cabrera again, a figure she loathed and who wouldn't make old bones if a #MeToo storm ever hit the police.

A little further away she spotted Sorbier, on his own with a phone to his ear. He beckoned her over.

'The examining magistrate's gone AWOL,' he grumbled as he hung up.

A bit like you, when you buggered off and left me.

As he was leading her off towards the custody suite, he turned to point at the group behind them.

'Everyone's falling over each other for a slice of the glory, even though the case is far from closed. The Nice lot, the third-district crew, us . . .'

'Fill me in, boss. Where are we up to?'

'The girl's nowhere to be found. The biker who tracked down the Audi in Tournon-sur-Rhône is adamant that Langford didn't stop once, the whole time he was tailing him.'

'What about the motorway CCTV footage?'

'We've scoured it all. We know Langford filled up in the Drôme, at the Saint-Rambert-d'Albon services. He stopped there for a good quarter of an hour. We've gone through everything with a fine-tooth comb, interviewed the pump attendants, the shop staff, the cleaners. No joy.'

'And the other services, before Tournon?'

'We've put out alerts, but it's Christmas Eve . . .'

'Where's Langford now?'

'Here,' Sorbier replied, nodding at the custody suite.

'Aren't they taking him back to Paris?'

'That was the hope, yes. But the stinking weather,

Christmas and the urgency of the situation have all put a spanner in the works. In the end, we've started the interrogation here. Come and see for yourself.'

At the end of the corridor, he turned and led her through a door that gave onto a small, dimly lit room. The only equipment was a one-way mirror allowing them to observe inside the interview room.

'Is that him?' Roxane asked in surprise, moving closer to the glass.

Amyas Langford looked different to how she'd expected from the photos she'd seen of him. Sitting at a long table, opposite two detectives, he seemed almost lethargic. Elbow propped on the table, head resting on his closed fist as if he had no interest in what was going on around him.

'Doesn't he have a lawyer?'

'He didn't want one.'

'What about his injury?'

'It was just a scratch.'

'What have they got out of him?'

'So far, not much.'

'Could I have a go on him?'

'You know full well you can't,' replied Sorbier. 'Officially, you're not part of this investigation.'

He walked out of the room and closed the door behind him. With a sigh, Roxane dumped her bag on the small desk and flopped onto one of the two chairs.

She narrowed her eyes to get a better look at Langford. Although he was in his forties, his features still had a youthful quality. He was sporting a green cord blazer over a white mandarin-collar shirt, and his mid-length hair was meticulously groomed. His almost Romantic pose reminded Roxane of old photos of Oscar Wilde or, on a different note, The Divine Comedy's *Absent Friends* album cover.

The guys in the interrogation room were trying to get him to spit out the passwords of his phone and laptop, which were laid on the table in front of him, but it was as though Amyas couldn't hear them. Roxane massaged her temples. She could feel a migraine coming on, in stealthy waves and at the worst possible moment. She rummaged in her bag for a tablet, swallowed it dry, then mechanically checked her phone which had been in flight mode since the helicopter ride. The same number had tried to reach her three times. There were no voice messages, but the caller had left an SMS:

Good evening, please phone me back urgently. P.-Y. Le Hénaff (SCRC).

The name vaguely rang a bell. Le Hénaff must be some kind of analyst or legal specialist from the Gendarmerie's Criminal Intelligence Information Service. She dialled him back immediately.

'Roxane Montchrestien. You've been trying to—'

'Yeah,' he cut in somewhat boorishly. 'Valérie Janvier gave me your number. I've got some intel for you.'

The guy was patently at a Christmas Eve bash in Brittany. Behind him she could hear a godawful rendition of 'All I Want for Christmas' being belted out to the wail of Breton bagpipes. Christ.

'About ten days ago, I worked with Marc Batailley to trawl the DSC database for crimes that could have a mythological inspiration,' the Breton began.

In her mind Roxane tried to join the dots.

'Like those in Avignon and Stratford, you mean?'

'With the figure of Dionysus as the common thread,' Le Hénaff confirmed. 'I told Marc I'd carry on digging to see if I could find anything from further back, as well as trying to gather any cases from abroad.'

'And? Have you found another case?'

'Not just one more,' he replied. 'I've come across at least six.'

Roxane groaned inwardly. Someone else with designs on 'her' serial killer.

'Are you sure you're not getting ahead of yourself?'

'Think what you like. The fact is that in the past three years, there have been six more murders linked to the cult of Dionysus.'

'How was the link not spotted earlier?'

'These murders all happened abroad. The Balkans, Greece, Italy, India, the States. And I'm sure there are others.'

Dubious, Roxane said nothing. But Le Hénaff was on a roll.

'When you look at the staging of them, there's no doubt about the Dionysus connection. The ivy wreath, the goat-skin, the thyrsus, the vines . . . it's all there. And in each case, the victims were symbols of law and order and author-ity – police, magistrates, soldiers, et cetera.'

'What are you thinking? The same murderer operating in different countries?'

'Course not. More like several groups or individuals who've been brainwashed by pagan beliefs and ended up down a radical rabbit hole. Dionysus is one of the few Olympian gods whose cult involved human sacrifice. These loons are out to recreate the ritual orgies that sometimes culminated with a kind of Eucharist. Communing with the god by feasting on human flesh.'

That was it. She'd officially lost Le Hénaff. The guy was blasting into tinfoil-hat territory. Given the time of night, chances were he hadn't just been on the apple juice. Sensing he could turn nasty, she tried to bring him back to earth gently.

'And you think they're in contact with each other?'

The Breton gave a protracted sigh of exasperation, then picked up where he'd left off.

'Fabio Damiani, an Italian professor from the University of Perugia, was arrested early this week on suspicion of murdering a Carabinieri officer, in a ritual that had some parallels with the Stratford murder.'

More silence from Roxane.

'The case has caused a real storm in Italy. Haven't you heard about it?'

'No,' Roxane admitted.

Le Hénaff became increasingly narked.

'One of my Italian contacts has given me access to a summary of Damiani's confession. He completely cracked in custody before trying to kill himself.'

'And what's the upshot?'

This time, it was the Breton who was silent for a moment before replying.

'I saw on the news that you've arrested Amyas Langford . . .'

'That's right. Was it Batailley who mentioned him to you?'

Le Hénaff cleared his throat.

'The Italian police seized Damiani's PC. Amyas Langford's name comes up multiple times. They were communicating over forums.'

'Do you have transcriptions of—?'

'Haven't I spoon-fed you enough, dammit? Something very ugly's going to happen this week. So you lot had better pull your fingers out!'

'*What's* going to happen? A coordinated action?'

'I suggest you hand this over to Major Crime, now. The touchpaper's been lit and it's all about to blow up in your faces. *Paour Kaez Parizian!*'

With the slur he slammed the phone down. When Roxane turned around, she saw that Sorbier was back in the room. The Breton had been sounding off so loudly, she hadn't heard him come in.

'Who was that?' her skipper asked.

'Pierre-Yves Le Hénaff. Do you know him?'

'The guy they used to call "the brain of Fort Rosny"? A prize wanker, but a sound copper.'

'"Prize wanker"? That sounds like him.'

'What did he want?'

She relayed her conversation with the analyst. The more details she revealed, the grimmer Sorbier's face became.

'Le Hénaff isn't wrong,' he declared once she'd finished. 'This case is a shitstorm if ever there was one. I have to find a way of reaching the examining magistrate.'

'Before you do, let me have a go on Langford. Nobody knows this case better than me.'

Sorbier scratched his right cheek nervously, as if trying to gouge out chunks of his skin.

'Ten minutes. That's your lot.'

RAPHAËL

5.

Paris, less than an hour before midnight

'Ho ho ho! Ho ho ho!'

The house was bathed in darkness. Stuffy. Sad. Slightly unsettling. Fluorescent tape and a plastic tarp were still barring access to the south side. I'd dozed off on the sofa, my phone within arm's reach, while waiting for news. About my dad or from Garance.

'Ho ho ho! Ho ho ho!'

The repeated trill jolted my eyes open. Father Christmas was advancing across my lawn, jingling a bell as he went.

This day can't end soon enough . . .

A prankster? A Christmas Eve reveller? In any case, the guy was drawing closer with each cheery tinkle.

'*Have yourself a Merry Christmas!*' he boomed in English.

In his free hand, the jolly red man was brandishing a small gift-wrapped parcel. He looped around the house to plonk himself in front of the glass door.

'Chronopost! Delivery for you, Mr Batailley!'

Over his white beard he was sporting a hideous mask, a carbon copy of the one worn by Alex DeLarge in *Clockwork Orange*. A dark wolfish face protruding into a huge phallic red snout.

'Chronopost!' he repeated, as though chanting 'Open sesame.'

Pull the other one. It would be headline news if La Poste had started delivering parcels at 11 p.m. on 24 December.

I wasn't letting the Big Bad Wolf huff and guff his way into my house.

'You can leave it on the step,' I told him.

'As you please, Mr Batailley.'

He duly deposited the packet. My relief was short-lived, though.

'I'll just be needing a teensy signature,' he chortled, flourishing a pad and pen from his pocket.

Get lost . . .

The manoeuvre stank of a trap, yet part of me was still curious to know more.

'Do you have the name of the sender?'

Without removing his absurd face covering, he held the parcel to his eyes. He peered at the address label, laboriously deciphering each syllable.

'Ma-da-me Ga-ron-ce Ka-ra-dek.'

Maybe he was a genuine postie after all.

'OK, I'll sign the damned thing.'

Warily, I opened the door a crack, poised to slam it shut at the first sign of trouble.

Setting down his wicker basket, he proffered me the parcel.

'Chronopost thanks you for your custom and wishes you a Merry Christmas.'

'Who forces you to dress up like that?' I asked him as I signed the slip of paper.

The guy finally peeled off his mask to wipe the beads of sweat from his forehead. He looked exhausted, like he hadn't had a square meal in days. I felt a sudden pang of guilt at my mistrust and frosty welcome.

'Those bastards at the top, who else?' he grimaced. 'They

say the customers like it, especially the little 'uns. Anything to boost their profits. Human dignity doesn't get a look-in. Here's your receipt, sir.'

'Thanks. Can I get you a coffee or anything to drink?'

'I wouldn't say no to a quick bracer. If you've anything in, of course.'

I left the door ajar and headed to the other side of the living room. In my dad's shagreen bar cabinet there was an open bottle of Chartreuse. I poured a glass for the postie, then handed it to him along with a **ten euro** tip.

'Thank you. That's very kind.'

He pocketed the banknote and downed the drink in one.

'Aah! That's cleared out the old sinuses! Do you mind if I . . . ?' he gestured to the bottle.

'Be my guest.'

'So you're all alone on Christmas Eve, Mr Batailley?'

'It's no big deal. I'm finishing a novel at the moment. I've got my characters for company, up here.'

'I often get voices in my head too,' the guy admitted. 'Anyway, I hope you like your present. I won't keep you any longer. I've a shift to wrap up!'

'Good luck.'

He replaced his mask and beard, then bent over his basket.

'And this . . .' he said, ' . . . is a gift on the house.'

Before I could blink, he'd whipped out a sort of long truncheon.

He swung a blow at my stomach that hit me just under the ribs, then a second at my neck, in the same place as my injury from the previous day.

'With compliments from Dionysus's Troupers!' he brayed, as he landed a hook that hurled me to the floor.

A kick to the face knocked the last of the consciousness out of me.

'Ho ho ho! Ho ho ho!'

6.

I stayed down for a good ten minutes, my body crippled with pain, my head all over the place, my thoughts a blur.

Father Christmas, my arse.

By the time I struggled to my feet, the guy had vanished. I wondered about calling the police, but what could they do? I wished I'd been more careful. I should have armed myself with my dad's gun, for which I'd located the ammo earlier that evening.

I picked up the parcel from the floor and shook it next to my ear in the hope of divining the contents.

What have I got to lose . . .?

I took the plunge and opened it. Nothing blew up in my face. Just a basic cardboard box, carrying the logo of the children's clothing brand Bonpoint. Then, inside, a pale-pink envelope and a pair of tiny, milky-white cashmere baby slippers.

Why?

I unsealed the envelope. It contained a photo of Garance de Karadec wearing a radiant smile, her gaze trained on the camera lens, her hand resting on her naked stomach. With a knot of apprehension, I turned it over to find a handwritten note: *Raphaël, you're going to be a daddy!*

Rooted to the spot, I tried to keep a sense of perspective, not to give any weight to some sick joke. But I knew it was more than that. I hunted under the tissue paper in the box, in search of another clue. Nothing. Finally, I discovered it inside one of the booties, in the form of a metal USB stick.

Sitting down at my computer, I plugged in the device and double-clicked on the icon to launch a QuickTime file. With my stomach writhing and a lump in my throat, I set the video playing.

7.

Within seconds I recognised La VillAzur hotel, on the tip of the Cap d'Antibes.

I'd only been there once – the previous September. A producer had shot an adaptation of one of my books, which was set in the region. To celebrate the end of filming, he'd invited me to an intimate private do, for which he'd hired out the hotel's rooftop bar. I'm not a party person. I never know how to behave, haven't a clue how to enjoy myself, and don't recall a single positive experience. That party was no exception.

I leaned into the screen to study the footage more closely. Who'd filmed it? You could see me there, drifting half-heartedly from one group to another, drinking coupe after coupe of Krug and Jacques Selosse to the beat of the dross being pumped out by some upstart DJ who was universally hailed as 'a-*mazing*'.

Even if my heart wasn't in it, the setting was incredible. Overhanging the Mediterranean, looking out towards the Îles de Lérins across the waves.

'Will you come swimming with me?'

My sister, Vera, had burst into my mind and slap-bang into the middle of the terrace. She was in her swimming costume, wearing a novelty bathing cap, snorkel goggles, and an inflatable duck around her waist.

'Come on, Raphy!' she insisted, pointing to the pool that was hollowed into the rocks. 'It's the best time. Everyone's gone home and the water's still warm.'

As always, I'd declined.

'No thanks, Vera.'

'Why?'

'Because you only exist in my head, and I'd look like a bit of an idiot blathering away to myself in a swimming pool.'

'It doesn't matter what everybody else thinks, does it?'

'The problem isn't everybody else. It's that you're dead.'

'You'll die too, one day,' she'd shrugged before scampering off.

I was left alone. Leaden. Captaining a ship that was flailing off course. Crushed by a sudden, overwhelming fatigue. I wished my dad would come and pick me up. That he'd carry me up to bed, tuck me in and hug me goodnight with his usual 'Sleep tight, champ.'

Instead, a woman had appeared from nowhere. Cultured, spirited. Perhaps part of the film crew, though I'd never noticed her before.

Back in Rue d'Assas my eyes were inches from the computer screen, my retina searing with the painful memories that the stolen footage resurrected.

How had we got chatting? Everything was out of focus. Kaleidoscopic fragments of conversation. A Paul Valéry verse – *For I have lived for waiting for you, / And my heart was only your footsteps.* A few anecdotes about the famous guests that had previously graced the hotel. Platitudes about the thousand shades of the sunset.

Still floating in my twinkly champagne-induced haze, sensations overrode thought. Lulled by the soothing lapping of the waves, I sank deeper into my new friend's blue-green gaze. By the time the sun disappeared below the horizon, I could barely keep upright. Incapable of clear thought, I'd followed the girl to her room. Watching the scenes on the sex tape now unfurling on my screen, I was appalled. Nothing in there – the drunkenness, the loss of control – was me. I was no longer my own master. A puppet who'd relinquished his free will to another.

When I woke the next morning, it was past 8 a.m. The room was flooded with sunlight. I had no memory of the previous night. A total blank. Alone with my shame, I left the hotel without further ado and resolved to return to Paris immediately.

On the way to the airport, I'd stopped to throw up. I was shaking all over. Nobody had stolen my money, I wasn't injured, I hadn't been mugged or beaten up. Yet the not remembering anything was unbearable. To set my mind at rest, I turned off at A&E at La Fontonne hospital, outlined what had happened, and asked them to run some tests. I waited until early afternoon for the results.

'You've experienced what we call a "G hole",' a junior doctor informed me.

'A kind of blackout?'

'Yes. A coma triggered by ingesting GBL or GHB.'

'But I didn't take any drugs or meds.'

She shrugged.

'Somebody must have spiked your drink. And when

mixed with alcohol, the drug acts as a sedative that can provoke a loss of consciousness. It's become commonplace, unfortunately.'

In the hospital car park I'd felt myself teetering, but, like so many times in my life, I'd pulled myself back from the brink. Burying the episode deep in my mind, I'd decided it simply hadn't existed. But now, this ill-digested morsel of my past was spewing back at me on steroids.

Back in the video, the timestamp showed 7 a.m. While I remained collapsed on the bed, a figure drew the curtains of the hotel room, then walked over to a dressing table topped with an oval mirror. The scene was filmed from a phone balanced on the small washstand behind it. Armed with cleansing wipes and a cotton pad soaked with micellar water, the woman removed her wig, her make-up, her false eyelashes, her contact lenses. One dab at a time, the unmade face of Garance de Karadec reappeared in the mirror. She winked at me and blew me a kiss.

And that's when I realised the child Garance was carrying could be mine.

Friday, 25 December

16

THE WORLD IS A THEATRE

ROXANE

1.

The new police station, Nice

The only window in the interrogation room shuddered as another thunderclap rattled through the skies. It had rained all night. An apocalyptic storm that had pounded the city, flooding the streets, uprooting palm trees and ripping off roof tiles. Though it was now 7 a.m., it was still pitch-black. At midnight, just when Roxane thought her chance had come to interrogate Amyas Langford, the actor had complained of stomach pains and his custody had been suspended. He'd been transferred back to L'Archet hospital, and had spent most of the night there before being returned to the station.

Meanwhile, tensions in the police ranks had ratcheted up. Despite intensifying the search effort around the motorway and the service stations, nobody had managed to gather a scrap of information relating to Garance de Karadec's disappearance.

On a drip-feed of coffee, Roxane had spent the past few hours swotting up on her mythology books. Just as dawn was crawling in and she was about to flop from exhaustion, the door opened at last. The Englishman entered in handcuffs, escorted by Serge Cabrera. With his bull neck, strapping frame and fuzz of long dark hair, the Parisian cop was one of the heavyweights of the third-district crew and clearly intended to wield his clout here.

'I'll give you ten minutes with him, OK sweetheart?' he blared in his French-Algerian accent. 'Then you let us boys take things from there.'

Roxane glowered at him in silence. With his chain bracelet, waxed cowboy boots, and pale-pink shirt exposing his hairy chest, Cabrera oozed boorish self-satisfaction. He clamped his hand down on Langford's shoulder to force him into a chair, before finally losing his rag.

'What's up, darling? You want a photo?' he shot at her, then swaggered out of the room.

Once alone with Amyas, Roxane remained standing for a moment opposite him, drumming her fingers on the screen of the laptop that was still poised on the long metal table. The BRI guys had recovered it from the passenger seat of the Audi, and, rather than sending it off to specialists who'd take several days to search the device, the investigation team had reasonably opted to keep hold of it in the hope of getting the password out of Langford while he was in custody.

'I suppose you're another one hoping I'll give you the password? Do you honestly believe that will help you find the girl?'

With his shackled hands the actor repositioned his corduroy blazer, which was now draped over his shoulders like a cape. Pinned to the buttonhole was a horrific spider brooch that reminded Roxane of the Louise Bourgeois sculpture, with its wasted body and monstrous vertical legs.

'I don't give a toss about your password,' Roxane replied. 'All I want is to understand.'

'Understand what?'

Amyas Langford had an odd voice. Smooth, but inflected with an English accent with a strong hint of German. Somewhere between Jane Birkin and Christoph Waltz.

'Truth is, I'm struggling to get this obsession of yours.' As she spoke, she set down the *Great Dionysia* book on the table and slid into the seat opposite him.

Langford sneaked a glance at the title.

'I'll make this easy for you, Amyas. I know you were involved in the Avignon and Stratford murders. I've enough evidence to have you charged, and even in France the courts won't hesitate to send you down for twenty years. The game's up.'

'You're right. It almost is,' he replied in English, before switching back to French. 'But I've saved the best until last.'

'So this is what gets you hard, then? The cult of Dionysus.'

Langford stretched his arms in front of him and cracked his knuckles. On the underside of his left wrist, there was a quote in Gothic script: *Totus mundus agit histrionem*. 'Everyone's playing at being an actor.' Or, more famously, *All the world's a stage*. The motto of Shakespeare's Globe. Having followed Roxane's gaze, Langford pounced with his question.

'Are you a fan of the theatre?'

'Not really. The classics send me to sleep and the modern stuff makes me cringe. It's all either too long, or too inane.'

Amyas gave an approving smile.

'The worst part is that you're not far wrong!'

'How about you, anyway? What is it you see in the theatre?'

Keeping up his ploy, the Englishman replied with another question.

'Are you satisfied with your life? Your relationships? Your job?'

Roxane shook her head.

'Not remotely. It's a shitshow on all fronts.'

'And what's your strategy for escaping the dissatisfaction?'

'Erm . . . Lexapro, weed, caipirinhas, Chardonnay . . .'

'Aha! And do they work?'

'They do the job. For a few hours . . . And you?'

'Me? What makes *me* happy is the ACTING, the STAGE-CRAFT, because they allow you to create an alternative reality. That's the true power of Dionysus: showing you the path to destroy reality and set yourself free.'

Roxane leant back in her chair wearily.

'But what do you actually want to free yourself from?'

'From the state, authority, hypercapitalism, from a world that alienates us from ourselves.'

'Not very original, is it, this little Marxist creed of yours?'

She did an exaggerated impersonation of his German twang:

'*Und zo, to free yourzelf from zee schtate und hybercapidalism, your idea of ein kood time is to ko around murtering beople? Vat himbeccable logic!*'

This time, Langford gave every appearance of laughing along heartily.

'Do you know the etymology of the term "tragedy"?'

'Yeah, I read about it in there while I was waiting for you.'

She indicated to the book. 'See? I've done my homework. Literally, tragedy means "goat song".'

He nodded in a simulation of impressed assent.

'Very good. It stems from the animal that was killed to honour Dionysus during the ceremonies of antiquity.'

'You'll have to forgive me, but I'm struggling to see the appeal of butchering a goat. Other than to eat it.'

'It's a symbolic sacrifice. Killing the goat at the end of a performance regenerates theatre. It revives the euphoria of the drama, the only outlet for purging the pains of our existence.'

'So that's how you get your kicks, is it? Every year, you treat yourself to a little sacrifice – a little murder *to honour Dionyzus und regenerate zee zeatre.*'

Assured that he was in the driving seat, Amyas kept his smile fixed in place. His hour of reckoning was clearly unfolding exactly as he'd intended. And that impression troubled Roxane.

'Have you ever killed anyone?' he asked suddenly.

'No,' she lied.

'You really should try it.'

'I'll bear that in mind.'

'Taking someone's life to give as an offering – there's nothing more simultaneously exciting and rewarding.' The last part was delivered in English.

Roxane tugged up the zip of her jacket. She was chilled to the bone. To make up for the defunct heating system, an ancient portable radiator had been installed which could only muster sputters of tepid air. In the inky light of day-break, she stared back at Amyas Langford's wolfish smile. In all the time she'd been interrogating him, she hadn't learnt a thing. Behind the mirror, her so-called 'colleagues' must be having a good laugh. And they weren't altogether wrong. The guy had got her dancing to his tune. He was in performance mode, coolly playing out his show.

But who was his audience?

She lingered on her theatre analogy. To perform his role, Amyas needed both an audience and an acting partner. And right now, it was she, Roxane Montchrestien, who was providing his cue. The Englishman again cracked his knuckles with his cuffed hands, so forcefully he might have been trying to snap the joints from their sockets, and once more she glimpsed his tattoo. She knew full well the gesture had been choreographed and that she was part of the spectacle. She knew Langford wanted to draw her attention to the inscription, to cajole her into wondering, *And what if that's the password?*

She knew full well that through such reasoning, she was allowing herself to be manipulated. That she was willingly coming onstage to act out a role someone else had written for her. She knew this was precisely Langford's intention. She knew it full well . . . but still she went ahead.

She grabbed the silver MacBook from the other end of the table. As Langford watched on avidly, Roxane punched in what she thought were the magic words: *Totus Mundus Agit Histrionem.*

Failure.

TotusMundusAgitHistrionem.

Failure.

She tried again without the capitals. This time, the device unlocked and connected to Wi-Fi instantly through the dongle in the USB port.

The horde of waiting cops surged into the room to con-
gregate around the laptop. The first window that popped up
on the screen was a real-time video conferencing platform,
which was configured to show all participants. At that point
in the meeting, ten attendees were online. Five men and
five women, in black tie and cocktail dresses. Though their
torsos were human, from the shoulders up each was sporting
a prick-eared horse head.

Like inverted centaurs. Human reason fused with animal
instinct.

The terrifying spectacle had all eyes riveted to the screen.
The room fell into deathly silence, until one of the cops
noticed the little green light that had appeared.

'Fuck, it can't . . . the thing's recording us! The bastards
can see us!' he cried, just before Roxane slammed the lid
down.

RAPHAËL

2.

Paris, Christmas Day, 12 minutes past midnight

A deafening blare shattered the silence of the night. Loud
enough to wake half the neighbourhood, like a devoted
football supporter's horn. I shot a glance out of the window,
fearing that 'Father Christmas' or one of his cronies was
back. Not a soul in sight. Maybe it was just a group of revel-
lers who'd had one too many, stumbling along Rue d'Assas.

But the horn kept on blasting, and the sound was too close for comfort. *Shit* . . .

I pressed my nose to the window. Everything was inky black. The lights in the house were dimmed, and half of the outside spotlights were dead. I jumped as the siren screeched again. *Fuck* . . .

I raced to my dad's office. From the drawer I retrieved his MR-73. After loading it with six .38 Special cartridges, I slung on my coat and ventured out into the night.

At the end of the lawn, near the bamboo hedge, something was blinking. Turning on my phone torch, I edged closer. It was a drone. An orange-and-black quadcopter equipped with a plastic horn, which was evidently the source of the din that had woken me. I surveyed it for a couple of minutes, but the craft gave no flicker of movement. I was on the verge of heading back inside when the thing sprang to life, first taking off vertically, then swerving off towards the botanical garden. To begin with I just watched it go, then, after a moment's hesitation, I charged after it to keep it in sight.

For a second it did leave my field of vision, but I soon found it again in the street, perched on the pavement by my car. There was no one around, but a device like that could easily have been pre-programmed. The Alpine was unlocked. I slid into the driver's seat. Someone had coiled an ivy branch around the screen of the satnav. When I switched it on, there was a route waiting for me.

That's right, throw yourself to the wolves . . .

But at this point, did I have any choice? What could be more important than *understanding*? After checking that my wallet was still in my coat pocket, I buckled up and slammed the door. I wasn't interested in thinking, in weighing up the pros and cons, in elaborating hypotheses and arguments. The cogs of my brain were all seized up. I *needed*, simply, to understand. To follow the story through to its conclusion, whatever the dangers might be.

I exited Paris at the Porte d'Orléans and let myself be led like a zombie, mindlessly following the itinerary on my screen: down the motorway towards Chartres, through the Perche, a petrol stop in Le Mans, then on to Laval and Vitré.

3.30 a.m. Over a coffee break in Rennes, I rang the on-call doctor at the Pompidou who'd left me his number. My dad's condition was unchanged. A second operation, on another of his vertebrae, was scheduled for the following day, but there'd be no further attempts to wake him any time soon.

I continued towards the western tip of Brittany: Saint-Brieuc, Guingamp, Morlaix. The Christmas night seemed to be unfolding outside the reaches of time. A journey into a one-way tunnel with no way out. I was lost. In my mind. In my past. In what my life could be from now on. I thought of the child Garance de Karadec was carrying, a child who had every chance – every misfortune – of being mine. I thought of the monstruous chain of events that I'd set in motion as a ten-year-old, through my lies, and which had devastated everything in its path ever since.

It was almost 7 a.m. when I reached my destination. The satnav had led me to a pierside, which had loomed suddenly from the morning mist somewhere between Roscoff and Saint-Pol-de-Léon. An odd choice of terminus. After pulling up in the deserted car park, I made my way along the jetty through a ghostly haze of spray. My legs were tingling all over with pins and needles, my back and sides aching from the six-hour drive. I felt drunk with tiredness. The lack of sleep over the previous days was blurring my thoughts and vision. In that detective novel-style setting, surrounded by cloud-swathed ribbons of treacly sea, I had the sense that, at any moment, a sinister creature might surge from the deep and swallow me whole.

3.

Three fresh horn blasts, like the three raps of the dramaturge's staff at the start of a play, announced that I wasn't alone.

Out of the pea-soup fog, a man's silhouette emerged. He looked to be in his sixties, with a short, stocky frame, and a cap emblazoned with the French Customs insignia obscuring his balding head.

'Mr Batailley?'

'That's me.'

'Let me introduce meself. Fred Narracott, at your service.'

He was wearing the regulation customs officer trousers, with a bright-red stripe down the leg – or 'Garance' red, as it was known in the trade. His features seemed frozen in place like a mask, except for one cockeye that kept veering inwards and twitching like a deranged insect.

'You were expecting me?'

He scratched his chin, most of which had been claimed by a rampant salt-and-pepper goatee.

'Yessir. I'm your captain. It's me who'll be sailing you to the island.'

'Which island?'

'The Karadec island, of course.'

I remembered Garance once saying something about a small private island that had been in her family for generations. The Breton fiefdom of the Karadec clan.

'Do you want to see the beast?'

I followed him to the end of the jetty to meet the 'beast' in question. A semi-rigid Zodiac that was about 25 feet long, with an aluminium hull and an inflatable collar.

'But who asked you to take me there?'

'Erm, you did!'

'Me?'

'A bloke rang a couple of days ago. Said his name was Raphaël Batailley and that he wanted to book my boat for a trip out to the island on Christmas morning. Was that not you?'

Realising it would be pointless to try angling for more details, I decided not to argue the toss.

'Is it far from the shore, this island?'

'About three quarters of an hour by boat.'

'Right, a fair trek then. Is it a good idea to be setting out in weather like this?'

'What weather? It's looking pretty nice, wouldn't you say?'

You think I was born yesterday . . .

'So the island belongs to the Karadec family, then? Do you know if they still live there?'

The customs officer sniggered.

'Nobody's stepped foot on that rock since the two old soaks died in the early 2000s. They certainly liked their plonk and their shoot-ups, that pair.'

'What are the main draws of the place?'

'Solitude, if you're into that. But I won't pretend mooring up's part of the pleasure.'

He produced a liquorice stick from his pocket and began chewing on it like a quid of tobacco.

'Well, it's your call! I've other things I can be getting on with.'

With a nod, I consented to follow him aboard. After handing me a life jacket, Narracott assumed his place on his bolster and fired up the motors and the two small display screens. The steering console was some way from the passenger benches. Hunkering down near the back of the boat, I sheltered as much as I could behind the polycarbonate windshields. Since I was a teenager I'd suffered from terrible seasickness, and, obviously, I didn't have any anti-nausea tablets on me.

'Will it be choppy?' I asked.

Narracott adjusted his customs officer's cap and put on a pair of diving goggles.

'You bet, kiddo,' he bellowed as he cranked into gear. 'All hell's about to break loose!'

ROXANE

4.

For a long while, time and space had stood still. As horrifying as it was fleeting, the image of the ten torsos with their horse heads had made the atmosphere suffocatingly tense. The cops were floored, paralysed with fear, stunned by the diabolic army that had exploded from its box. His face set in a broad smile, his eyes gleaming, Amyas Langford was relishing every moment.

As a barrage of lightning bolts streaked past the window, the men were finally sparked back to life.

'Who were they, those people?' Cabrera demanded.

His question remained unanswered, echoing off the icy walls. In a spurt of rage, he grabbed Langford by the scruff of the neck.

'WHO WERE THEY, THOSE PEOPLE?' he roared again.

But the harder the cop shook him, the more pleasure Amyas seemed to take. Everyone could see the balance of power had shifted. Sorbier stepped in to restrain the third-district skipper.

Detached from the action, her forehead resting against the streaming window of the interrogation room, Roxane watched the drainage channels of the flashy new HQ being overwhelmed by the torrents of rainwater. A fitting metaphor for the present situation.

'It's all very well acting the big man now,' the Englishman remarked once Cabrera had released his grip. 'You weren't so clever when you found yourself on the other side of the bar.'

His German accent had completely disappeared. The chameleon had slipped on a new skin to fight another round.

'What fucking "bar" are you on about?'

'In front of the JURY.'

'You're the one who'll be facing the jury in court, you smug bastard. And they'll kick your fuckwitted arse all the way to the slammer.'

At the word 'jury', something clicked in Roxane's mind.

Abandoning the window, she rushed to retrieve the book from the table and flicked back to a page that she'd read and annotated in the helicopter, about the organising committees of Great Dionysia.

Suddenly, everything fell into place. The drones, the spy cameras, the Troupers, the network unearthed by Le Hénaff, the Dionysian symbolism, the saga of the Stranger in the Seine, the sense of theatre that stalked the case from the start . . . The logic that had eluded her over the preceding days blazed into view like a pilgrimage shrine. The ten masked individuals formed an online jury that mirrored the one from Ancient Greece.

'It's all a drama contest, isn't it?' she asked, walking over to Amyas. 'Dionysus's Troupers are one of the three theatre troupes competing before the jury, like they used to do at Great Dionysia.'

Langford's smile grew even wider. At last, Roxane had delivered the line he was waiting for.

Suddenly there was a buzzing of notification tones, like a chain reaction tearing through the room at split-second intervals. One by one, as the plague spread, all the cops whipped out their phones. His face rigid, Sorbier stared at his screen for a long time before showing it to Roxane. *Le Parisien* had pursued its investigation, which was cited in an AFP press release headlined, *Could the Stranger in the Seine be the pianist Milena Bergman?* Though the newspaper was slightly behind the game, it was a sufficiently juicy story to have sparked a media frenzy. Picked up by every news and social media outlet, the initial dispatch had been spun out, retweeted, commented on and twisted so many times that it had gone viral.

It was clear the wildfire had triggered panic in the room. The media storm would demand a hunt for scapegoats. If the investigation was a disaster, sooner or later heads would roll. And once the guillotine was out, questions of truth, reasonableness and nuance wouldn't enter the equation.

Roxane saw that all eyes had turned to her. Her colleagues were out of their depth. Surpassed by a case whose whys and wherefores they'd never got a handle on. It was official. She'd won. And now, they had no choice but to put their fate in her hands. Like a queen in her ice palace, she surveyed them with all the contempt she could summon. Sorbier, who'd turfed her out five days earlier; that lump Cabrera, who looked like he was about to expire from an apoplectic stroke; the morons from the Left Bank JP crew; the Riviera yokels who thought they were Billy Big Bollocks with their dodgy accents and pastis breath.

As though communicating through some unspoken code, the rats began to jump ship, filing out until she was alone for her final face-off with Amyas Langford. The Englishman hadn't missed a moment of the drama, relishing the impending *mano a mano*. For the first time, he dropped the formalities.

'You're like a little chilli,' he mused as she reseated herself opposite him. 'The one that's going to spice up the dish I've prepared.'

Her mind was in overdrive. Langford patently considered her a useful and necessary accessory to the denouement of his grisly performance. But why? A detail suddenly came back at her.

'In Ancient Greece, Great Dionysia went on for five days, didn't it? It's Friday morning now. The Stranger in the Seine stuff kicked off in earnest on Monday, which means . . .'

'. . . that the end is nigh. Nothing gets past you, my dear.'

'So it's time for the fireworks, is it?'

'You couldn't have put it better.'

'What's keeping you, then? Why don't you get the party started?'

'It already has started, hasn't it? If I'm not mistaken, all over the world the media are talking about us . . .'

'Yeah, but that's just froth. To win your contest, it will take more than that. Recreating the sacrifice of the goat, that's the idea, isn't it?'

'You're finally catching on. To win, we have to recreate the ultimate sacrifice.'

'Enlighten me.'

With a grimace he inhaled loudly through his nose, as if snorting an invisible line of coke. His whole face was convulsing. Roxane could sense in him a suppressed violence, just waiting to explode.

'Does the Battle of Salamis mean anything to you?'

Once again, memories of her foundation year flooded back in vivid detail. 1997. Lycée Louis-le-Grand. Tuesday evenings, 5 to 6 p.m. Classical Culture with Miss Casanova. The answer shot from her lips as if she were responding to an exam question.

'One of the naval battles between the Greeks and the Persians.'

'The Greco-Persian Wars, bravo! You're pretty clued-up for a copper. Salamis was a crucial battle. Not just in the history of Greece, but for the whole of humanity. You know why?'

'I'm all ears.'

'Many historians believe that if the Persians had won, Ancient Greece's development would have been so hampered that we'd never have seen the birth of Western and world culture as we know them. Just think, the fate of our civilisation hinged on the outcome of a single battle!'

In a heartbeat, Langford's features had transformed. His gaze was now penetrating, his pupils distended, his smile ferocious, his face and neck muscles tensed like a predator primed to pounce.

'At one point in the battle, the Greeks, led by Themistocles, were down to only 200 ships – against over 1,000 on the Persian side! Defeat looked inevitable. So, to reinspire his troops, the Greek general decided to surrender his most precious prisoners of war and ordered the sacrifice of three Persian princes in Dionysus's honour.'

'So that's the "supreme sacrifice", then? Three sacrifices?'

'Yes, three murders.'

'Stop me if I'm wrong, but no one's been killed yet in this saga.'

Langford made a show of fighting for breath, gasping and panting uncontrollably. For a few seconds he remained with his head in his hands, his forehead bowed. When he re-emerged, his expression was even more horrific than before. His face had a rare malleability to it, a true modelling-clay mask. In his latest incarnation, his brows were arched like circumflexes and his hair was tousled to look like horns. Like a demented Beelzebub springing from a jack-in-the-box, or Jack Nicholson in certain scenes from *The Shining*.

'No one's been killed? Hang on a minute! Aren't you forgetting the dear mummykins who was flattened by that Japanese dyke, leaving behind a poor baby orphan? Oh, just you watch when the media get all over that – and the police cock-up that allowed it to happen!'

'You're not seriously claiming that one! Her death was collateral damage you could never have foreseen.'

Langford retorted through a faceful of sweat.

'But that's the magic of total theatre and improvisation! You sow the seeds, then watch them grow!'

'And the second murder?'

His sneering smile contorted, his eyes giving way to two furious flames. He was visibly tipping into madness.

'The second victim is me.'

'You?'

'I have to sacrifice myself, you see?'

'All I see right now is a guy in handcuffs with a dozen coppers watching over him.'

'You can't watch me forever.'

With his face gnarled in a grotesque rictus, he began grinding his teeth as though spasming into a mystic trance.

This time, Roxane felt a stab of fear. She knew his deranged demeanour wasn't an act. As she reached for her Glock, she could see a scramble of activity in the room behind the mirror.

'Don't blink,' Langford advised her through his delirium.

At once, with all the violence he could muster, he rammed his head against the metal edge of the interrogation table. The first blow exploded his nose, breaking clean through the bone and unleashing a geyser of blood. The second sliced his forehead from left to right, as if someone had tried to plunge a cutlass through to his skull bone.

On cue, the army of cops burst into the room and leapt on Langford to restrain him.

'Someone call an ambulance!' Sorbier ordered.

As the blood poured down his face, Amyas carried on grinding his teeth in a frenzy.

'Why's he doing that, the nutter?' Cabrera demanded once it seemed they had the Englishman under control.

Like a flash, Roxane remembered what the casting director had told her: *A few years ago, while playing a Second World War Resistance fighter for a TV film, he got so into the role that he had a fake tooth implanted that contained a genuine cyanide pill! You get the measure of the guy . . .*

In that moment, she realised the fake tooth had just shattered. The wild rictus on Langford's face froze as the poison spread through his body. Barging Cabrera out of the way, Roxane tore over and grabbed the actor by the hair.

'Who's the third victim, Amyas?'

Leaning over him, she pressed her ear up to Langford's mouth in the hope of gathering his final confession. She could feel her hair sticking to the blood that was snaking down the dying man's face. She could feel his hot, ferruginous breath, trying to form the words.

Then she jerked to her feet and stopped still, suddenly seized from head to toe with goosepimples. She'd spent the past two days trying to convince herself that her big moment had come, that she'd at last landed the case of her life, and that she was on the verge of cracking it. The case that she'd stopped dreaming would ever come, and which would get her life back on track. But she'd blown it, once again.

She reopened the laptop. The torsos in the horse masks were long gone. She clicked on a window that was minimised in the corner of the screen. Footage from a series of drones flashed before her. At first Roxane thought the landscape looked Greek. Then she realised the images were showing the island of Karadec in Brittany, off the coast of which a dinghy was currently mooring.

An electric charge shot down her spine. The third and final murder was about to take place. And she was over 600 miles from the scene of the action.

17

THE STRANGER IN THE SEINE

RAPHAËL

1.

The Zodiac's advance through the waves came at the cost of relentless pitching and tossing. At the helm, still chomping on his liquorice stick, Narracott was in his element. Just as at home in the swells as I was petrified by them. The journey to the island seemed interminable. Out on the raging sea, everything inspired me with dread and revulsion. The suffocating pearly mist, the spray with its stench of rotting seaweed, the icy breakers tirelessly battering the dinghy.

To add insult to injury, it had started to rain. All the swaying was making my stomach heave. The danger was ubiquitous. With each new breaker, I felt like a dark hand was about to surge from the depths and wrench us under. Hunched on the back seat, clenching the metal rail, I screwed my eyes shut and tried to block out the ordeal. While I waited for the storm to pass, the best I could do was grit my teeth and let my mind drift into a milky fug, too formless to engage conscious thought.

I couldn't say how long the rest of the crossing lasted, but when I opened my eyes again, the landscape had transformed.

Perforated by the morning light, the curtain of mist had begun to lift to reveal Karadec island. I shaded my eyes to get a clearer view. My immediate association was the cover of Hergé's *The Black Island*. There was no ribbon of sand, just rocks and a swathe of heathland encircling a crag topped with a small medieval-looking fortified tower.

'Not too shabby, is it?' Narracott yelled.

The Zodiac had started to lose speed. Though the wind had got up, the weather was almost set fair.

'Are we docking on the other side?'

''Fraid not. The only way onto the island is here, to the south,' he explained. 'The other side's even steeper.'

As the dinghy pulled closer, I realised the journey ashore was going to be perilous. No real provision had been made for boat access, other than a fairly stubby jetty and a concrete ramp that had half crumbled away.

Narracott was struggling. The strong winds kept changing direction, forcing him to adjust the propellor pitch constantly in a vain effort to stabilise the boat.

'Could you jump out here?' he asked, after judging he couldn't get any nearer.

I took a run-up and launched myself out of the boat, then promptly fell flat on my face on the ramp. Hauling myself up, I kept walking until I reached a shingle shoreline.

'Well done, kid!' the customs officer exclaimed in English. 'And now, it's up to you!'

He gave me a final wave, then fired up the engine and vanished from sight.

2.

After an initial swathe of fern and gorse the heathland gave way to an Irish-style landscape, with lumps of rock erupting from a bed of boggy peat moss and climbing like a sort of Giant's Causeway to the top of the fortress.

At its highest point, the island must have clocked in at a good 130 feet. After making my way up the 'stairs', I found myself in front of a quadrangular tower with two projecting turrets – a kind of stately pile-cum-military outpost that reminded me of the tower houses I'd seen in Scotland. But the Karadec family's former stomping ground had long since fallen into ruin. Part of the roof had been blown off by the wind, the glass was gone from the windows, and the southern bartizan looked like it might collapse at any minute.

As I skirted the building I spotted another path in the distance, leading down through the rocks and vegetation to the opposite side from where I'd come up. I followed it along until I reached a rocky plateau, which jutted out to offer a panoramic view over the hidden face of the island. Narracott hadn't been lying. Overrun with broom, the other flank was even more abrupt, and apparently a haven for falcons, sparrowhawks and puffins.

I returned to the path, heading for the eastern tip, but soon met with a rusty chain that cautioned against continuing any further. An old enamel sign rammed home the warning: EXTREME DANGER AHEAD.

'Hi, Raphy!'

I spun around at the sound of my sister's voice.

'Hi, Vera.'

This time she was again seven or eight, as she had been in all her appearances over recent weeks. She was dressed in khaki shorts with a bright-yellow T-shirt, and carrying a small water bottle attached to a hiking rucksack.

'You look tired,' she observed as she pulled up in front of the sign.

'It's true, I didn't get much sleep.'

Scrutinising me through her heart-shaped sunglasses, she frowned as she noticed the bruises on my face.

'Who did that to you?'

'I had a fight with Father Christmas.'

'Raphy! I know he's not real!'

The sun was now fully up and beginning its ascent through the sky, splashing the horizon with labile pools of light as it jostled with the clouds. Vera set off to perch herself under a pair of mimosa trees, then proffered me her bottle with a beaming grin.

'I've brought Banga! The apple one with the monkey on it! D'you want some?'

'Go on, then.'

I joined her and took a couple of swigs, letting myself be swept along on the sugary hit of childhood. Then I sat down next to her, watching her laughing, singing and hooting with glee as the wind whipped up her bunches.

I'd seen countless shrinks, tried every drug going, completed course after course of therapy. Yet still never a day went by when I didn't think of my sister's death. When I didn't picture Vera's screaming face, trapped inside that metal furnace. I was painfully aware that she must have called to me to save her. It was always me she went to when there was a problem. When her bike got a flat tyre, when she got her foot stuck while scaling the garden fence. She called, and I found a way to make the problem go away. I was her hero. And that's exactly how I wanted it to be.

'I've already told you there's nothing you could have done,' she said, as though reading my thoughts.

Every time we replayed the same conversation, almost word for word.

'I shouldn't have left you with Mum. I shouldn't have written that anonymous letter.'

She shrugged with an oddly stoical frown.

'You were ten. You didn't have any choice. There's no point in beating yourself up about it.'

'But why do you keep coming back, then? Why don't you leave for good?'

She ducked my question and pulled a silly face. I persevered.

'You'll never leave, will you?'

'No,' Vera replied.

'Why?'

'Because you'll never let me.'

A solitary tear rolled down my cheek. For a few minutes, neither of us spoke. We just stared out at the landscape, watching as the clouds streaked by giddily fast overhead. All was well. The wind was humming through the branches of the mimosas, the light changing constantly as though God were clowning around with a giant light switch. In the space of seconds, the rocks could transform from white to grey, from the cliffs of Étretat to the scarps of Dunnet Head.

I would have liked the moment to last forever, but the

magical interlude was broken when Vera got to her feet and picked up her bottle.

'I have to go.'

'Where?'

'To see Daddy.' She hitched her rucksack onto her back. 'We've agreed to meet on a little beach not far from here.'

'There are no beaches for miles, Vera, and Dad isn't here. He's in Paris, in the hospital.'

'Not for much longer.'

She retied a trailing shoelace, then stepped over the chain that was barring the path.

'Wait for me!'

I wanted to go after her, but I sensed she was already slipping away. When I looked a moment later, she was gone.

MARC

3.

Paris, Pompidou Hospital, Christmas morning, 8.28 a.m.

'Doctor, there's a problem with the patient in Room 18.'

'Marc Batailley? What's the issue?'

'We're losing him.'

'That's not possible. He was perfectly stable when I just checked on him!'

'Well, he isn't anymore . . .'

'OK, I'm on my way.'

I'm still comatose, yet I can hear them talking. I can sense them flailing around me. I can see them desperately trying to revive my spent hulk. CPR. Defibrillator. Electrode pads. Two hundred joules through the ticker to get the old beast pumping again. But it's no use. I'm on my way. My bags are packed and I'm getting out of this godforsaken place. Out of this lifeless existence. Like a wild salmon, I'm heading back upstream to catch my final rays. Adrenaline. Cordarone. It's a waste of time refilling the tank, scrambling to change the batteries. The cells have given up the ghost. This rust bucket's not for restarting. I'm off. Thank God. Don't hold me back. I've taken all I can take. I've nothing left to give. Let me go. *Let me go!*

'Daddy?'

I turn around, but I'm no longer in the hospital. I can barely see for dazzling sunlight. A salty breeze is whipping my face. The sand is the colour of gold.

'Daddy!'

'Vera . . . ?'

I've never dreamt about her. Ever since I lost her, to be sure of not running into her in a nightmare, the only way I've slept is with my nightly dose of pills. Knocking myself senseless to escape being battered by the pain.

'Come on, Daddy! The water's perfect for swimming!'

As I make my way across the shore to join her, she throws herself around my neck and appears through beads of sunlight. Crying and laughing, with every ounce of me I cling to her. Her scent, her mica eyes, her peals of laughter.

And I know that this time, I'll never let anyone take her from me again.

RAPHAËL

4.

Karadec island

Since leaving Vera, I'd been skirting the cliffside along a narrow path, hewn out where erosion had eaten the rocks away. The view from all sides was dizzying. Although the water was sparkling, the crashing of the waves against the sheer cliff face was a reminder of the peril that lurked behind the slightest misstep. As I rounded a bend in the path, a blinding glare of sunlight hit me like a jet of hot mercury. Shielding my eyes with my forearm, for a moment all I could see were black spots. When the dancing stopped, I was floored by the landscape that met me. Within skimming distance of the waves, someone had erected a small, ancient-style amphitheatre, like a giant shell blooming from the rock.

How long had it been there? The arena had been built on the slopes leading down to the sea. A semicircle of stone steps enclosed a small orchestra, which was dominated by a full-body statue of Dionysus. A little further on, raised by a few feet and covered over with wooden slats, was the stage. And right in the middle of the boards, tied to a chair made of branches, the unmistakable figure of Garance de Karadec. Caped in an animal skin, and exposed to the elements with all the markings of a sacrificial victim.

I scanned the perimeter, but saw no one. Drawing the MR-73 from my pocket, I cocked the hammer and advanced down an aisle towards her.

'Garance!'

The moment I climbed onstage via a set of side steps, a swarm of drones appeared overhead. Four, five, then six of them, patrolling the skies with their cameras.

'Raphaël!' Garance shouted, her terror palpable even through the scarf that was knotted around her mouth.

I untied the gag and the cords binding her hands and ankles. The animal skin she was wearing smelt as repulsive as it looked: a genuine fur pelt, crowned with a goat's head.

'Who did this to you?'

'I'll explain later. We have to get out of here, now!'

'But how?'

'There's a boat moored to a pontoon, just behind the path.'

'Watch out!'

The drones whirring above us were getting dangerously close, prowling in concentric circles as if they'd been pro-grammed to attack. Hoping to ward them off, I pointed the gun skywards. With a clammy palm and my fingers tensed on the trigger, I tried to shoot one of them down. Inevit-ably, never having used a gun before in my life, I was way off target. Garance took the weapon from me.

'Let me try.'

As if she'd been doing it all her life, she gripped the MR-73 in both hands, swept the barrel overhead and fired two shots, each exploding one of the drones. The remaining four immediately beat a retreat.

Satisfied with her handiwork, for a moment she remained motionless. She smiled into the sun, its light giving her blue-green eyes a manic intensity.

Keen to get away, I held out a hand to her, but she refused it.

'You need to beware, Raphaël.'

'Of what?'

'Of me.'

While I stared at her in confusion, she spun the revolver at me and blasted a bullet into my thigh.

5.

My cry was lost in the echo of the shot. I was hurled back by its force, but my fall was broken by the branch chair. Instinctively, I touched the wound to check my kneecap was still there. The impact had been so ferocious, it felt like a chunk of my leg had been ripped off.

'Why . . . ?' I murmured.

For a few seconds, I was convinced my body had lost all sensation. Then the sluice gates opened to the pain.

'Why? Why would you do that?'

'Because you're the third victim. The third sacrifice to Dionysus.'

I tried to understand and catch my breath all at once. Part of me thought I could make her see sense. Another part told me I'd only land up getting my brains blown out quicker.

'Come on, Garance. This isn't you. It's Amyas that's swept you along in all this. He's the one that's put these crazy ideas in your head.'

'Of course, it's always the men who are to blame. And we're just the poor innocent victims of patriarchal oppression. Ha ha ha! But Amyas is nothing but a pathetic anarchist,' she fumed. 'A nobody who did whatever *I* told him to do.'

Her smile had given way to rage. Having cast off the

goatskin, she now revealed beneath it a striking mirrored dress, made up of hundreds of tiny fragments throwing back reflections of sky and sea.

'None of it makes any sense, Garance.'

'Freedom doesn't make any sense?'

'Where does freedom come into it?'

'The only route to freedom is through intoxication, drugs, fantasy, dreams, theatre, disguise – anything that releases us from the role society wants to assign us. You know that in Elizabethan times, the Puritans called theatre "the house of the devil"? They thought it drove people to sin and degeneracy, because it defied the normal way of things.'

The sun was dazzlingly bright now, sitting high in the sky as Garance stood commanding the stage below, reciting her script like a queen in her summer palace. Straining for breath, I tried again.

'Sorry, but I don't see the connection.'

'Oh, but you do,' she replied, her tone almost maternal. 'Because we're the same, you and me. I could tell from the first time we met. Life's intolerable for us. We're constantly looking for escape mechanisms, to stop the reality from killing us. We can only cope by finding ways to mitigate the pain. For you, it's writing and all the lies you've told your father all these years. For me it's acting, taking on different identities, distorting and manipulating. We don't live in the real world, Raphaël. We go around in our own "virtual reality" that we've created to compete with it. Did you know the term was first used in relation to the theatre?'

She had an aura of breezy relish, watching me dying without a hint of empathy or remorse.

I gritted my teeth. The pain was excruciating, worse than

anything I'd ever experienced. It felt like my femur was dis-integrating inside my leg.

'If . . . if I'm the same as you, why . . . why do you want to kill me?'

'Because that's the essence of tragedy, my love. You're the hero, vainly fighting against his destiny.'

'And you? What's your role?'

'I'm the merciful force that comes to free your repressed spirit. The armed hand of fate, who destroys you so you can be reborn.'

'Reborn . . . ?'

Gathering all my strength, I made a last-ditch effort to get up and snatch the gun from her. But she easily stepped aside, and blasted out a fresh shot that hit me in the thorax.

With my arms crossed over my chest, I collapsed into the centre of the stage, while the four drones whirred back over-head to capture my final moments.

6.

Warm, salty tears stream past my half-closed lids. Through their translucent gauze I see – or I sense – Garance de Kara-dec flashing me a final smile as she exits the stage. Then my vision blurs almost completely, and my eyes drift shut.

I hear the deafening roar of the rising tide. The jeering laughter of an avenging god. I'm drenched in sweat, cold then hot. I feel the veins of my neck swelling and pulsing with warm blood, then a rush of soothing images and sen-sations. Lush foliage, silvery clouds, a gentle sun breaking through.

Then everything lurches, like an axis has been flipped, and suddenly I'm in brilliant daylight, barefoot on a beach.

My body feels implausibly light, unburdened of all its woes. I'm ten years old again! I take a few joyous steps along the damp sand.

'Raphy!'

I turn at the sound of my sister's voice.

'I knew you'd come!'

Vera and my dad were already there.

Waiting for me.

Roscoff – Maritime Gendarmerie Rescue Mission on Karadec Island

25 December 2020 – 11.52

Maritime Gendarmerie coastguards in Roscoff (Finistère) called out to rescue gravely injured man on Karadec island

The six-strong military crew arrived on the southern tip of Île d'Enez-hunvreadell – better known as 'Karadec island', after the family that owns the islet – early this morning, after the alarm was raised by Captain Roxane Montchrestien of the Brigade Nationale de Recherche des Fugitifs (BNRF).

The island, which has been uninhabited for several years, is reported to have been the scene of a shooting. Though the circumstances are still unclear, the incident is believed to have resulted in at least one casualty, a man in his forties, who sustained multiple shots to his thorax and leg.

The victim was evacuated by helicopter to the military hospital in Brest (HIA Clermont-Tonnerre). His injuries have been described as extremely concerning, and he remains in a critical condition.

More updates to follow . . .

ABOUT THE AUTHOR

Guillaume Musso is the number one bestselling author in France. He has written eighteen previous novels, including the thrillers *Central Park; The Reunion,* which was made into an international TV series; and *Afterwards...,* which was made into a feature film starring John Malkovich and Evangeline Lilly. He lives in Paris.

Also in paperback by Guillaume Musso

The Reunion

"A fast-paced thriller, set on the Côte d'Azur, packed with a glamorous missing girl, a dead body, and enough references to *Twin Peaks* and raves and Belle and Sebastian to tickle anybody who came of age in the 1990s...Musso is not just a popular author but *the* number one bestselling novelist in France. So you're bound to emerge more *branché* than those people you see on the beach reading home-grown potboilers."

—Lauren Mechling, *Vanity Fair*

Central Park

"Musso spoons out details and misdirection with brio...The initial conceit provoked plenty of interest...The opener is a doozy."   —Sarah Weinman, *New York Times Book Review*

"Sure to please those who like to use reading as their cardio."

—*CrimeReads*

Back Bay Books
Available wherever paperbacks are sold